Inside the Kill Box

A Novel

Michael W. Romanowski

To Brad— Best wishes!

Foremost Press
Cedarburg, Wisconsin

Published by Foremost Press

ISBN-10: 1-936154-19-6
ISBN-13: 978-1-936154-19-7

For Evangeline

CHAPTER 1

Washington International Airport
(2100 hours – Monday, 21 January 1991)

Peter Vermeer had been at the gate for nearly thirty minutes when the last flight from London Heathrow arrived.

Vermeer had been in government service for too many years to count, and felt his days playing Agency chauffeur and errand boy were long behind him. Only a personal request by a very old friend had brought him here without complaint.

The terminal was crowded with servicemen headed to posts both stateside and overseas. He watched as the jet-way was maneuvered into place at the side of the British Airways 747. Minutes later the first passengers began to deplane in a steady stream.

Soon Vermeer spotted Tariq Saadoun, and waved to draw his attention. The two had known one another since Vermeer's days as a field officer in Beirut ten years earlier.

He thought his old friend looked tired. "It's good to see you, Tariq. How was your flight?"

"Fine."

The Iraqi expatriate looked frail, anemic, as if unaccustomed to life beneath the open sky. He had round features and small, damp hands, and wore the mantle of clerk or other minor functionary like a suit of medieval armor.

The two men said little else as Saadoun took his lone carry-on and headed toward Customs.

* * *

The rain came pouring down as Vermeer led the way to his vehicle, a government fleet sedan. Once Saadoun's bag was in the trunk they were on their way, motoring for CIA headquarters in Langley, Virginia. The trip would take less than twenty minutes all told, Vermeer knew, especially at this time of night.

Saadoun did not break his silence until Vermeer paid the parking fee and headed north into Arlington.

"Deputy Director Farraday is expecting us?" he asked.

Nicholas Farraday was the Central Intelligence Agency's Deputy Director of Operations, and Vermeer's ultimate superior. "He's waiting for us now," Vermeer answered. "But why . . . ?"

"Do you remember Mohammed Halabi?" Saadoun asked.

"He's a member of Saddam's inner circle, right? And a Sunni from Tikrit. Last I heard he was twisting thumbs for the Mukhabarat."

"Not any more."

"What do you mean?" Vermeer asked.

"Halabi wants to defect." Saadoun's voice was tight. "He knows he's on the wrong side, and that Saddam is doomed. Now he wants out before American tanks roll into Baghdad."

Vermeer doubted such a thing would ever come to pass, but knew better than to press the matter. "Go on."

"He doesn't trust the Agency, Peter. Not yet. That's why he contacted me through my people in Damascus."

Vermeer's fingers were tight on the wheel as he headed for the freeway entrance. "How do we know this is legit? Halabi is an old-time Ba'athist. I find it hard to believe he'd ever turn traitor, UN mandate to liberate Kuwait or no."

"A lot of prominent Iraqis are running scared. Halabi is one of them. That's why he's willing to give you a present before he comes over. Have you ever heard of something called Project Backgammon?"

They were two hundred yards from the freeway entrance. The road was lined with gas stations, convenience stores and small businesses. The well-maintained slopes of Arlington National Cemetery were two blocks distant. He came to a halt as the stoplight turned crimson.

"It was part of an intelligence-sharing program we had with the Mukhabarat during the Iran-Iraq war," Vermeer replied. "We were in bed with Saddam then, and did everything we could to help him. I seem to remember Dupont even helped set up a chlorine factory in Ba'qubah sometime around '82, '83. They use it to crank out mustard gas by the ton.

"It was all a big bust, though. The bastards rarely listened to us, or did anything useful with the intel we gave them. The program was shut down sometime before the end of the war with the Iranians, and never amounted to much. Why?"

"You're wrong," Saadoun insisted. "There was more to it than that. Halabi was our Iraqi contact with another portion of Backgammon. He called it Operation Bed Check, and says it involved operations against anti-Saddam radicals living outside Iraq. They had people murdered, often with direct U.S. assistance."

"I've heard this before, Tariq. I was part of the commission that investigated the original allegations."

"What did you find?"

"Not a damn thing." Vermeer shrugged. "It was nothing but smoke and mirrors, all right? Something the editors at the *Washington Post* ran with to sell newspapers."

Saadoun paused long enough to light a cigarette. "Halabi says different. What do you think would happen if . . ."

"Wait a second. What's that?" A dark colored sedan had pulled up to their left, in the next lane over. Vermeer saw the passenger door open, and a man in dark clothing climb out. He wore a black *balaclava* and brandished a Kalashnikov assault rifle.

"Son of a bitch!"

"Peter?"

Vermeer punched the accelerator and sped out into oncoming traffic. A look in the rearview mirror showed a muzzle flash flare against the night.

There was a tap-hammer rattle as high-velocity slugs punched into automotive steel. Saadoun shouted a needless warning: Vermeer saw the headlights of an onrushing delivery van as it careened toward them at high speed. The panicked honking of a car horn and the scream of rubber on wet pavement came to him, with the crash following in inevitable succession.

* * *

Gunter Zaisser watched the sedan fishtail from the impact of his bullets and crash. The Ford sedan twisted as it was jerked sideways by the impact. The oncoming UPS truck fared little better, its driver surely dead as the mangled wreckage that entangled him slid to a halt just beyond the scene of the crash.

"Heinrich! Follow close." Zaisser swapped magazines in his weapon and loped out into the rain-swept intersection, ready to finish what he had started.

* * *

For just a second Vermeer thought he was back in the Iranian desert, pinned in the remains of a burning C-130. The smells were right: hot metal, spilled fuel. Fresh blood. His head throbbed, his neck ached, and the sound of a distant scream echoed in his ears.

Then he remembered Tariq, and opened his eyes. He found himself covered with broken glass, and slumped behind the steering wheel. A woman was visible through the shattered windshield, speaking animatedly into a nearby payphone. He hoped she was calling 911.

"Tariq?" Everything was smashed all to hell. The stink of spilled gasoline came to him as he leaned over, and pulled Tariq Saadoun close.

His hand came away sticky with blood. Saadoun's neck was twisted at an odd, altogether impossible angle from where it had hit the dashboard. A sudden whiff of loosened bowels made Vermeer's stomach tighten.

"Look out! He's got a gun!"

The shout washed across Vermeer like cold water. He reached down between the driver's seat and the center console, and felt his fingers brush cold steel. He pulled the Detonics .45 automatic free and undid his seatbelt.

He climbed out of the car on unsteady legs. Everything wavered, jerking sickly, as he steadied himself. The taste of blood was thick on his tongue.

There was movement off to his left. It was the masked gunman, coming in fast with his AK braced and ready to fire.

Vermeer brought up his weapon and squeezed the trigger. He felt the pistol kick, and a red halo surrounded the guy's cranium as his first shot found its mark.

He dropped as if smacked in the head with a shovel. Vermeer tracked right, centering his sights on the sedan following close behind. He emptied the pistol into the windshield, and heard glass shatter. The driver clutched at his chest and screamed, a broken, brittle sound.

Someone yowled in unthinking terror. It was the same gal he had seen calling 911. Other gawkers were gathering nearby. He dumped the spent mag, and stooped to get a spare from inside his vehicle.

"Oh my God! He shot that guy!"

Vermeer reloaded as he limped over to the now-halted Mercedes. Broken glass crunched underfoot as he leaned in to inspect the man behind the wheel. Blood bubbled from a bullet wound to his right lung. Air rasped weakly as he struggled for each breath.

Vermeer pressed the .45 into his cheek, finger on the trigger. Police sirens sounded in the distance.

"Who sent you?"

"Fuck off."

His eyes were dark, angry, and slack with oncoming shock. He reached for a holstered sidearm, but the weapon was hopelessly tangled in his seatbelt. Maybe they didn't save lives after all, Vermeer thought. His mind was racing quicksilver fast.

Police sirens howled. "Last chance, buddy."

"Fuck you!"

He had an accent, Vermeer noticed. German, Swedish maybe, Euro-trash chic. Blood oozed through his clenched fingers, pulsing weakly, to dribble slowly away to nothing. There was little Vermeer could do to save him. By the time the first police cars arrived the guy was already dead.

* * *

Three hours later Michael Erich Litke walked into a 24-hour diner just off I-695 and ordered coffee and apple pie. He was a tall, fairly nondescript man with a receding hairline and faded blue eyes. The pie was production line quality, almost tasteless, like most of the food Litke had sampled since coming to America. Luckily the coffee was somewhat better.

The television behind the counter was tuned to CNN. He took a moment to watch as the contrail of a ballistic missile bisected the dark Saudi sky, followed by a brilliant flash as an American Patriot rose to intercept it. A fat general in desert camouflage replaced the image, and the Pentagon briefing continued.

Soon a woman sauntered over to join him. Elise Shilling had dark eyes and winsome features that few men could resist. But there was steel behind that lovely gaze, Litke knew, shining and pure.

"How did it go?" she asked.

"Not well. The contract is closed, yes? But Heinrich and Gunter are both dead."

Shock flitted briefly behind those beautiful eyes. Somehow Litke managed a small, sad smile. "The fortunes of war, Elise."

"Yes." She licked dry lips. She and Zaisser had been good friends, he knew, and sometimes more.

"What now?" Litke prodded.

"We leave for Paris in the morning." She passed him an envelope. Inside he found an airline ticket. "From there we head on to Amman, and wait for further orders."

"Why?"

"Control believes the Americans may try to bring Halabi out of Iraq," she said. "He wants us in place to assist as needed."

"I was afraid of that."

He eyed the television once more. The thought of journeying to Saddam Hussein's doomed madhouse held little appeal for him, but duty was duty after all.

"What is it?"

"Nothing." Litke shook himself out of his reverie. "I'll tell Willi. We can be at the hotel in fifteen minutes."

"I'll meet you outside." Elise headed for the door.

Litke waited a little longer, watching the images of war march across the television screen. Then he stood and gathered his jacket. Before he departed, however, he made sure to leave his waitress a generous tip. He of all people knew how important it was to reward good service.

CHAPTER 2

Northwest of Kibrit, Saudi Arabia
(1800 hours – Tuesday, 29 January 1991)

The approach of twilight found the sky muddied and black, and roiling behind a wall of smoke and flame. Great clouds hung on the wind, creating a petrochemical haze that blotted away the sun and turned day into night.

The marine helicopter skirted the worst of the conflagration as it neared the border, flying hard and fast against a stiff headwind. A journey of no longer than fifteen minutes followed as it plunged onward, over the bleak, undulating surface of the deep Saudi desert.

Gunnery Sergeant David Sweet's stomach churned as he felt the CH-46 Sea Knight bank sharply to the west. The cargo compartment was filled with the roar of the helo's jet turboshafts. His view of the desert tilted as they slipped to port. Little else was visible against the viscous miasma that cloaked the sky for miles in every direction.

He sighed. The oil-stench seemed to permeate everything, the chopper, his skin, even his sweat-soaked desert utilities. A finger wiped across his cheek would come away black, as if coated with thick summer molasses.

He had never seen anything like it. Sweet knew that Saddam Hussein had ordered all the oil wells and petro-facilities in occupied Kuwait to be put to the torch, partly out of some sense of petty revenge, but also to leave nothing for the Coalition to liberate once the ground war began. It was a scorched-earth policy on the grandest scale, almost too big to grasp, and wasteful beyond his ability to comprehend.

Sweet shared the cargo compartment with the helo's crew chief, a teenage W-M from supply, and a mountain of consumables including ammunition, fresh water and MREs.

They had taken his recon team away from him, of course. That skinny prick Barilotti had explained it was standard operating procedure, and suggested that Sweet's recent promotion had forced Colonel McCurry's hand. Team leader was a staff sergeant's billet after all. At least Recon 2/4 was in good hands, he thought. Staff Sergeant Bill Marino was as good a marine as any Sweet had ever served with.

He had always suspected there would be a price to pay for his affair with Jessica. The colonel had been kind enough not to charge either of them under Article 134 of the UCMJ. Considering the fact that Jess was still married, Sweet knew he should count his blessings. The last thing he'd wanted was to hurt her.

Now, in payment for his sins Sweet had been assigned as NCOIC to a logistics unit in Kibrit. There he'd spent the last week handing out beans and bullets, and going slowly mad in the process. He had hopped this supply flight out of simple desperation, mainly in a bid to get back into the desert to see some of his old buddies from Force Recon.

He saw the girl from supply was asleep, slumped atop a stack of Meals, Ready to Eat. The crew chief stood over the .50 Browning mounted in the starboard hatch. He looked to be no more than eighteen, Sweet thought, pimples and all. He bent over for a moment as com-chatter filled his headset.

"What is it?" Sweet had to shout to be heard over the roar of the engines.

The kid shouted back. "The pilot wants to know if you have a GPS set on you."

This perked Sweet right up. "Are we lost?"

He shrugged. "Probably. This is Lieutenant Metcalf's first run out here, Gunny."

Sweet grunted a reply. He had seen pilots lose their bearings over the rolling, hilly terrain of Camp Pendleton on more than one occasion, flying routes they had supposedly followed a hundred times before. And the lay of the land was considerably different here, he knew. Flat as a pancake, and as desolate as a high school valedictorian's chances on prom night.

"Give me a headset."

Sweet and the young, slightly unsettled helicopter pilot had a nice little chat over the intercom. No, he did not have a Global Positioning System receiver. The cool little satellite navigation aids were too expensive, Sweet had explained, and too hard to come by to be in the possession of a mere supply NCO. But yes, he did know the area, and offered to help if he could. The pilot ordered him into the cockpit and handed Sweet his map board.

"We're headed for Observation Post Four, Gunny. It's here, right near the border." He pointed to an area just one thousand meters from occupied Kuwait.

"Yes, sir." He took a moment to review Lt. Metcalf's map. They were in the vicinity of a region the marines had dubbed 'the Elbow,' after the sharp right angle it created in the borderline between Saudi Arabia and Kuwait.

"We're already close to the border, sir," Sweet reported after a moment's thought. "Are you sure we're still on the Saudi side?"

"As sure as I can be . . . Wait one." The copilot was gesturing out the front windscreen. Sweet leaned forward to see what the fuss was all about.

Metcalf smiled in relief. "There! That's it, I think."

* * *

Major Rashid Maseri stood in the lee of an abandoned Kuwaiti border post and watched the American helicopter approach through a set of high-power binoculars. It was mottled green in color, and appeared to be a troop transport.

"Is it a reconnaissance mission, sir?" his executive officer asked. He too watched through binoculars.

"I think not." Maseri pursed his lips thoughtfully. "They have merely strayed over the border, Aboud. Order the anti-aircraft batteries to open fire."

* * *

It took Sweet a moment to figure out what the copilot had spotted. It was a small, dun-gray structure, like a stone Quonset hut, set by a barely discernable trail that stretched to the northern horizon. A number of men were visible, standing around an armored vehicle parked to one side of the structure.

Metcalf was trying to raise them over the radio. "Cobra Nine Actual, this is Biscuit One-six. Come in, please. Cobra Nine Actual, this is—"

"Those aren't our people." Sweet's mouth was dry. "Sir, that's not an American vehicle."

"Are you sure, Gunny? I—"

"Jesus." The electric buzz of a radar-warning receiver suddenly filled his headset.

* * *

Sweet would never recall much about what happened next. All that would remain were vague, disjointed images: smoke and flame, and bits of stinging metal that flayed his skin and set his nerve endings afire. Incoming tracers licking at the smoke-filled sky. The crew chief, banging away with his Ma-Deuce until a hit by a 23mm shell tore away his arm at the shoulder, sending bright arterial blood spurting.

There was more screaming, shouting. He saw the young PFC huddled on the compartment floor, pissing herself in stark terror. Blackness followed as the helo spun in to crash.

He felt a huge impact, jarring and painful. Hands reached in, grabbed him. Pulled him from the wreckage; the smell of avgas and burning flesh was all around him.

Voices spoke in whip-fire Arabic. Someone rolled him over, and stars exploded as a boot struck him in the ribs. He heard laughter and a woman's ragged cry.

Sweet opened his eyes and tried to sit up. His skull pounded, and blood oozed into his eyes from a cut on his forehead. It was hard to move, hard to think. Someone put a boot on his neck while others took his sidearm and lashed his hands behind him.

Things grew hazy as men hurled Sweet into the back of a purloined Toyota pickup. They wore the uniform of the Iraqi Republican Guard, red berets and French-pattern desert camouflage. An officer supervised, regarding Sweet with eyes of angry obsidian.

Another marine had survived the crash. She was already in the back of the truck, and under the eye of a Kalashnikov-toting Iraqi conscript. PFC Monica Evans was battered but alive. One side of her head was so bloody that it was difficult to make out her features. He could see she was terrified, however, her wild blue eyes staring out of the unruly mop of her tangled blonde hair.

More soldiers clambered into the back, and then the truck was off, motoring into the gradually approaching night.

The movement sent Sweet crashing back to earth. He felt dizzy, nauseous, and sick. He fought the urge to vomit. Then another sound came to him. A familiar sound he had heard often enough before, in the field on full-scale maneuvers.

It was the sound of diesel engines. The sound of trucks and tanks, the clatter and squeak of heavy treads. The sound of hundreds of engines roaring all at once.

He lifted his head and fought back the taste of bile. He saw them then. Unending columns of Iraqi armor: Russian T-55 main battle tanks, Chinese armored personnel carriers, self-propelled artillery and anti-aircraft batteries. He saw infantry both mounted and afoot, and trucks and jeeps of every description, a logistics train that stretched for miles beyond Sweet's rapidly blurring line of sight. Great plumes of dust rose skyward as they rumbled by, going in the opposite direction, to the south.

Toward Saudi Arabia, and his fellow sailors and marines that held the line south of the deserted city of al-Khafji.

CHAPTER 3

Al-Mishab, Saudi Arabia
(1835 hours – Tuesday, 29 January 1991)

Captain Jessica Seeley was at evening chow when she first saw him. Slow anger swirled in her belly, fanning a hatred that burned inside her like a bright, shining star.

Major Steven Barilotti was tall and thin, with flat, dark eyes that were red-rimmed from lack of sleep. He was seated with his usual coterie of sycophants. The group included the battalion sergeant major, as well as that asshole Markham from supply. Even Captain Solovsky, the colonel's new battalion S-2, was there. It disgusted her to think that she had once been one of them.

"Good evening, ma'am."

She looked up to find one of the drones from battalion admin standing over her. Wondering how much the little ferret knew of her current situation put Seeley into an even darker mood.

"What do you want, Neuberg?"

"Mail call, ma'am." He handed over a stack of letters before departing.

Her depression grew deeper as she examined each letter in turn. The one person she desperately needed to hear from would never write her. Not so soon after their mutual humiliation had come to light.

Instead she was surprised to find one from Scott. She tore the envelope open, and noted that the postmark was nearly a month out of date.

> Jessica,
> Hope you're okay. They've been working us hard to be ready for the big show. We've flown more sorties in the past three months than we did in a year during peacetime. It's good, hard work though. Keeps me busy.

There was more, of course. Mostly filler about mutual friends from his squadron, and how much he enjoyed duty aboard ship. Crap like that. Things you would put in a letter to a friend, or maybe a distant relation. Not someone you'd been married to for the past four years.

She knew Scott's ship, the USS *Saratoga*, was in the Red Sea. The two had not seen each other in nearly eleven months, a fact that had started to mean less and less to her as the weeks had passed. She knew her marriage would not be the first hammered into scrap on the twin anvils of duty and career, but somehow the knowledge did little to bring her comfort.

Seeley realized she was no longer hungry, and got to her feet. As she expected, Barilotti and his toadies pointedly ignored her as she stepped out into the cold, uncaring rain.

Minutes later she entered the tent she shared with another marine. It was dark, and smelled vaguely of damp canvas. The only sound to be heard was the rumble of combat aircraft circling overhead. For the first time she wondered if Scott was flying one of them.

Seeing Barilotti had not helped matters. Fresh ire flooded through her as she remembered the way he had summoned her like some naughty puppy caught pissing on the living room carpet.

Seeley had not needed to be told that adultery and fraternization with an enlisted man were chargeable offenses under the Uniform Code of Military Justice. In many ways the UCMJ seemed a creation of an earlier time, she thought. Like something out of the Victorian Age, with its corsets and ridiculous sexual mores. The only thing that had saved the two of them, she knew, was the fact that the colonel needed every marine in the field more than some strict adherence to military regulations.

Still, the thought that David had lost his slot with Force Recon flayed her skin like fire. All he had done was be there when she needed him most.

"Captain Seeley! Captain Seeley!"

Lance Corporal Neuberg's voice cut through her introspection. She came to her feet, instantly alert.

"I'm here, Neuberg. What is it?"

"The colonel wants all officers and staff NCOs in the battalion CP." The kid blundered into the tent and shined a flashlight in her face. "It's a general alert, ma'am. The Iraqis have crossed the border and are headed this way."

* * *

Forty-five minutes later Seeley stepped out of the CP and into a freshening drizzle. She shivered as the wind cut through her field jacket, cold and chill. She had heard someone on Armed Forces Radio call it the worst winter the region had experienced in decades. For days the sky had been inky midnight, producing a gritty rain that poured down on the thousands of Coalition soldiers waiting for the ground war to begin on this side of the border.

It had been like this long before Operation Desert Storm had kicked off two weeks earlier. Like many in the First Marine Expeditionary Force, Seeley felt as if she'd been stuck in the desert for far too long. Now she could hear manmade thunder booming in the distance. Colonel McCurry's briefing had been quick and to the point. Although intel was scarce, it was clear to Division that an entire Iraqi army corps had crossed the frontier, bringing with it four first-tier combat divisions.

Unfortunately Central Command had left the area largely unguarded. Only a sprinkling of Saudi National Guard, Recon marines and LAV scout companies had been staged this close to the border, too meager a force to do much against the oncoming Iraqi juggernaut. Coalition forces had been left naked all the way to al-Mishab, Seeley had been told.

As a result General Krulak had ordered every warm body into the field. Cooks, typists and mechanics, male and female both, would join their infantry counterparts at the front. Seeley had been given command of one such unit, and told to prepare a defensive line across the highway that ran north–south along the coast.

Eighty-four sailors and marines had been placed under her direct command. She found them in the motor pool, checking gear and loading magazines.

A figure appeared at her side as if by magic. "We're mounted up and ready to go, ma'am."

Gunnery Sergeant Lyle Halverson was part of battalion motor transport, and a reservist. Seeley barely knew the man, and found herself praying he would be up to the task as her NCOIC.

"Ammunition?"

"I have three hundred rounds per man, plus a thousand for each M-sixty. Best I could do on short notice."

It would have to be enough. "What about LAWs?" she asked. LAWs were single shot, disposable rocket launchers designed to kill tanks and other armored vehicles.

"The ammo techs gave us twenty, ma'am. That's it."

"All right, Gunny. Mount up."

Seeley clambered into her command Humvee, encumbered by her body armor, helmet and deuce gear. She kept a loaded M-16 close at hand.

The little convoy moved out, and headed up Highway One. A curious mixture of excitement and fear danced inside her. This was something she had trained for, hoped and prayed for, for her entire adult life. It was the chance to go to war, and fight in service to her country.

* * *

Within the hour her ad-hoc rifle company was in place, straddling the highway into Khafji. To their immediate flank was something the Bedouins called a *sabkha*, a swamp-like salt marsh that stretched for miles inland from the coast.

Seeley had her people divided into three under-strength rifle platoons, each supporting an M-60 general-purpose machinegun. She ordered them to dig in. It was still dark, and the rain cloaked her view of everything beyond the first defensive berm. She was short of night-vision gear, and therefore assigned all she had to her squad- and platoon-level commanders. By 0200 she knew her marines were as ready as they would ever be.

She stood atop the berm, peering through Litton night-vision optics. Her view of the world shimmered, an ugly green-on-black. Khafji was barely discernable on the far horizon, backlit by quick-strobe flashes that filled the northern sky. Seconds later the low rumble of heavy artillery reached her.

Something crackled from the radio in her vehicle. Seeley turned to see Gunny Halverson speaking hurriedly to someone on the other end of the line.

"Movement forward, ma'am. One hundred meters."

"Stand by." Seeley put the NV set back to her eyes and scanned the night. Perhaps it would be best to pop a few illumination flares, she thought.

"Gunny, I want—"

Gunfire! She heard the sudden *crack-crack-crack* of M-16s mixed with the dull thud of a belt-fed machinegun. Tracers arced through the night, skimming over the flat desert terrain. Seeley wondered what her people thought they were shooting at.

"Gunny! I need a situation report, damn it."

"Aye, ma'am." Halverson got back on the horn, speaking heatedly. The rifles continued to crackle. A minute later the report came back to her: "It's a camel, ma'am. Fucker wandered into our beaten zone."

"Cease fire." The rattle of small arms fire died away slowly, resentfully. "Did we get him?"

Halverson nodded. "Dead as a doornail, ma'am."

Seeley stifled a tired sigh. It was going to be one hell of a long night, she decided.

CHAPTER 4

Northwest of the al-Wafra Oilfields – Kuwait
(0845 hours – Wednesday, 30 January 1991)

"Gunny? Gunny, wake up. We've stopped."

David Sweet swam upwards through a pool of blackness. For a long, luxurious moment he could not remember where he was. But then the pain returned. His skull throbbed. He opened his eyes and saw, blearily, that he and PFC Evans were still amongst the living.

"Keep it down, all right? My head is killing me."

"Sorry."

Monica Evans sat in the rear of the truck, her hands tied securely behind her. Someone had treated and dressed her injuries. Sweet wondered if he had been given the same treatment.

Of more immediate interest was the fact that their guard was nowhere to be seen. Sweet tested his bonds. He decided that whoever had tied his hands had done a bad job of it. He felt a bit of slack, maybe enough to start working at loosening whatever they had used to tie him up.

"How long was I out?" he asked, still groggy.

"I'm not sure. One of them took my watch."

Evans sounded weak, dejected, as if she didn't have a friend in the world. He would have to work on that. Her morale might be vital to their mutual survival in the days ahead.

"Did they, uh . . . Did they hurt you?"

"No." She kept her expression carefully neutral, but Sweet could see the haunted look in her eyes nonetheless. "One guy put his hands on me, you know? Groped me while I was tied up. An officer stopped him before it could go any further."

"We're going to get out of this. Don't worry."

Sweet fell silent as fresh voices sounded nearby. He heard murmured conversation and a metallic clatter as the Toyota's tailgate was undone.

He felt the truck shift as someone clambered aboard. Hands grabbed Sweet and rolled him over. He looked up to see the young Iraqi who had been guarding them earlier. Another soldier, an officer, stood nearby.

The lieutenant gave an order, and other soldiers appeared.

"You, get up." His English was thickly accented, as if learned from a book.

Sweet did not respond. The Iraqi snapped another order, and the trio of guards pulled him to his feet. One clouted Sweet across the back of the head, staggering him. They then frog-marched him across a large, open field.

The air still held that foul petrochemical tang. In the distance Sweet could make out the skeletal frames of what appeared to be dozens of drill rigs. All were aflame, row upon row of them, he saw, burning, and spurting fire in an unending stream.

A road was visible in the near distance. Both lanes were clogged with traffic as yet another Iraqi column headed south. Sweet looked to the sky for a moment, trying to pierce the smoke for any sign of friendly aircraft. He saw nothing. Where was the Air Force? A pass or two from a single A-10 and that column would have been history.

A hand shoved Sweet from behind. "In here."

He saw a small building before him. It had once been some sort of storage facility, perhaps a tool shed to service the petro facilities he could see nearby. It now sat abandoned, a lonely sepulcher of rotting wood and rusted metal.

Several armored personnel carriers were parked nearby. Each was equipped with the myriad radio aerials needed by a battalion-level commander. His guards led him up the stairs and into the shed, dark after the wan morning light outside.

The air within was rank and still. A man in Republican Guard mufti sat at a nearby desk. He was tall and whippet-thin, with piercing brown eyes and the angry, angular features of a man who had gone too long without adequate sleep or rest.

"Sit down, Sergeant. I'll be with you in a moment."

The lieutenant guided Sweet to an old swivel chair and forced him to sit. It squeaked loudly as he put his full weight on it. The guards withdrew at a command from the seated officer. After a moment he looked to Sweet, his expression thoughtful.

"You are Sergeant Sweet, yes? I have your identification card here, as well as your dog tags."

His English was silky, Sweet decided. Perfect. He said nothing in reply.

Instead Sweet noticed a number of items scattered across the man's desk: military ID cards, dog tags, even photographs, religious medals and other bits of personal gear. They were items from the crew of the downed helicopter. Sweet remembered the Arab penchant for looting the bodies of fallen enemies.

"I am Major Maseri," the man said. "Escape is not possible. Please note this, and act accordingly. You will be treated in accordance with the Geneva Convention as long as you continue to behave yourself."

Sweet sat up straight. "Sweet, David L. Gunnery Sergeant, United States Marine Corps. Service number—"

"Yes, yes. I know this already." Maseri waved a hand dismissively. "There is something I would like to speak to you about, however."

Sweet waited. Maseri picked up an item from the collection before him.

"The aircraft you were on was shot down while on a supply run," he said. "We know this from documents recovered at the crash site. Every person on board had reason to be there, save you."

"Sweet, David L. Gunnery Sergeant, United States Marine Corps. Service number five three zero, eight five four—"

"We know you are not a supply sergeant." Maseri slid an object across the table. Sweet recognized it immediately.

"This photograph was taken from your pocket, Sergeant. Do not waste time by denying it."

It was a picture of Matt, the latest Laura had sent just weeks before. He had memorized every line, every detail, as if it were a painting hanging in a museum of fine art.

"This is your son, yes?" Maseri asked. "I cannot help but be taken by the fact that it was the only personal item you had with you."

Now eleven, Matthew had grown quite a bit since Sweet had last seen him. He had his mother's eyes, and her square, almost severe features, littered with a fine dusting of freckles. In the photo Matt smiled and held up what looked like a pint-sized catfish. His stepfather, Brian, sat at his side, sunburned and beaming.

"Look at the shirt your boy is wearing, Sergeant. It caught my eye, so to speak."

The shirt was a gift he had given Matt the previous Christmas. It displayed outsized representatives of the Combatant Diver Badge and Naval Parachutist Wings, both coveted symbols of Marine Force Recon. It also bore a legend, visible, if somewhat blurry, at the bottom of the photo:

SWIFT – SILENT – DEADLY
1ST RECON BATTALION - USMC

It had been a stupid thing to trip up on, Sweet knew. Something the rawest Recon candidate learns on his first day in the Fleet: never carry personal gear in the field. But Sweet had been careless, and forgotten he had the photo on him when he had hopped that supply run just hours before.

"Kids wear all kinds of stupid things, Major."

"Yes, this is true." Maseri smiled, displaying crooked teeth. "Unfortunately my orders are clear."

He began to pace the tiny, cramped room. "Reconnaissance marines are considered elite troops. I have orders to turn any suspected Special Forces personnel over to Directorate Seven of the Intelligence Service General Staff. Therefore you are to be taken north immediately."

"Sweet, David L. Gunnery Sergeant, United States—"

Maseri barked an order, summoning his guards. Sweet was hustled bodily from the room. The last he saw of Maseri, the major was examining the photo of Sweet's son minutely, as if he too wished to memorize it for all time.

CHAPTER 5

Andrews Air Force Base – Maryland
(1900 hours (EST) – Thursday, 31 January 1991)

Nicholas Farraday stood at the window and stared out at the dark, heavily overcast sky. It seemed like years since he had seen the sun.

The maintenance sergeant who normally inhabited this office was nowhere to be seen. Like so many enthralled by the drama unfolding overseas, he had a television tuned to a local news affiliate. Farraday only half-listened as the oft-repeated footage of the ongoing incursion into Saudi territory played out on media outlets all over the world.

To many it seemed a huge disaster. The press certainly acted as if the battle heralded the Apocalypse, although Farraday liked to think he knew better. At the moment the marines and their Arab allies seemed to have the situation well in hand. The line was holding in the vicinity of Khafji, with heavy fighting continuing on into its third day.

He spied headlights moving in the darkness. A car pulled up to the exterior of the hangar and stopped, emitting a lone figure. Farraday would have recognized that tall silhouette anywhere.

Minutes later the man entered the office, clad in casual attire and carrying a light duffle bag.

"Sorry I'm late." Peter Vermeer had not recovered from the pounding he had taken the week before, Farraday noted. His face was bandaged where it had been cut by broken glass, and he still walked with a pronounced limp. Otherwise Vermeer was a big man, simply mountainous, with a perpetually shaved scalp and bright hazel eyes. He and Farraday had known one another for more than twenty years, ever since the bad old days of Tet '68.

"Don't worry about it," Farraday replied. "There's something we need to talk about."

Vermeer eased himself into a nearby chair. "Shoot."

Farraday opened his briefcase and pulled out a series of file folders. "Here. Look at this."

Vermeer took a moment to examine the morgue photographs contained in each folder. "Not much to look at, are they?"

"Do you recognize either man?"

"No. Should I?"

Farraday took back the pictures. "The first is a German national by the name of Gunter Zaisser, age twenty-eight. The other fellow was Heinrich Molle, thirty. Both were a part of a covert action group known as Objekt-74. They were Stasi once, and wet-work operatives of the highest order."

"I've heard of Objekt-74," Vermeer replied. "They were responsible for the assassination of that NATO general back in '83. The one the Red Army Faction originally claimed responsibility for."

"That's right." Farraday produced yet another series of photographs. "The Brits sent these over this morning. They're from a Heathrow security feed, at the same gate where Tariq Saadoun boarded his flight to Washington."

Vermeer examined these pics as well. They showed a woman who was tall, willowy, and, Farraday thought, quite attractive. Her hair was short and dark, and cut into a flattering pageboy.

"Pretty girl."

Farraday snorted. "If you have a taste for rattlesnake, maybe. She's a former Stasi major by the name of Elise Shilling. Before Reunification she ran her own Objekt-74 cell, with black operations in both West Germany and the United Kingdom. Interpol's been on her tail for the past year."

"So she's gone freelance?" Vermeer inquired. "Shilling is working for the Iraqis now?"

"That's our best guess."

Vermeer rubbed a hand across his jaw, seemingly deep in thought. "How did the Iraqis know to come after Tariq in the first place? Publicly he's nothing more than a low-grade smuggler and arms dealer."

"We're working on that." Suddenly Farraday felt very tired. "I asked to see him personally, Peter. I believe he had information that would have been valuable to us, especially now."

"Mohammed Halabi."

"That's right." Farraday handed over another file. "I want you to head to Riyadh, and link up with our senior man there. Do you remember Jim Detloff?"

"We worked together in Libya, just prior to El Dorado Canyon. We're going after Halabi, right?"

"That's the plan."

Vermeer opened the folder. The photo inside depicted a heavyset man with dark eyes and the requisite Saddam mustache. Vermeer looked it over for a minute before replying. "Tariq mentioned a possible connection with something called Operation Bed Check. Did you read my report on the subject?"

"We're looking into it," Farraday said. "But I wouldn't get too excited at the prospect. Chances are it's just another tall tale Halabi is offering to sweeten the pot."

"Who else am I working with?"

"Grant Lattimore is handling the ops side of things. Right now the situation is a little fluid over there, but if Grant can get things locked down in time we'll send in a team to bring Halabi out."

Vermeer spent another moment perusing the file. "We know his movements that precisely?"

"To a point." Farraday suddenly felt the need to pace the room. "Commo intercepts suggest he's going to be in the south, interrogating Kuwaiti resistance members the Iraqis have captured. Langley thinks this might be the best time to bring him out."

"It's going to be a bitch, what with the air raids and all."

"I . . ." Farraday paused as a young airman entered the room. "Yes?"

"The flight you requested is ready, sir."

"Thank you." Farraday turned back to his old friend. "You'd better get a move on, Peter."

Vermeer regarded Farraday for a moment. His expression was no longer pleasant, only thoughtful.

"I'll be in touch." Vermeer picked up his bag and followed the airman out into the night.

CHAPTER 6

Near al-Khafji, Saudi Arabia
(0900 hours – Friday, 1 February 1991)

The Iraqi had died trying to escape his burning vehicle. He sat in the turret of what had once been a Russian T-62 main battle tank, now fire-blackened and smoldering from the wire-guided missile that had immolated it. The flesh had been burned completely from his skull, leaving only char-paper remains and empty, gaping eye sockets.

Jessica Seeley turned at the scream of approaching jet engines. A pair of marine AV-8B Harriers sped by, low and fast, their wings studded with Rockeye cluster bombs and other high-explosive ordinance. Air power had broken the Iraqi offensive. Once the Coalition had unleashed endless streams of ground attack aircraft on the approaching enemy, little could have been done to save them.

Conversely, Seeley's patchwork rifle company had never fired a shot in anger. Until today the only casualty she had seen had been the unfortunate camel that had stumbled into their free-fire zone at the start of the battle.

Now the marines and their Coalition allies were advancing steadily northward. Khafji had already been retaken with a minimal cost in friendly lives. At least that was what the latest scuttlebutt said. Seeley knew full well the local rumor mill had been wrong on more than one occasion.

At the moment Seeley's unit was assigned to prisoner detail. Enemy POWs streamed to the rear by the hundreds, often overwhelming the regular military police contingents assigned to guard them. As a result her marines now stood watch over an Iraqi unit that had surrendered the night before.

She turned from the dead tank and headed toward her company CP. Armored vehicles, Humvees and 5-ton trucks by the dozens still churned their way north, driving past her unit, past her, and apparently past her military career and any chance she may have once had at seeing her next promotion board.

The rumors had already started to trickle downrange. It seemed Colonel McCurry had finally cut orders for Seeley to be relieved of her duties pending a final hearing, and then she was to be sent Stateside. Case closed, thank you very much, end of story.

Gunny Halverson intercepted her just short of the main EPW encampment. Fifty filthy, bedraggled Iraqi prisoners huddled in the dirt there. Most gorged themselves on American MREs under the watchful eyes of Seeley's marines.

"Good morning, ma'am." Halverson looked dirty and tired.

"Gunny."

"Word just came down, ma'am. An MP platoon is on the way to relieve us. Once they're in place, we're to report back to al-Mishab for reassignment."

"Understood." She paused for a moment, considering. "Our people did a good job, Gunny. All of them."

"Every marine is a rifleman, ma'am." He saluted. "With your permission?"

She returned his salute with grim precision. "Carry on."

"Aye, ma'am." Halverson turned as if to leave, and then halted. "Oh, ma'am?"

"Yes?"

"There's someone waiting at the CP for you. Looks like a Recon marine to me."

* * *

Seeley found Staff Sergeant Bill Marino leaning against the bumper of her command Humvee. He was tall and gangly, with sharp Aztec features seemingly hewn from the darkest marble. She remembered David speaking of him often, for the two had gone through the Basic Reconnaissance Course at Coronado together nearly a decade before.

"You wanted to see me, Staff Sergeant?"

He stood. "Yes, ma'am."

Marino wore grimy desert camouflage. Something about the hard look in the staff sergeant's eyes made her feel distinctly uneasy.

"What is it? Is something wrong?"

"You could say that, ma'am." He paused as if gathering his thoughts.

"Go on."

"Two days ago my team was sent on a TRAP mission. We were already across the border, reporting enemy troop movements, when we got word that a supply helo had gone down. Higher wanted boots on the ground to look for survivors."

Seeley knew that TRAP stood for Tactical Rescue of Aircraft and Personnel, marine-speak for a traditional search and rescue mission. "Why are you telling me this, Staff Sergeant?"

"Dave Sweet was on that bird, ma'am. Along with four other marines."

"I see." Her world spun crazily for a bit, tottering, before straightening with a terrible abruptness. "What about survivors?"

"We found the crash site okay," Marino went on. "But no survivors, no dead bodies. It looked like the Iraqis sanitized the wreck before we could get there."

"I see," she repeated. The words were like ashes in her mouth.

"That doesn't mean he's KIA. If anybody could survive that crash, it would be Dave Sweet. You know that as well as I do."

"Yeah." But her own voice sounded vague to her, distant, as if coming from the bottom of a deep, dark well.

* * *

Seeley could not remember whether she ever thanked Marino for coming to see her. One minute he was there, the next, he was gone, and she was standing alone at the berm along Highway One.

Tanks, trucks and infantry carriers continued to grind their way north toward the border. Black clouds marred the horizon, dark as pitch and befouled with the stench of waste and of war. Her eyes watered from the smell of spilled oil, spilled blood, until Gunny Halverson came and told her it was time to move on.

CHAPTER 7

Az Zaubayr, Iraq
(0731 hours – Saturday, 2 February 1991)

David Sweet huddled in the back of the Iraqi armored personnel carrier. His muscles ached from shivering so much. He could not remember ever feeling this cold before now.

A long, rolling boom echoed overhead, telling Sweet the good guys were still in the war. Once in a while he heard Iraqis muttering outside the vehicle. They were scared shitless, he decided. The thought had given him strength, and lent him a certain resolve whenever his sleep-deprived brain wandered toward thoughts of escape.

The gash on his forehead throbbed, making it hard to think. So far they had made few attempts to actively interrogate him, although Sweet suspected that would change once they had him in a secure location.

The conversation outside ceased abruptly. A voice grunted a command, and the rear hatch of the carrier was levered open on rusty hinges. Gray light flooded in, admitting a familiar figure. Sweet's chief jailor was a fellow he had dubbed Porky Pig, and a sergeant in Saddam's crack Republican Guard. He was around forty-five, with broad, porcine features and a slight potbelly earned by the inevitable encroachment of middle age.

"Where are we going?" Sweet asked.

Porky Pig slapped him across the face and shouted. Another soldier stood with the sergeant, tensely cradling an assault rifle.

Sweet blinked rapidly as they dragged him into the light. They had loaded him into this armored personnel carrier two days before, bound, guarded and finding little chance of escape. Sweet had worried constantly that some U.S. jet jockey would spot the column and drop a laser-guided bomb on his head.

Now it looked as if that time had finally come. The Iraqis had stopped at a major roadway, bordered for much of its length by shabby looking palm trees. Rows of equally shabby buildings were visible in the near distance, probably the outskirts of a larger town somewhere to the north.

Blots of fresh smoke clouded the horizon, as if the Air Force or Navy had just smacked someone down hard. He could hear the not-so-distant rumble of approaching jet engines.

There was more shouting. Porky Pig prodded him onward, causing Sweet to trip and fall.

He was dragged to his feet by the two guards, and the trio tumbled into a muddy drainage ditch. The bottom was filled with scummy water that stank of fresh sewage. Sweet crouched low as the sergeant bellowed at him in meaningless Arabic.

An olive-drab shape jetted by at that moment, flying low and popping decoy flares. It was an Air Force A-10 Warthog. Sweet recognized the bird's long, graceless slab wings, forked tail, and ugly blunt profile. The plane was so low that Sweet could make out the helmeted silhouette of the pilot seated in his titanium-armored cockpit.

An Iraqi private brought his AK-47 to one shoulder even as the Warthog sped by. Hot brass rained down on Sweet as the kid triggered off a long burst.

Now other guns were sounding from the stalled column. Sweet saw rifles, anti-aircraft guns, even the contrail of a shoulder-fired surface-to-air missile or two. Tracers lanced through the sky like emerald fire.

None of it would make a bit of difference in the end, he thought. Sweet watched as that beautiful-ugly bird circled around, jinking past AA-fire, and rolled in for its first gun-run. A great, roaring purr shook the earth as the jet opened fire with its nose-mounted, seven-barrel rotary cannon. The world dissolved into a nightmare cacophony of fire, heat and sound. Iraqi vehicles disintegrated as a series of explosions swept through the column like the passage of a giant fist. The ground tilted crazily, savagely, and Sweet felt as if he had been thrown aside by the horns of some massive bull.

Vehicle after vehicle burst into flame, erupting skyward. Men ran, screaming, only to be cut to pieces as 30mm depleted uranium shells detonated all around. Sweet hunkered down and prayed.

It was then that he felt something sharp and metallic cut into his right hand.

His long ago SERE training came to him in a flash: escape and evasion, an operator's first creed when held prisoner. Sweet fought to recover whatever it was that had dug into his flesh. A moment's effort brought it to his fingers: a sharp piece of metal, possibly a bomb fragment from an earlier strike.

The Iraqis had tied his hands with strong rope. Sweet rubbed his bindings against the metal, working quickly. At the moment both of his guards were too busy firing at the Warthog to worry about him.

He felt the rope part cleanly. He massaged his bruised skin to get some feeling back, and turned to look at the two enemy soldiers. Both watched as the attack jet followed up for yet another devastating run.

Porky Pig kneeled at the edge of the ditch, looking toward the wildly maneuvering jet fighter. The other man crouched nearby, clumsily reloading his rifle. Neither soldier so much as glanced in Sweet's direction.

He turned his gaze to the service pistol hanging from the sergeant's belt. Both Iraqis cringed as a nearby APC erupted into flames, its onboard store of fuel and ammo igniting with a bright, hoary flash of light and sound.

The flap on the military holster was already open. Sweet reached out, grasped the weapon, and tugged it free.

The pistol was an old Browning Hi-Power, worn from decades of hard service. He pulled back the slide to bring a round into the chamber and pressed the pistol against the back of the sergeant's head. There was a flash, a pop, and Porky Pig pitched forward, dead. Sweet tracked right and brought the weapon to bear on his second target. At first the kid did not react. He just sat there, stunned, with bits of gray matter clinging to his face. His eyes were filled with fear.

He started to plead. But Sweet remembered the face of another young man, the crew chief of the downed helo, and the sudden, terrible way he had died. A second gunshot sounded, closing those dark eyes forever.

* * *

Sweet took the dead sergeant's AK, spare ammo, and pack before scurrying off into the chaos stirred up by the waning American air strike. He dashed across the road, threading his way between the burning vehicles. The Warthog had moved on by now, its onboard ammunition likely spent. This left the Iraqis milling about like confused children, many still firing blindly into the rain-swept sky. None seemed to notice Sweet as he headed across the fields bordering the highway, the sporadic crackle of their guns following him every step of the way.

CHAPTER 8

The outskirts of Basra, Iraq
(1605 hours – Saturday, 2 February 1991)

Hours of hard walking brought David Sweet to the main road into Basra. Signposts in both English and Arabic showed him the way. The Shatt al-Arab Waterway, paralleling the major highway into town, was visible only as a winding black ribbon to the north. He knew he was perilously close to Iraq's principal seaport, with its massive military garrison and attendant anti-aircraft defenses.

The presence of so many enemy troops made Sweet nervous. Recon marines normally preferred to operate under the cover of darkness, and avoided built-up areas like the plague. But the hasty nature of his escape had forced his hand. He needed to put as many kilometers as possible between himself and his erstwhile captors, thus necessitating this journey in broad daylight.

The thought of enemy patrols had barely slithered across his mind, snake-slick, when the sound of approaching diesels came to him through the rain. Sweet went to ground as dim vehicle headlights appeared on the road to his right.

It was almost as if they were herding him toward the city, Sweet thought. He could just make out the column of military vehicles through the murk. The closest was barely three hundred meters distant.

Moments later he heard a tailgate slam open, followed by the clatter of boots on blacktop. Sweet watched as a number of shadowy forms left the trucks and began to approach his position.

He eased back, ever so slowly, and crept into the brush lining the road. He rose to a low crouch and began to make his way around the patrol.

He heard something, the clatter of equipment, a softly spoken word, off to his left. Sweet froze in place, heart pounding, as a second column appeared, moving quietly along a flooded *wadi* twenty meters from the road. He was close enough to see the Republican Guards' badge on the squad leader's beret.

Sweet waved to them, the fear flowing through his veins like heavy oil. The squad leader waved back, casually, before continuing on. Sweet's camouflage uniform was similar enough to the enemy's that he had evaded detection for now. Chill water flowed down his face as he waded across the stream and ducked into a nearby stand of reeds.

He quickened his pace as voices sounded from the road. More soldiers, he thought, searching for anyone trying to ford the river. He was nearing the waterway, the reeds thick, and matted together like a closely woven hedge. He pushed through one last thicket, expecting to see the waterway. Instead he came face to face with a startled enemy soldier.

Sweet reacted without conscious thought. He moved in, his bayonet whispering free of its sheath. He clamped his hand over the man's mouth, and plunged the blade into his sternum, once, twice, three times. The Iraqi struggled, thrashing fingers prying at Sweet's arms, his face, clawing desperately. Seconds passed, and Sweet felt his struggles lessen. He pulled the knife free and lowered the body to the ground. There was no time for anything fancy, he thought. Sweet dragged the body to the river, and rolled it into the dark, murky water.

More voices came from the left. He eased out of the reeds and continued on his way. A series of gray concrete buildings were now visible in the near distance.

It was the outer suburbs of Basra, he soon realized. Here the streets were filled with drab shanties, shops and low-rent apartments. The buildings were gray brick, dusty and forlorn. Sweet crouched behind a wall and surveyed the area, looking for any sign of human habitation. He saw nothing, but the familiar grumble of heavy diesels forced him into motion. Sweet vaulted the wall as the first of several armored vehicles trundled down the street.

He waited as one of the Russian-built BMP armored personnel carriers came to a halt directly across the way. Armed men began to emerge from inside. Sweet crept toward a nearby apartment building and slipped through a door that had been left ajar.

He could hear men talking as he moved into the corridor beyond. Somewhere outside he heard a dog barking, followed by more voices.

Decaying plaster hung from the walls like strips of dead skin. Sweet spied a door to his right and tried the knob. It was locked. He slammed his shoulder against it, hard, and felt it give slightly. More voices outside. Footsteps. He rammed his shoulder into the door again, and it gave way, sending him tumbling into the apartment beyond.

The place seemed dark and deserted. The living room was dingy and cramped, and done up in faded red-on-white striped wallpaper. The furniture looked like something out of a dentist's waiting room, except for the portrait of Saddam Hussein on the wall opposite the door. He saw plates in the sink, and smelled the distant rot of spoiled food. He heard footsteps in the corridor outside, soldiers searching, calling to one another.

He moved into the bedroom. There Sweet found a small chest of drawers and a mattress, stained from hard use.

The voices grew louder. Sweet noticed the dresser was placed at an odd angle in relation to the bedroom's inner wall. He tugged the chest aside to see a large, gaping hole in the plaster, blocked by a set of old cardboard boxes.

Sweet pulled one of the cartons aside. The hole fed into a crawlspace within the wall itself. He crouched and scurried inside before dragging the chest back into place. He gripped his rifle tensely as more voices came to him through the walls, murmuring, questioning. Fresh terror swirled in his belly. The darkness shielded him, true, but for how long? How long until the enemy came for him, and dragged him back into the light?

* * *

King Khalid Military City – Saudi Arabia
(1915 hours – Saturday, 2 February 1991)

Peter Vermeer tended to favor charcoal, especially with faces. Tonight he worked steadily, rapidly outlining the features of a woman he had never met. The image he had used as a start had come from an old passport photo included in the files on Elise Shilling and the rest of her team. Mostly he sketched to relax, to allow his mind to wander, and consider options he might not have seen otherwise. Now he sat and regarded the sheet of paper before him: Shilling had long, almost equine features, pretty but harsh, as if she had lived a hard life, with little in the way of luxury or kindness.

He checked the time. They should have reported in by now. He was reaching for a cigarette when the telephone on his desk began to ring.

He picked up. "Vermeer."

"Wishbone is overdue." He recognized the voice of Grant Lattimore on the other end of the line. "You'd better get over here, Peter. Lindsley looks like he's about to have kittens."

"I'm on my way."

The sound of turboprop engines assailed Vermeer the moment he stepped into the night. A Hercules transport taxied onto a nearby runway as he walked past sandbag revetments, guard towers and endless rows of steel Connex boxes. Tactical aircraft thundered overhead. Vermeer knew that while no aircraft were permanently stationed here, KKMC was still a major rearming/refueling point for the entire Coalition air effort. As a result the airspace above the base was crowded with circling military aircraft twenty-four hours a day.

The command bunker dedicated to Special Operations Command was located just beyond Runway 3-1 west. Vermeer checked in with the sentry before descending a set of concrete steps into the bowels of the earth. The room beyond was packed with flickering computer screens, radar repeaters and SATCOM uplinks. Lattimore met Vermeer at the door and handed him a cup of coffee.

"We've been waiting for forty-five minutes now," Lattimore said. "Lindsley is starting to make noises about pulling the plug. Talk to him, will you?"

Lattimore was Vermeer's senior operations manager, and third in command of the task force ordered to recover Halabi. He was also one of the New Breed the Agency seemed so hell-bent on recruiting: educated, thoughtful and intelligent, but with little real-world experience. He wore his Stanford class ring like a badge of honor, and carried a certain youthful arrogance and sense of entitlement that often irritated his older colleagues to the core.

Vermeer sampled the coffee, grimaced, and set it aside. "Where's Detloff?"

"In the shitter again." Vermeer looked a question at him, and Lattimore shrugged. "I told him not to drink the water."

Vermeer headed across the room. A number of military types were crowded around one of the satellite uplinks, waiting for word from the team sent to contact Mohammed Halabi.

Senior amongst them was Lieutenant Commander Steven Lindsley, United States Navy. The four Navy SEALs that made up the recovery team were under his direct command.

"Any word yet?" Vermeer asked.

"Nothing."

"These things take time, Commander."

Lindsley jacked a thumb toward Grant Lattimore, still at his self-imposed spot by the door.

"Tell that to your buddy over there," he said.

Vermeer wished for another cigarette. "That was condescending of me. Sorry."

"I guess we're all on edge," the commander said. "I—"

"Wishbone Six to Lima Actual. Lima Actual, do you copy? Come in, over." The words hissed from an overhead speaker.

Lindsley took up a headset. "Lima Actual, go."

"At Rally Point Candle. No contact. I say again, no contact."

Vermeer frowned. The pickup team had arrived on-site and waited for more than the prescribed thirty minutes. Now the Iraqi was a no-show, and the mission commander was asking Higher for instructions.

"Stand by." Lindsley looked to Vermeer. "I don't like it. There's too much enemy activity in the area, and our primary LZ is close to at least three triple-A emplacements. I'd rather abort now, before first light."

Vermeer turned to an ops map set up nearby. His eyes traced the lines of roadways and built up areas that surrounded As-Samawah, a city of 200,000 on the banks of the Euphrates River. It was at least two hundred kilometers from As-Samawah to the Saudi border. If they missed the extraction bird it would mean a long walk for the team, especially if the enemy were somehow alerted to their presence. Vermeer hoped that whatever Halabi knew was important enough to risk the lives of four good men.

"I'm sorry, Commander. We wait. Order your team to make another circuit of the primary and secondary meet sites, and then have them report back in at zero-six hundred."

CHAPTER 9

Basra
(2300 hours – Saturday, 2 February 1991)

Nightfall found the city's skyline illuminated by fire.

Amina Jabouri stood in a trash-strewn alley, watching the anti-aircraft tracers burst far above her with startling ferocity. Shrapnel clattered onto the shop awning over her head like bits of steel confetti. A smaller, more vivid glow etched a horizontal line across the sky. It was an American cruise missile, speeding unerringly to its target despite the darkness and the foul weather. She saw a sudden flash, followed by a stupendous thunderclap of sound, and knew instinctively what the Americans had just hit. A local annex of the Special Intelligence Ministry was located just a few blocks away, in a compound bordering Basra Maqal Airport. How many Mukhabarat lackeys had just died, she wondered. If it was God's will the death toll would be enormous! She prayed that it be so, and watched as the flames shot skyward, tainting the horizon for kilometers in every direction.

Part of her abhorred this destruction, this wanton murder. Part of her relished it, and cheered to see the hated Ba'athist regime torn down and shattered! If only it was not the hand of the Great Satan that did the work, she thought. Still, it could only be the will of God if the Americans were destined to be the instrument of Iraq's liberation.

The skies seemed to have quieted, so Amina decided to move on. She kept mostly to the shadows. The rain had stopped hours before, leaving the road muddy and well-churned by the passage of dozens of military vehicles. Eventually a dark outline appeared before her, low against the horizon. She knew it to be the cemetery that paralleled Abu Khasib Boulevard. Rude stone crypts stood before her, while the towers beyond were actually the minarets of a nearby mosque.

The growl of approaching diesels froze her in place. Fear burned within her anew as she scurried into the cemetery and went to ground at a nearby crypt.

Military vehicles clattered by, most piled high with soldiers. But Amina remained unseen: her black *abaya*, which preserved her modesty during the day, now served to conceal her by dark of night. Once the vehicles had moved on she emerged from cover. She had just enough time to reach her destination, recover what she sought, and return before dawn's first blush could taint the distant horizon.

Upon arrival she discovered that the apartment door had been battered inward.

Should she go in? Or just leave? Need won out over fear as Amina shined a flashlight around her miniscule flat. She had not been here in weeks. Other members of her cell had used the place as a safe house instead. One look at the ruined kitchen told her they were just as lazy and messy as her older brothers had been growing up.

Thinking of Ismail, Hafez and Ibrahim brought a torrent of memories welling up inside of her. She'd been all of thirteen when the soldiers had come for her father, for all the boys. They'd lived in Baghdad then. The officer in charge had told Mother they would be at Abu Graibh for questioning only. Amina had never seen them again.

Their only crime, she knew now, had been being born poor and Shi'a.

Shaking herself, Amina moved past the living area and into the bedroom. She wondered what they had done with her furniture. At least her dresser hadn't been moved, she thought. Amina extracted one of the boxes hidden in the crawlspace, and noted its weight with satisfaction. She opened the container and took a moment to inspect the dozen or so medicine bottles inside, a veritable treasure trove that included codeine, Percocet and Penicillin.

"Quite a collection you have there."

Amina reacted as if physically struck, and nearly dropped her flashlight. A man's voice, speaking in English! She spun about, heart pounding, to face him. Her light fell across a shadowed figure standing in one corner of the room. Her mouth went dry as she realized she had passed right by him and never suspected a thing.

A nameless dread gripped her by the throat. She shouted at him, angrily, and told him to get out. The saltiest curses in the world had sprung from her native tongue, after all. If only her knees would stop shaking so!

"Stop pretending you don't understand me. I found this earlier, when I was looking for something to eat."

He held a book in his hands. She recognized it instantly, of course: an English-language anatomy textbook, now worn from years of heavy use.

"I'm not going to hurt you. I was just looking for somewhere to hide."

She stopped herself from eying the rifle he carried. "You have no right to be here. This is my home."

"If that's the way you want it. But I have questions first."

He came fully into the light. His face was lean, she thought, with a hard, unsmiling mouth. His piercing gray eyes seemed to bore into her very soul, like sunlight after a fierce spring rain.

"Do I have a choice?" she asked him.

"Of course you do. I was just wondering how you came to speak English so well."

She stood a little straighter and scowled at him. "I went to University in America. Most of my family lived there once."

He indicated the medical supplies. "Are you a doctor?"

She felt anger welling up inside her. "A nurse. I work at the teaching hospital . . . Well, I used to. You bombed it last week. Many innocent people were killed."

He picked up a bottle of pills. "So what's this for? Are you thinking of opening a free clinic?"

Her anger burned brighter. She took the bottle and shook it in his face.

"Damn you! Food is scarce. Medicine is scarce. Bush and his sanctions are killing us slowly, bit by bit. Sometimes I sell these things in the Market to make ends meet."

"I see."

She resisted the urge to spit in his face. "Is there anything else?"

"Just this."

He reached into a pocket and removed a small cardboard box. Her stomach clenched as he upended it, sending a stream of lacquered-steel rifle cartridges spilling to the floor.

* * *

David Sweet matched the girl stare for stare. She seemed to have nothing to say, so he decided to plunge onward. "The ammo is Russian, and the case of rocket-propelled grenades I found in the crawlspace is from Czechoslovakia."

He saw her eying the doorway, as if considering whether or not she could make it out before he put a bullet in her spine.

"What do you want from me?" she replied.

"I'm not your enemy, lady. Saddam is. I have no idea who you work for, but somehow I doubt it's someone who wants to see him remain in power."

She shook her heard emphatically. "I have no idea where these things came from. Now let me go, okay? I just came for the medicine. There are many injured people at the mosque down the street. I must return before my—"

"Quiet." Sweet raised a hand, stopping her in mid-sentence.

"I—"

"I said shut up." He took the flashlight from her. The room plunged into inky darkness.

There it was again, Sweet thought. Voices, probably in the hallway outside.

He went to one knee, dragging her down beside him. He had already unslung the AK and snapped off the safety.

He placed his head next to hers, and smelled the sweat in her hair. "Stay quiet. Do as I say." The words came out as barely a whisper.

"Y-yes."

Sweet put her out of his mind. The last thing he wanted to do was open fire. In Recon, firing your weapon usually meant failing the mission. You were supposed to get in, do your thing, and leave the AO exactly as you had found it. Now it looked as if Sweet was about to be reintroduced to the pointy end of the stick.

* * *

The American was crazy, Amina thought. Blood-mad, stupid, out of his head. She could feel him kneeling next to her, tensely fingering his weapon. Eager to kill, to maim. She also heard the soldiers outside, and knew the terrible danger they were in. She reached for the cardboard box containing her medicine. All this would be for nothing if she failed to return with it in time.

Madness. It was all madness, and waste. Thoughts of poor dead Ismail came to her now. There were times when she had trouble remembering his face, and the odd, snorting way he had laughed, like some lovesick hyena.

No. There was simply too much at stake, she thought. Too much at risk. Standing, Amina strode past the crouching American and began shouting for help at the top of her lungs.

She stepped into the hallway, shouting of thievery, murder, and worse.

A half-dozen flashlights pinned her in place, and a man gruffly ordered her to halt. The brilliant glow dazzled her. She caught a vague impression of uniformed men, assault rifles, and dark, curious eyes peering at her from the shadows. It shocked her to note that she no longer felt afraid at all.

"You there! Go back inside. We are searching for dangerous criminals."

Amina steeled herself. "You are soldiers, yes? You are here to protect the people? Someone has broken into my flat, and stolen everything I own!" She gestured to her sundered door for effect. "I want to know what you're going to do about it."

The lead soldier grunted. "Sergeant El-Qaisy."

A figure came forward. "Sir!"

"Secure both ends of the hallway, and see to it that a squad searches the apartments upstairs. No one in or out. I'll handle this."

"Sir!"

The officer stepped closer. Amina saw that the man was a *Naqib*, or captain of the elite Republican Guard.

"You say your apartment was broken into, miss? Where is your husband?"

"At the front, along with my two brothers." She lowered her eyes in humility, ever the picture of the dutiful spouse. "I was not here either, but upstairs, visiting with neighbors."

"And your father? Or any other male relatives?"

"All dead. Killed in the war with the Iranians."

He scowled. "There is a curfew, miss. From dawn to dusk. Why were you not at home?"

"I was lonely, and afraid. The bombs fall so close at night, do they not? The hospital I work at was destroyed just last week."

He entered the apartment and played his flashlight about, examining her few meager possessions. "I will need to see your identification."

"Of course." She handed over a document folder. The name inside was false, of course. She had several different sets of ID, all expertly made up from the names of women long dead.

Amina watched him go over her papers, all the while aware of the silent, darkened bedroom behind her.

After a moment he handed them back. "Private Fawzi."

"Sir?"

"Search the area. Make sure the thieves are not hiding nearby."

Amina waited as the soldiers performed a very cursory inspection of her flat. Luckily the American had known enough to pull the dresser back into place over the crawlspace opening.

"Nothing, sir. There is no one here."

"I'm sorry, miss. We don't have time for anything more. Try the regular police in the morning, if the telephones are working."

Amina complained, of course. Bitterly. But her objections fell on deaf ears. Minutes later she was alone again, save for her unwelcome visitor.

"Just what the hell did you think you were doing?" the American snapped the moment the dresser had been pulled aside. It pleased her to think he was the one feeling frightened, frustrated. Not in control.

"Saving your life." She gathered the medicine she needed. "Now come along. There are people I want you to meet."

CHAPTER 10

Basra
(0244 hours – Sunday, 3 February 1991)

David Sweet played his flashlight around the edges of the gaping wound in the earth. The air wafting up from the open manhole stank of dampness and decay.

"Inside, quickly," his new friend said. She still refused to give him her name. "I've never seen the streets so heavily patrolled at this time of night."

He put one foot on the ladder leading down. Moments later he was clambering hand over fist into the darkness. The stone walls around him were slick with fresh condensation. The girl followed close behind. A descent of at least thirty feet followed before Sweet reached the bottom. He panned his flashlight around, noting he now stood in a passage of rough brick construction. The place had the feeling of ancient bones, long buried.

"What is this place?" he asked. "Is it part of the sewer system?"

"Follow me." She led the way with Sweet close at her heels. As they walked fingers of darkness seemed to press in on them, grasping and close.

At first he thought she had decided to ignore his earlier inquiry. Then she looked over her shoulder and began to speak.

"These tunnels date back to Tamerlane," she explained. "The Ottoman Turks expanded on the original construction years later. Sometimes we use them to smuggle people and contraband in from Abadan, all under the noses of the secret police."

Sweet eyed the surrounding darkness. "We?"

A scowl flirted with her tired expression. "You Americans are not the only ones to oppose Saddam! You came here as mercenaries to protect Saudi oil. My friends and I, however, are Shi'a. Once we fought the British, and before that the Turks. Now, we fight Saddam and his Ba'athist pigs."

She fell silent as his light fell upon an opening in the stone wall.

"Is this it?" he asked.

"Yes."

He followed her inside. Beyond the tunnel a staircase climbed to a large, low-ceilinged stone chamber. A dozen folding cots were arrayed against one wall, with piles of wooden crates stacked opposite. The image of a bearded man in the garb of a Persian *mullah* looked down from above, grim and disapproving in his aged severity.

Sweet recognized him immediately, of course. He knew the late Ayatollah Khomeini was considered a grand figure in the eyes of the Shiite people, and the leader of the Islamic revolution that had forced the Shah from power. He had also possessed no great love for the United States government, or its people. Seeing his image displayed so reverently sent butterflies dancing somewhere deep inside Sweet's already churning insides.

"You see? You are safe enough here." She brushed past him, busying herself with the medicine she had brought from the apartment.

He looked away from Khomeini's picture. "Yeah."

"You know first aid?"

"Yes."

"Come with me."

She hurried past the cots, past the Ayatollah, and into a cramped space just beyond. It had been taken over as a makeshift hospital, with two cots arrayed side by side. There was a blanket-bundled form on one of them. The girl peeled back the blanket, exposing the pale, bearded features of a man of about forty. His eyes were open, staring. Vacant. The coppery stink left by congealing blood hung in the room like a cloud.

"Was he alive when you left him?"

"Yes." Her expression was troubled as she covered the dead man's face. "But his wounds were very serious. I feared I might not make it back here in time."

"What happened?"

"An ambush." Her eyes took on a haunted mien. "I think it was the Mukhabarat, with government troops in support. Most of our people were killed outright."

"I guess that explains the soldiers I saw earlier."

She struck a match to a kerosene lantern. Its saffron glow filled the underground chamber like oil spreading across still water.

"I was not there, or I would be dead as well. Several of our people survived the attack, however. They brought the wounded man to me, and then left to see if there were any other survivors. They have yet to return."

"I'm sorry." Sweet didn't know what else to say.

"It was God's will." She gathered her things. "Come. I'll fix you something to eat."

It turned out her larder was nearly bare. Sweet had to make do with warmed-over lamb stew, dark tea, and cinnamon-seasoned rice of questionable origin.

She watched as he cleaned his plate. "Do you want more?"

"If you can spare it, yeah."

She was pretty, Sweet thought, with a deep olive complexion and eyes so dark they verged on the purest ebony.

She handed him another plate. "So why are you here? In Basra, I mean."

She nodded sagely once Sweet had finished telling her an abbreviated version of how he had come to be in her apartment.

"When is the last time you slept?" she asked.

He shrugged. "I can't remember."

"Come then, and rest." She led him to one of the cots at the other end of the room.

"I'll keep watch, and wake you in a few hours." She smiled at him. "Then we must leave. I have learned it is best not to stay in one place for too long."

"Thanks." Sweet settled in with his rifle close at hand. Darkness closed in as she cut the lamp at one end of the chamber, easing him into a deep, exhausted slumber.

CHAPTER 11

King Khalid Military City
(2225 hours – Sunday, 3 February 1991)

Peter Vermeer watched as the USAF special mission helicopter chattered out of the darkness like some massive green insect. The Sikorsky MH-53J Pave Low circled into the wind before flaring out to make a perfect landing on the runway tarmac. Aircraft handlers ran forward before the chopper's engines could begin to spool down.

Commander Lindsley's men de-assed the helo in short order. First on the ground was the mission commander, a tall, lanky fellow from central Kansas with bright green eyes. He was clad in desert BDUs, black face paint, and carried a suppressed 9mm submachine gun.

"Lieutenant Jerome?" Vermeer had to shout to be heard over the helo's dying jet turbines.

"Yes, sir?"

"This way, son. We need to talk."

Vermeer handled the debriefing personally. Once he had the Wishbone team settled in, he asked Lt. Walter Jerome for his mission report.

"Sir, the area appeared to be empty of enemy personnel beyond the few units normally stationed inside As-Samawah. From what we could see it looked as if the Iraqis had decided to deploy the bulk of their troop strength farther south, where they would be closer to the Saudi border."

Vermeer offered Jerome a cigarette, and then lit one of his own. "What about militia, or plainclothes security types? Is it possible the Mukhabarat had the place staked out, and you just didn't see them?"

"No, sir." Jerome traded a guarded look with Lindsley, who shrugged. "We were in place for two days, and saw more goats than people. If Halabi had been there, we would have spotted him."

Vermeer knew there wasn't much to say after that. Jerome provided the rest of his report, noting enemy troop strengths, locations, and all the other bits of military trivia U.S. Central Command would want after any deep penetration raid into enemy territory.

"Thank you, gentlemen. That will be all. And Commander Lindsley? I'll inform Admiral Mollar that you and your men have been released to SOCOM for further assignment."

"Yes, sir." The SEALs stood and filed out of the underground briefing room. Soon only Vermeer and Grant Lattimore remained.

"Where's Detloff?" he asked.

"Still sick." Lattimore grimaced. "We may have to send him back to Langley. He's pretty messed up."

"I guess it doesn't matter now. Tell him to get some rest. We're about done here anyway."

"All right." Lattimore paused as if expecting something more. "What about Halabi?"

"My guess is he's either dead, captured, or on the run. Unless we hear something from our sources in-country, we may never know for sure."

Once Lattimore had departed, Vermeer stood and stared at the Wishbone ops map that Jerome had used for his debrief. He knew there was still much to do before his team could leave the Gulf. For starters he had to write up his final mission report, and transmit it via secure-com satellite to various parties in the U.S. intelligence community. One copy, he knew, would go directly to Nick Farraday's office at Langley. From there Vermeer had no idea what would become of it.

CHAPTER 12

Basra
(1150 hours – Monday, 4 February 1991)

"Follow me, and do exactly as you are told."

David Sweet and the girl had departed their underground bolt hole just after dawn. They had spent the morning moving cautiously from building to building in the city's southwest quarter, never staying in one place for long. It was grim, demanding work, and left him nervous and exhausted.

They were now creeping through a series of seemingly abandoned tenements west of al-Hamour Boulevard. The buildings here were old, all crumbling brick and rusty corrugated steel. Dogs barked, and somewhere just ahead Sweet thought he heard a baby crying.

They entered one of the buildings and took a short staircase to the second floor. The hallway at the top was dark, and smelled heavily of rot and mildew. She led him about halfway down before knocking at the door to Apartment 212.

A man's voice answered. She called back, speaking quickly. Sweet heard door locks click open. Light appeared as the door was opened. A man stood in the doorway, regarding them with sullen hostility. He was young and lean, and wore a filthy woolypulley and matching cammie trousers. There was a pistol in his hand.

More words passed between the two. "Inside, quickly," she said, leading Sweet onward. The room beyond was gloomily lit. Sweet smelled a mixture of body odor and stale cigarette smoke. The young Iraqi glared at Sweet and fingered his weapon.

He heard another voice, speaking animatedly. The girl led Sweet into a living area that was lit by guttering candles. There several men waited, including an older fellow in a silk shirt, dark slacks, and expensive Italian shoes. The others wore an assortment of Arab *mufti* and careworn Western attire. Most fingered

Kalashnikovs and eyed Sweet with something akin to well-earned hatred.

The older man asked a question. She replied, meekly Sweet thought, and the old guy nodded. There was a 9mm automatic stuck in his waistband. His fingers brushed against it absent-mindedly as he regarded Sweet through half-lidded eyes.

"You are American?" he asked. His English was very good.

"Yes, sir. Gunnery Sergeant Sweet, United States Marine Corps." Sweet extended his hand.

"I did not ask your name."

He turned to Wooly-pulley and growled an order. Men grabbed Sweet. Wooly-pulley shoved his pistol into the side of Sweet's skull as two of his friends bound his wrists with electrician's tape. The leader pulled a foul-smelling pillowcase over his head, shutting off the light. It grew hard for him to breathe.

"Do not resist us," the leader said. "I will speak with you shortly."

Someone jerked at his arm and led him from the room. The last thing he heard was the girl arguing with them, her tone strident, and perhaps even a little afraid.

* * *

"Kill him now, and be done with it." Assef Moammar Hassan's eyes glittered with a dangerous light. "It is too dangerous to keep him alive, especially now that the Americans have betrayed us."

There was anger and maybe a little madness dancing behind those black eyes, Mohammed Halabi thought. It was a fever brought on by the twin storms of passion and unchecked religious fervor.

"I think not, Assef." Halabi lit a cigarette. "This is not the time."

He turned to the girl. "Explain yourself, Amina. Quickly."

The girl told her story without undue embellishment. Halabi thought she actually seemed concerned about the American soldier's welfare.

"So he just fell from the sky?" Assef spat. "Bullshit! We have been betrayed and abandoned. Kill him now, and send his head to the Americans in a box."

Halabi grunted. "I will talk to him first, Assef. Then we'll see."

Amina laid a hand on his arm. Her eyes seemed to implore something of him, Halabi thought. She would bear watching from here on out.

"Please Colonel. We—"

"Not now." He shrugged her off. "Go to the kitchen, will you? Make us coffee, and something to eat. I need to think."

CHAPTER 13

Basra
(1305 hours – Monday, 4 February 1991)

"Take off his hood."

David Sweet blinked in the sudden light. He had been stripped to his skivvies and tied to a wooden chair. After a moment he saw the Iraqi leader and Wooly-pulley standing over him, their eyes aglitter in the glow cast by a kerosene lamp.

"Untie him, Assef, and leave us."

Wooly-pulley cut Sweet free and placed a set of counterfeit Nike sweats on the bedroom nightstand. He glowered darkly before leaving the room. Moments later the two men were alone.

Sweet rubbed his wrists and stared at Assef's retreating back. "Nice guy."

"I apologize for the way you've been treated. It's disgraceful, I know." The Iraqi handed Sweet the clothing and motioned for him to get dressed. "My current associates often view the world in terms of black and white, good and bad. The more pleasurable aspects of modern life are not easy for them to understand, or appreciate."

"I'll have to take your word on that." Sweet stepped into the sweats before pulling on a matching T-shirt.

"Are you hungry? Thirsty?"

He reached inside his jacket and produced an unopened pint of what Sweet took to be good, old-fashioned Kentucky bourbon. He broke the seal and held it out to Sweet.

"Please, I insist."

Sweet took the bottle. Drank. The liquor was a warm, smoky fire as it worked its way into his belly.

"I thought alcohol was banned here."

"In Saudi Arabia perhaps. Not here." He smiled. "As I said before, black and white. Good and bad. The real world rarely aligns itself into such convenient designations."

The man took the bottle and sipped at it. Smacked his lips.

"I am no religious fanatic, Sergeant. I've given thirty years of my life to Saddam and the Party. And how does he reward me? War and misery. Death. My oldest son is dead, killed in the war with Iran." He sighed. "Now Iraq is involved in another pointless war, this time with America. No, the world! And as you have no doubt noticed, it is not going entirely to plan."

"So you want out," Sweet said.

"In a manner of speaking, yes." He pulled a gold-embossed cigarette case from his jacket. "Cigarette?"

"No, thank you."

"Filthy habit." He fired one alight. "I contacted the CIA, of course. Just after you Americans began to arrive in August."

Sweet flew back to those initial weeks in Saudi Arabia: memories of white sand and blast furnace heat. He scowled as he remembered the way his marines had been positioned as mere 'speed bumps' against any planned Iraqi incursion.

"I have information." The man exhaled, sending pungent smoke skyward. "Vital information your government will pay dearly for! I was supposed to be taken out yesterday, yes? But something happened, and my people were ambushed."

Sweet considered this for a moment. "I ran into Republican Guard patrols outside the city. They were looking for you, weren't they?"

He offered Sweet a crooked grin. "In all likelihood, yes. We were betrayed, Sergeant. Someone told the Mukhabarat where to find us. I have no idea who it was, however. That's where you come in."

"Sir?"

"We go together, preferably after the shooting stops. Go to the Americans. This war cannot last forever."

Sweet nodded. "What then?"

"We have false identity papers, foreign passports. In the ensuing chaos it should be a simple matter to slip out of the country, preferably somewhere along the border with Saudi Arabia."

Sweet found himself reaching for another drink. "What do you need me for?"

"I have no way of contacting U.S. forces. We have to assume my contacts within the CIA are compromised now. I need you, my friend, to talk us through any American checkpoints we encounter."

"I've seen the old tunnels under the city," Sweet replied. "There are secret ways into Iran, or so the girl told me. Why not go out that way?"

He laughed. "The Persians and I are not on the best of terms. I show my face there, and boom! A bullet to the back of the head. You'd fare little better, I think. The Iranians would never let you out of their hands."

Dull thunder rumbled as American jets maneuvered far overhead. "What's to stop Assef and his friends from turning us in anyway?" Sweet asked. "Last I heard the Iraqi Shi'a were in tight with the Ayatollah."

The older man laughed again. "I have been planning this for years. To that end I have been feeding Assef information, and protecting his people from detection by the security services. We are safe enough in their care, I assure you."

"I suppose you know best, sir." Sweet took one last pull on the whiskey before handing back the bottle. "Just one thing, though. What is it you know that's so damn important?"

"You're better off not knowing. Beyond that you'll just have to trust me."

* * *

An hour later Sweet stood in an alley off to one side of the tenement building. He had insisted upon the return of his uniform, which now lay bundled in an old suitcase at his side.

"Take this." Assef handed Sweet the same 9mm Browning he had liberated from Porky Pig. He motioned for Sweet to climb into the big Isuzu delivery truck that had been parked nearby. Sweet did as he was told.

There he found a number of rusted 55-gallon oil drums, crates containing color television sets, and a pair of plain wooden coffins. Sweet looked a question at the old Iraqi.

"This is the best way to smuggle us out of the city," he replied. "There are checkpoints at every major roadway and intersection, but soldiers are unlikely to search a coffin, especially with the grieving widow so close at hand."

He gestured to the girl Sweet now knew as Amina. She stood veiled and silent, her eyes downcast.

"There is a cemetery just a few blocks away, at the edge of town," Assef added. "Once we get there, we put stones in the coffins, and a sympathetic imam buries them with all due ceremony. You come with me to another safe house outside of the city. From there you get false papers, and prepare for the journey south."

Sweet eyed the nearest coffin. "When do we start?"

Assef took up a hammer and nails. "Now."

Sweet climbed gingerly into the rough wooden box, and waited as Assef fitted the lid into place. There was barely enough room for him to breathe. Then darkness fell as the Iraqi began to hammer the coffin shut.

CHAPTER 14

The Persian Gulf
(1755 hours – Friday, 8 February 1991)

Peter Vermeer felt the small turboprop slam hard onto the flight deck of the USS *John F. Kennedy*, the impact stunning, ferocious. He grunted as the C-2 Greyhound hit the second arresting wire and came to an abrupt stop, the impact throwing him against his seat harness.

The rear clamshell doors of the aircraft were opened immediately. Vermeer gathered his document bag and was on his feet, fully recognizing the need to be off the plane and into the bowels of the ship as soon as possible. This was no time to be caught sightseeing on the deck of a United States' aircraft carrier. An endless roar came to him the moment he stepped into the open. The stink of aviation fuel, the thunder of turboprops and jet engines, and the carefully controlled chaos of active flight operations: it all hit him full in the face, sharply, like an open-handed slap from a beautiful woman.

An enlisted plane handler directed him and the other passengers through a hatch leading into the depths of the ship. Once beyond that portal the sounds of the flight deck became muted and indistinct.

"Mister Vermeer?" The speaker was a young lieutenant in sweaty service khakis.

"That's right."

"Welcome aboard, sir. If you'll come with me?"

He followed the lieutenant into a confusing warren of passages, headed ever deeper below decks. Minutes later he led Vermeer to a closed hatch. The compartment beyond was red-lit, and fairly hummed with frenetic activity. The throb of overworked air conditioners warred with frequent radio chatter, the hush of muted conversation. Crewmen crouched over radar screens, monitoring strike packages destined for targets deep inside enemy territory. Vermeer took a moment to let his eyes adjust to the dimness before heading over to speak with the man he had come to see.

"Peter! Good to see you." Rear Admiral Norman Mollar had wide features and sandy brown hair shot through with streaks of gray. The coveted SEAL trident was pinned to his rumpled desert utilities.

"Glad to be here, sir." Vermeer took a moment to eye their surroundings. "Is there somewhere private we can talk?"

The admiral's flag wardroom was just off the ship's Combat Information Center. Mollar ordered his steward to bring them some coffee before offering Vermeer a seat.

"What brings you here, Peter?"

"An update on Wishbone." Vermeer opened his document bag and handed over a weighty file folder. "It's been five days, and still nothing out of Iraq. No word from our people in Baghdad, or any of our operatives in-country. It's as if Halabi simply fell off the face of the earth."

"Hmm." Mollar took a moment to peruse the contents of the file. "Any chance he's been captured? Maybe the Mukhabarat are holding him somewhere."

"It's possible, of course. But the latest intercepts out of Fort Huachuca tell a different story. I think the Iraqis are still looking for Halabi too. Hell, Admiral. They're beginning to think *we* have him."

"So he's gone to ground." Mollar lit a cigarette for Vermeer with his battered silver Zippo. "God knows there's a healthy anti-Ba'athist movement in Iraq right now. Chances are someone in al-Dawa or one of the Kurd groups has taken him in for the duration."

Vermeer took a drag on his cigarette. "You sound pretty sure about that. Neither al-Dawa or the Kurds have any great reason to help an old-hand Ba'athist like Halabi."

"Experience, Peter." Mollar's expression grew cloudy. "This is my third war here, remember? I buried a son after that so-called 'peacekeeping' mission in Beirut. If anyone can tell you a thing or two about how these bastards think, it's me.

"Look at it this way: if Halabi were dead or in the bag, there'd be intercepts telling us as much. The Mukhabarat would trumpet it to the Four Winds. After the mess Iraqi intelligence made of things, telling Saddam the West wouldn't fight for Kuwait, that Americans couldn't fight in the desert . . . They need a victory in the worst way. Otherwise Saddam will be lining up some very important people to be shot after this war is over."

Vermeer had to admit the admiral had a point. If nothing else the Iraqis were not known for stellar communications discipline.

"There's something else I wanted to talk to you about, Admiral. It's Commander Lindsley and his men."

"Oh?" Mollar stubbed out his cigarette. "Is there a problem?"

"Not really. I was just wondering why you never reassigned them after the end of Wishbone. As of right now they're just cooling their heels, waiting for something to happen. It seems like a waste of good talent."

Mollar's answering grunt was noncommittal. "I've talked things over with Nick Farraday, and he agrees. We'll keep Lindsley on site just in case Halabi turns up after all. That way our asses are covered both ways."

* * *

Aboard USS *Saratoga* (CV-60), somewhere in the Red Sea: Lieutenant Scott Seeley clambered into his rack, still clad in his soiled flight suit. He felt exhausted, both mentally and physically. He couldn't remember the last time he'd slept more than a few short hours at a time. That last sortie had been pretty hairy. His bird had come back all shot up by triple-A, leaving Seeley and his navigator with some much-deserved downtime.

He'd been driving A-6 Intruders for four years now. There was nothing he loved better, except maybe Jessica. Now his marriage was in ruins, like the pieces shot from the starboard wing of his aircraft.

As he rolled over he felt her letter crinkle in his pocket. Awake now, he snapped on an overhead and began to read.

I'm sorry Scott. I didn't mean for things to work out this way. Please find it in your heart to forgive me. Creative writing had never been her strong suit.

He'd gotten the letter just the day before. Rumors had reached him long before that. Pilots talked amongst themselves, and spread scuttlebutt like rats carrying the Plague. Sorry, guy. Didn't you know? Your wife's banging an enlisted man.

Now she was asking for a divorce. He hadn't told CAG yet. He was worried the Old Man would pull him from the flight roster. He also believed it would be better to wait until the shooting stopped before going public with this. He just hoped they'd throw the book at her. New rumors had already begun to circulate that Jess had been relieved of duty and sent back to the States. Her letter mentioned none of that, however. He found himself praying it was so.

"Scotty!" Seeley saw Lieutenant (j.g.) Tom Kress, his bombardier/navigator, standing in the hatchway. "Great news, buddy."

"What is it?" Seeley carefully folded the letter and put it away.

"I just talked to Chief Noble. He's got a bird for us. Preflight briefing in thirty."

Seeley reached for his boots. "All right. See you up top." With that Kress was gone. Seeley wondered if he had time to get a cup of coffee from the mess deck. Already he was looking forward to getting back in the air.

CHAPTER 15

Amarah, Iraq
(2245 hours – Thursday, 14 February 1991)

"Sergeant! Sergeant Sweet!" David Sweet awoke to the sound of someone knocking frantically at his door.

"Come in." He sat up, blearily, as Amina stormed into the tiny cubby he now called home.

"What is it?"

"Something's happened. You'd better come with me."

Sweet needed to piss but knew better than to argue. Instead he followed Amina up the concrete steps that fed onto the farmhouse's cramped kitchen.

The farm was located a few kilometers outside of town. They had once grown rice and barley here, in green, marshy fields flooded seasonably by the nearby Tigris. The house was small, and built of the same tan brick Sweet had seen on buildings in Basra and al-Qurnah. A corrugated metal roof kept out the wind and the rain. Though furnished, the place looked like it had been abandoned for some time. Amina had told him the man who had lived here moved away after his sons died. There were two bedrooms, walled off from the rest of the house by a partition of simple wooden planks.

They found Halabi and some of the other al-Dawa fighters who'd taken refuge at the farm huddled over a small transistor radio. At the moment it was tuned in to the evening BBC radio news broadcast.

Sweet was about to ask what was going on when Colonel Halabi shot him a warning glare. He stood next to Amina and whispered his query to her instead.

"The Americans bombed an air raid shelter in Baghdad last night. It was filled with women and children. Many were killed."

A cold, clammy dread crept into Sweet at hearing this. He looked at the men gathered around the radio, noting the tense air that seemed to fill the room. Assef turned and saw Sweet. His eyes were perpetually dark, angry, but took on an odd, almost feral light whenever Sweet was in the room. He stood now and beckoned for Sweet to join them.

"Come, sit. You should hear this."

A space was made for him at the table. The other Iraqis huddled in closer to listen.

"*Iraqi government sources claim that at least five hundred civilians were killed in the attack, and insist that the bunker complex at Amiriyah was a civil air raid shelter, and not a military facility as initially reported. Independent confirmation has been difficult to secure. This is Andrew Hutchins, reporting from Saudi Arabia.*"

Sweat prickled on Sweet's skin. "Look, I'm sorry this had to happen. I really am. But it was probably just an accident, a mistake. I—"

Assef was on his feet in a flash. There was a 9mm pistol in his waistband.

"A mistake?" His expression blazed hotter. "This is hardly the first time Americans kill Arabs to take their land, to take their oil! Is it an accident when Americans give the Zionists missiles to kill children in Gaza? Is it an accident when you sell Saddam weapons to kill my people?"

Everyone began talking at once: shouting, hurling insults. One guy raised a fist, and Sweet felt his fingers curl around the butt of the Browning concealed in the pocket of his field jacket.

"Enough!" Halabi's shout cracked like a gunshot. He put a restraining hand on Assef before turning angry eyes on Sweet. "Go back to your hole, Sergeant. Please. Perhaps I'll come see you later."

* * *

Sweet did as he was told. His hiding place was a concrete-lined cellar directly beneath the farmhouse. They'd kept him in the cramped storage room, forced to share his space with an old cot, a pile of cardboard boxes, and mops, brooms and wash buckets left over from God knew when. Sometimes in the dark he could hear rats scurrying to and fro. The light from a kerosene lantern exposed the line of hash marks he'd scratched onto a nearby wall. By his count seven days had passed since his arrival.

Soon there was a timid knock on his door. Sweet sat up and eased the pistol into his lap.

"Who is it?"

"Amina."

He allowed himself to relax. "Come in."

She poked her head in. "Am I bothering you?"

"Not at all." She slipped inside.

She had some dates and a pot of the bitter dark coffee Iraqis favored so. He thanked her and offered her a seat, not really expecting her to stay. Ever since they'd come into contact with her friends, she'd treated him as if he had some communicable disease. Instead she perched gingerly on the cot beside him.

"Your boy Assef needs to learn some manners," Sweet said. "The colonel might not be around next time to keep things civil." He set to work on the dates and the tea. He was surprised to discover just how famished he was.

"He was angry." Amina shrugged. "You have to understand, we have little to thank the Americans for. During the war with Iran you helped Iraq, and gave Saddam money and weapons. That kind of thing is hard to forgive or forget."

"We're not on good terms with Saddam now." Sweet finished the last of the food and set his plate aside. "You'd think that would make a difference."

"As I said. Some things are hard to forgive." The two were silent for a time. The only sound to be heard was the rumble of fast-movers passing far overhead.

"How long have you been a soldier?" she asked.

"Almost sixteen years."

She seemed to consider something for a moment. "You like it then? War and killing?"

Sweet's cup paused halfway to his mouth. How to answer such a question?

"I don't like it, no. But my dad was in the service, and so were most of my uncles. So in a way I guess it's a family tradition."

She nodded. "I hate Saddam. He killed my father and my brothers. Now I have nothing: no family, no home. No future."

Another rumble sounded above them. He watched as she settled comfortably beside him.

"You could always leave," Sweet said. "You used to live in the United States, right? Go back. At least you'd be safe."

"No. This is my home, and these are my people. I will stay, and fight."

"Even if it kills you?"

A shrug. "If it is God's will, yes."

"Ah, Sergeant! Amina! There you are." Halabi came into the room suddenly, all smiles and warm handshakes. Amina pulled away before busying herself with the dirty dishes.

"Walk with me, Sergeant." The two men headed upstairs and out into the night.

"You shouldn't be alone with her like that." Halabi spoke quietly so only Sweet could hear. "This isn't America. If the others saw you it would be bad for all of us."

"I didn't mean anything by it. We were just talking."

"A woman's reputation is a fragile thing. Remember that."

His words brought another woman to mind, and another reputation, shot all to hell. "Yes, sir," Sweet replied dutifully.

"Good." Halabi smiled once more. "You can stay if you like. The BBC will be on again soon, with news of the war. I could use the company."

"What about Assef?"

Halabi frowned as he lit a cigarette. "He's gone to bed for the night."

Sweet followed the older man back inside. "I'm causing you problems, aren't I?"

"It's nothing you need concern yourself with. Friends argue all the time, but in the end we always come to an understanding."

Sweet nodded, feigning agreement, and said nothing more. The Browning was a dead weight in his pocket as he followed the older man into the kitchen, eager to listen for any fresh news of the coming storm.

CHAPTER 16

Basra
(1405 hours – Tuesday, 19 February 1991)

Congealed blood stained dirty white tile. The prisoner hung by his wrists, shackled to eyebolts in the ceiling. Somewhere in the distance a gasoline generator hummed.

"No more, please." The man had been taken in a raid just the night before. At the moment he was sobbing, his body wracked with pain. His jailors had worked him over for hours before asking their first question.

"Have mercy, please! I swear to you I know nothing."

"We shall see." The chief inquisitor was a Mukhabarat major by the name of Hasim Awad. He stood now, scanning a sheet of paper attached to a clipboard. A low, deep rumble sounded far overhead, sifting dust from the ceiling.

"You're certain the man you saw was Mohammed Halabi?" Awad said. "Absolutely certain?"

"That is what our leader called him." The prisoner choked down another sob as fresh agony lanced through his body. "But he was not there for very long. Two days, maybe three. Once the American came, he and the others left for one of our safe houses in the country."

"An American?" The agent looked up from his clipboard, his interest piqued. "Why didn't you mention this sooner?"

"You did not ask about an American." He licked dry, cracked lips. "Water. May I have some water?"

"Sergeant." Another man came forward and gave the prisoner something to drink. Once he had pulled back, the major continued his line of questioning.

"Who was this American?"

"He was a flyer, or escaped prisoner of some sort." He sobbed once more. "We were not allowed to interact with him."

"Go on."

"They left with Assef Hassan and some of the others," the prisoner said. "I think they headed for Amarah, but that was more than two weeks ago. I haven't seen them since."

There were more questions, of course. But the prisoner knew the answers to none of them. In the end Awad told the guard sergeant to unchain the man and return him to his cell. A few moments later he met one of his lieutenants in a hallway outside the interrogation room.

"You think he was telling the truth?" Lieutenant Qassim Abdul Zahra asked.

"We'll soon find out." Another low detonation sounded far overhead as the two retired to a nearby office. "You remember the reports we received of an al-Dawa safe house located near Amarah?"

"Yes." Zahra indicated a spot on a map fixed to the wall. "As I recall it is located here, on the outskirts of town. I was going to send men to investigate as soon the air raids let up."

"Send them immediately." Awad took a seat behind the desk. "Call all area militia and Army commanders. Do whatever it takes to drum up the men you need. I want that location raided as quickly as possible."

* * *

David Sweet watched the rat as it crept across the cellar floor. It was gray, with mangy fur, red eyes and a pink, twitching nose. Sweet sat on his cot as it edged ever closer to the piece of stale bread he had placed near the door. The creature squeaked once, indignantly, before seizing its prize.

Soon Sweet grew tired of watching his new friend. He had been stuck down here for hours. He had just decided to go upstairs, Halabi's rules be damned, when there was a knock at his door.

"Come in."

"Hello." Amina slipped inside. There was a weighty volume in her hands. Sweet realized it was a photo album, and made room for her on the bunk.

"Assef and the others aren't back yet. The colonel is starting to get worried." Sweet remembered that Assef and some of the other al-Dawa fighters had gone into the city to buy provisions.

"When are they due back?"

"Later this afternoon. I tell Colonel Halabi not to worry, but he never listens."

Sweet glanced at the door. "Where is he now?"

"Don't worry, he won't bother us." She pursed her lips in sudden disapproval. "It's shameful. I think he's been drinking again."

"So what's this?" He gestured to the album.

"Old photographs. Here, look."

She opened the book to the first page. Sweet saw a pair of pretty teenage girls, both mugging for the camera. One was Amina, clad in a University of Michigan sweatshirt. Other photos showed the same pair, hurling snowballs, or riding a rollercoaster at some gaudy theme park. In none of them did Amina wear the abaya.

"This is my roommate, Leila." She flipped to another page. It showed Amina in various settings: a cluttered apartment, at the student union, studying at the campus library. She looked so young, Sweet thought. It was hard for him to associate the fresh-faced child in the photos with the determined militant he'd met in Basra weeks before.

"Who is this?" Sweet pointed at a time-faded Polaroid of three grinning young boys. All had her dark hair and eyes.

"My brothers." Unkind memories seemed to settle across her like a blanket. "The oldest is Hafez, while the twins are Ismail and Ibrahim. They were good boys. Naughty at times, yes. But good boys nonetheless. I loved them dearly."

"Do you want to talk about it?"

"No, I . . ." A pause. "My father and brothers died in prison. It was God's mercy that my mother did not live long after that."

Amina closed the book and gently set it aside. "I've been alone ever since. Except for my brothers and sisters in the Cause. They are my family now."

"I'm sorry."

She turned her eyes away from him for a moment. "I don't mean to burden you, Sergeant. I—"

"David."

She blinked. "What?"

He felt himself smile. "You should call me David."

It was good to see her smile in return. "I . . . All right. David it is."

* * *

That night fires burned in the darkness, glimmering brightly. Sweet huddled atop a ridge three hundred meters from the road into town. His body was cloaked head-to-foot by a dark wool blanket.

He'd watched the convoy head out just before nightfall, moving rapidly toward Basra. Soon friendly F-111s had streamed in, deploying cluster bombs and slaughtering at will. The Iraqis must have been desperate to be somewhere else, Sweet thought. You'd either have to be desperate or stupid to move in the open right now.

He heard movement behind him, the soft scrape of shoe leather on bare earth. Sweet waited patiently as Amina appeared from the surrounding shadows.

"What are you doing?" she asked.

"Counting trucks." He shrugged. "I guess old habits die hard. What are you doing here? I thought the others were keeping you pretty busy."

"Assef has returned." She crouched at his side. "You must come with me. Colonel Halabi and the others want to speak with you."

Sweet felt tall grass swish against his pant legs as the pair quickly made their way across the broad, empty field between the road and the farmhouse. Once in the kitchen he found the others busily gathering food, stocking equipment and readying their meager supply of weaponry.

"What is it?" Sweet asked Halabi. "What's going on?"

"Assef brought news when he came back from town." The colonel stood slotting cartridges into a Kalashnikov magazine. "The police raided our safe house in Basra. Several of our people were killed. Others were captured. We're moving out just in case we've been compromised, too."

A lead weight seemed to settle in the pit of Sweet's stomach. "What do you need me to do?"

"Help Amina." He indicated a nearby stack of cardboard boxes. "Find what food you can and load it into the cars. I want to be on the road within the hour."

* * *

Sweet grunted as he lifted the last of the group's food and water into the trunk of a battered Mercedes sedan. Amina stood nearby, illuminating his efforts with a small flashlight.

"Is that the last of it?" he asked.

"I think so." She clicked off the light.

Sweet watched as shadowy figures moved along the row of cars parked on the road leading into town. Here and there he saw a cigarette flare, and heard low voices murmur against the darkness.

"What will you and the others do now?" he asked. "None of you can go back to Basra again."

"*Insha'Allah*. My life will be as God wills it, David. As you well know."

There was fatalism in her words he found irritating. It was that bullshit Shi'a pragmatism again. God wills this, God wills that. Sometimes he felt as if he were talking to a wall.

"Do you think the authorities will come after you now?" he said. "After I'm gone?"

"I don't know. Probably."

"You could come with me." His eyes were very intent on her now. "When Halabi and I head for Saudi, I mean. You saved my life. I'm sure the U.S. government could swing some kind of deal for you, get you sanctuary or something."

“We’ve talked about this before,” she said. “You know I’m staying, no matter what. This changes nothing.”

“None of this is worth dying for.”

He spoke without thinking, and immediately regretted it. She turned and stalked away, heading for the house. The set of her shoulders told him she was angry.

“Amina! Look, I’m—”

Suddenly Halabi was by his side. “Get ready. We’re leaving soon.”

“Yes sir.” Sweet gathered up his rifle and pack before heading for the car Halabi had assigned him to. Amina was traveling in a separate vehicle, closer to the rear of the column. Maybe some time alone would allow her to see the wisdom in his words.

* * *

Peter Vermeer was watching a news report on Tariq Aziz’s recent trip to Moscow when Grant Lattimore stormed into the duty lounge, note board in hand.

“I think we may just have dug up something on Detloff. Look at this.”

Vermeer took the message flimsy Lattimore held out to him. It was a signals intercept, straight out of an American listening post in Turkey. The intercept had been brief, but fortunately one word in particular had caught the attention of the Agency station chief in Ankara: ‘Watershed’ was thought to be the Mukhabarat code phrase for Mohammed Halabi.

“Get Lindsley and Jerome,” Vermeer said. “I want a pre-mission briefing in thirty.”

“They’re staged and ready to go,” Lattimore replied. “Admiral Mollar has already given us the green light to go ahead. All I need now is your say-so.”

“You have it.” Vermeer got to his feet and shrugged into his jacket. “Let’s get moving.”

* * *

Less than an hour later Vermeer and Lattimore stood at the airfield perimeter, watching as Walter Jerome and his men strode up the ramp of a waiting Hercules transport. Lieutenant Commander Lindsley stood nearby, pacing irritably.

"They'll be on the ground in a little over two hours," Lindsley said. "Whether or not they'll be able to reach the final rally point before dawn is hard to say."

Vermeer checked his watch and noted the time. "We'll go on the assumption they won't be able to make contact with Halabi before daybreak," he said. "Have them go to ground at Hide Site One as soon as they land."

"Aye, sir."

"Do you think they'll make it in time?" Lattimore asked once the SEAL commander had gone.

"I hope so." Both watched as the big turboprop began to taxi onto a nearby runway. Brilliant station-keeping lights glimmered against the night as the engines revved to takeoff speed. Minutes later Vermeer saw the bird lumber into the sky, to be silhouetted briefly against the clouds before disappearing altogether.

CHAPTER 17

Amarah, Iraq
(0008 hours – Wednesday, 20 February 1991)

"Take the front seat. I'll drive."

David Sweet did as Assef indicated. Rain tracked across the elderly Fiat's windshield as Sweet settled his rifle into a more comfortable position. Moments later the four-vehicle convoy moved out with the little Italian sedan in the lead.

Another of Assef's al-Dawa fighters sat in the back. Sweet saw that the cars trailing them were also on the move, headlights jouncing as they lurched over ruts in the surface of the dirt road. There was a sudden clearing in the rain and the mist, and the black outline of what had to be the Tigris appeared to the right, visible but dimly against the night. Soon the group was northbound on the highway into Amarah, paralleling the river and moving quickly under the cover of darkness.

"Where are we going?" Sweet asked.

"Into the city," Assef replied. "That's all you need to know for now. Just do as you are told, and keep an eye out for patrols."

Sweet turned his attention to the passing darkness. Now and again a row of lonely palms would appear at the side of the road, but otherwise the world seemed devoid of life. Even the moon was hidden completely by the clouds overhead. Minutes later an iridescent glow appeared on the road before them. Sweet tensed a bit as Assef slowed, and soon spied the cause of his discomfort: a line of smoldering vehicles, jeeps, trucks, military equipment of all manner and description, blazing merrily in the pouring rain. The air was thick with the stink of burning fuel and melted rubber. He wondered if it was the same convoy he had seen destroyed earlier that night.

Sweet kept mute as they drew abreast of the ruined convoy. Dark human forms lay by the side of the road, unmoving. For a time no one spoke. A light flared as the guy in the back lit a cigarette, and began to hum nervously. It was a weak, wordless little ditty, harmless really, but soon it began to get on Sweet's nerves. He was about to say something, to tell the guy to knock it off, when the sky before them was engulfed in a spasm of brilliant white light.

Sweet shielded his eyes against the sudden glare. As he watched, a trio of parachute flares floated far above, and shed a bright, garish glow upon the surrounding terrain. Stark shadows slithered across the road, snakelike and furtive.

Assef hit the brakes even as an army checkpoint became visible ahead. Sweet saw five-ton trucks, camouflaged fighting positions, and several low, hulking shapes parked just across a mud-churned field: Iraqi tanks draped with camouflage netting against possible discovery from the air. The indistinct figures of dismounted infantry could be seen in support. He opened his mouth to speak even as the first flashes of incoming tracers lit the night.

Sweet watched those flickering strobes reach out to strike them. He heard metal on metal contact, and saw glass shatter as heavy slugs sparked across their hood and windshield. He felt the Fiat shudder, and saw their sole remaining headlight swerve as Assef steered directly for a ditch by the side of the road. A palm tree reared up before them like some dark pagan monolith. He felt himself lifted bodily by the impact, slamming shoulder-first into the dashboard. The collision jarred the breath from his lungs and sent stars bursting before his eyes, stunning him.

Sweet slowly became aware of the deep throbbing inside his skull. The air stank of blood and piss. He looked over to see Assef slumped over in his seat. The back of his head had been blown open by a direct hit.

Sweet looked back to see the Marlboro Man was also dead. He kicked open the passenger-side door and crawled into the rain. The deafening thud of a heavy belt-fed gun sounded to the right. With a start Sweet realized that only seconds had passed since the beginning of the firefight.

He had to find the others! Headlights glowed from back the way they had come, bracketed by flickering muzzles and the steady growl of rifles on full automatic. Sweet dropped to his belly and began to low-crawl through the mud. As he did so the flares above began to sputter and die. Soon the outline of yet another bullet-riddled sedan appeared before him. He spied furtive shadows crouching behind the engine block. As he scurried to join them, another flare rocketed skyward.

It took him a moment to realize they were already dead. Voices came to him, barking hurried orders. Sweet sought cover behind the Mercedes as more figures moved about at the edge of his vision. The closest Iraqi soldier was less than fifteen meters away. Heart pounding, Sweet brought up his AK and opened fire, leaning into the rifle as it rattled off on full automatic. Indistinct figures tottered and fell, others shouted, and answering muzzle-flashes sparked at him from the road. He was up and moving, jinking left and right, as more slugs hissed past him. Green tracers crackled overhead.

* * *

The Iraqi sniper was atop a low rise nearly two hundred meters from the road. He peered through the scope mounted atop his Russian Dragunov and spied a running figure as it darted across a muddy field.

The figure ran on, moving quickly. The sniper centered his sights, and expertly adjusted for windage and elevation before taking up the slack on the trigger. He mouthed a silent prayer, and felt the rifle go into recoil against him. A hit! He saw the man stagger drunkenly before going face-first into the mud.

* * *

Less than an hour had passed since the first gunshots had pierced the night. Now all was quiet as Amina Jabouri crouched in a filth-strewn ditch, listening intently to the night for signs of pursuit. Her heart fluttered within her chest as the sound of soldiers calling to one another came to her through the rain.

She still clutched the automatic pistol she had taken from a dead man. If the soldiers came for her, she'd save one bullet for herself. None of those animals would be allowed to touch her, to rape her, God willing. Memories of the tracers burning the night, men screaming, guns firing, all came to her through the rainy dark. She didn't know if any of her comrades had survived, and felt sudden shame to think she might be the lone survivor.

She froze in place as someone barked a short laugh just a few meters away. This was followed by more voices, whispering now, and the sound of heavy boots clomping through the tall grass.

"Pick him up, Sergeant. The road is this way."

Amina's heart continued to pound as she peered over the edge of the ditch. Another illumination flare had popped in the far distance, shedding a weak glow across the scene. She saw uniformed soldiers, mud-splattered, filthy, carrying some heavy object between them. One stood guard while the others dragged their burden across the uneven ground.

It was a man, Amina saw, faceless against the dark. He hung limply between two of the soldiers, unresponsive, unresisting. A blood-soaked bandage had been wrapped about his right thigh.

Her pulse raced more quickly as the group drew parallel to her. It seemed they were heading for the highway. Amina followed just out of sight as the soldiers crossed the field. Soon she made it to the tall berm that divided the fields from the road. Now Amina heard the rumble of heavy diesels. She went to ground as a shout went up from the road nearby. Peering forward, she saw the men she had followed waving, shouting again. The soldiers on the road spotted the group and seemed to beckon them forward.

Amina crawled on her belly amidst the tall grass. Soon she was a mere twenty-five meters from the road and the cluster of armed soldiers. A flashlight was shined into the face of the bound prisoner they carried between them. Even at this distance Amina recognized David's bruised features. The light went out, plunging the fields back into night's comforting embrace.

"Who are you?" The sound of a fist striking bare flesh came to her despite the dark. David said something in reply, something

Amina did not hear, and the soldiers began to murmur excitedly in turn.

"Put him with the others." She watched as David was lifted up into a nearby truck. Moments later the soldiers clambered into their vehicles and begin to move out. The rumble of diesel engines was loud in her ears as she slinked back into the night, shivering in the cold, wet wind.

CHAPTER 18

Amarah, Iraq
(1845 hours – Wednesday, 20 February 1991)

David Sweet's leg throbbed dully, as if someone had jammed rusty metal deep into the muscle. At least they'd given him something for the pain, morphine perhaps. Even now he floated on crimson-tainted clouds, drifting far from this place of madness and death.

The cell they had put him in reeked of urine. At the moment he was alone, shivering in the chill dark. Now and again he would drift up toward partial lucidity. It was then he would think of Jess, or sometimes poor Amina. At least Jessica was safe. What of Amina? Had she survived the ambush? What would the bastards do to her if they did have her in custody?

His thoughts were turning down a very dark, dangerous path when he heard the clatter of a key in the door to his cell. Heavy steel squealed on protesting hinges. Several figures appeared in the glow of the dim bulb in the hall outside. A guttural command sounded, and a man was hurled inside. Like Sweet he was clad in a bright orange prison jumpsuit.

The door clamored shut. "Sweet? Is that you?" It was Mohammed Halabi. Sweet saw that the older man's face was bloody and mottled with fresh bruises.

"Yeah." Sweet licked his too-dry lips and wished for some water. Halabi bent low and checked the blood-soaked bandage at Sweet's thigh.

"Have they given you medicine for this?" the Iraqi said. "Or let you see a doctor?"

"Somebody came in to change the bandages, and give me a shot," Sweet replied. "But that's it. Are you okay?" Sweet could only dimly make out the battering the older man had taken.

"The Mukhabarat have sent someone here to interrogate us," Halabi said. "He's just a junior officer, however, so I doubt he's authorized to use excessive force on us. That privilege is usually reserved for senior interrogation specialists."

"I suppose I should feel honored." Sweet tried to smile, and failed. He felt dizzy and weak.

"You should rest. They'll be coming for us soon." Halabi settled onto the other cot in the tiny, cramped space, and said little else as night fell outside, leaving them both in absolute, clinging darkness.

* * *

Amina Jabouri had spent the last eighteen hours cowering like a dog in the rain and the mud. She now sat, shivering uncontrollably, as the sun sank below the horizon and yet another dark night came upon the war-ravaged countryside.

The farm they had used as a safe house was nearby. In truth she hadn't known where else to go. The locations of the other bolt holes her people used were unknown to her. The fact that most of her comrades had already been captured or killed had done nothing to encourage Amina to be bold in exploring her other options.

She'd seen much activity earlier in the day. Now the main house was dark. Nothing had moved in any of the outbuildings for several hours, suggesting the authorities had been here, searched the place, and found nothing of interest. But she also prayed that the farm would hold hidden treasure of a different sort.

Now hunger and a nagging fear of hypothermia drove her onward, gun in hand. The pistol's weight reassured her, though only four bullets remained in its magazine. Her earlier thoughts about what to do in case of capture weighed upon her as Amina crossed the field and approached the darkened farmhouse.

Nothing moved in the night as she made her approach. No dogs barked, no Mukhabarat agents emerged from the shadows with guns drawn. Amina reached the back door of the farmhouse and tried the knob. She needn't have bothered. The door had been smashed in, and now hung haphazardly by one hinge. She crept cautiously inside before snapping on her small penlight.

The floor was littered with the odd items they had left behind. Clothing, discarded shoes, broken furniture, all sat forlorn and abandoned. She began to dig through a pile of discarding clothing in search of something to change into. In the end she chose a pair of gray sweats. One of the headscarves she had forgotten lay in the remains of her old bedroom. After settling it in place she headed back to the kitchen in search of something to eat.

A pair of dark shadows stood by the door, waiting for her. Amina froze in place as her light played across dirty camouflage and black gunmetal. Vivid green eyes gazed back at her from the lead soldier.

"Don't be afraid. We won't hurt you." His Arabic was terrible. Amina let her flashlight fall to the floor and slowly raised her hands in surrender. One of the men came forward with his submachine gun ready and took her by the shoulder.

"On the floor, face down." This man spoke with a slow drawl that was difficult for her to understand. She did as he commanded, and gritted her teeth as the American shamelessly patted her down for concealed weaponry.

Moments later he handed her gun over to the group's apparent commander.

"Let her up." The leader had kind features, Amina thought, despite the fact that they were blackened with camouflage paint. He turned a chair over and wordlessly offered her a seat.

"Do you understand English?"

"Yes." There were at least three of them, Amina now saw. The third soldier stood by the kitchen window, peering into the night.

"We're looking for somebody," the leader said next. "Perhaps you can help us."

* * *

His name was Walter. He didn't bother to introduce the rest of his men. Instead they questioned Amina thoroughly, and told her they'd come to meet with someone very important.

"It's the colonel, isn't it?" she asked. "Colonel Halabi, I mean. You're here for him."

Walter tensed visibly at this. "Do you know where he is?"

"What about David?" she asked instead. "Have you come for David as well?"

The two traded confused looks. "Ma'am?"

"Sergeant David Sweet. He is an American like you, like all of you." She found it difficult to speak without having the words tumble over one another in the rush to be free. "He came here two weeks ago, after escaping from the army. I saw soldiers capture him, along with the rest of our group."

"Slow down. Start from the beginning." She told them everything she knew, from beginning to end. Word that she had been part of the group that had sheltered Halabi stoked their interest noticeably. Walter listened patiently, never interrupting. In the end he asked more questions, wanting clarification in this, making her add details to that, before handing over a few sheets of notepaper and a pencil.

"You know the location of the local police station?" Walter asked. She nodded in reply. "Good. Sketch out what you know of it. Try not to leave anything out."

She did as he asked. Eventually she provided a rough outline of the building, which she had seen only from the street outside. She also guessed there would be at least twenty Iraqi National Police officers stationed there full time, with light weapons only. Walter took careful notes, again asking a few questions to clarify several items she had not thought to mention.

"Fifteen minutes, Mister Jerome." They were the first words the man at the window had spoken.

Walter checked his watch. "Saddle up. Gehren, you take point."

"Aye, sir."

Moments later the Americans led her back out into the wind and the rain. She asked him where they were going.

"East, to someplace safe." His hand was firm on her arm as he steered her through the night. "Now keep quiet, all right? There are patrols all over this area."

* * *

"Situation report from Wishbone Six, sir."

The Air Force technical sergeant handed over a secure-com document folder and departed. Peter Vermeer read the brief missive and quickly digested its contents. He handed it over to Grant Lattimore, who grunted sourly.

"Looks like we're done here."

"The hell you say." Vermeer snagged a telephone receiver and dialed the number to Steven Lindsley. A few minutes later, both he and Lattimore met with the SEAL commander in one of the facility's many underground briefing rooms.

Vermeer took a moment to regard the ops map tacked to the wall. "Jerome's team can't possibly take on an entire police detachment by themselves. Not with just four men. What assets do we have available for immediate deployment?"

"Just a second." Lindsley regarded a copy of the XVIII Airborne Corps Quick Reaction Force roster. "There's a Ranger company stationed at al-Kharj. We can have them in the air inside of two hours if we make the call right now."

"Get it cleared through CENTCOM." Vermeer lit a cigarette, and began puffing away thoughtfully. "I want boots on the ground before midnight tonight, gentlemen. And Commander? See if you can get Lieutenant Jerome back on the horn. We have a rescue mission to get up and running."

CHAPTER 19

On the outskirts of Amarah, Iraq
(0059 hours – Thursday, 21 February 1991)

The grumble of distant aircraft engines reached the ears of the men waiting in the tall grass. The highway into Amarah was just visible in the distance as an occasional cluster of fast-moving automobile headlights. Lieutenant Walter Jerome checked his watch before nodding to his radioman.

"Red Cap, this is Wishbone Six. Come in, over."

"This is Red Cap Actual. Send your traffic."

"In position Rally Point Tango." Boatswain's Mate Louis Gehren spoke slowly and distinctly into the RT pickup.

"Inbound now."

Like the rest of his men, Jerome wore night-vision goggles. Looking westward he saw a number of ghostly figures rise from cover and approach, outlined in vivid green-on-black.

A platoon of U.S. Army Rangers had been sent to assist the SEALs with Halabi's rescue. The senior man was First Lieutenant Amos Castillo. He seemed grimly businesslike as Jerome outlined the details of the coming raid. Minutes later the combined task force moved out, hidden now behind a fresh rainsquall that had swept in from the marshlands to the northwest.

* * *

"This is wonderful, thank you." Qassim Abdul Zahra sipped the coffee one of his men had offered him, and smiled. The night's labor had been grueling, almost painfully so, and he'd needed something to rejuvenate himself. He turned back to the man he'd been interrogating for the past four hours.

"Please, Sergeant! You cannot expect me to believe you are here by chance. Tell me the truth, so we can end this now."

David Sweet sat tied to a nearby chair. Zahra knew the man's last dose of morphine had long since worn off, leaving his wounded leg drenched in fire. The American looked up through abuse-swollen eyes and struggled to form his reply.

"Sweet, David L. Gunnery Sergeant, United States Marine Corps. Service Number—"

"Sergeant al-Jaafri." The burly Iraqi carried a leather-wrapped truncheon. He lifted it now, and slammed it across Sweet's shoulders with brutal efficiency.

"How many soldiers were sent to rescue the traitor Halabi?" Zahra asked. "What is your unit designation, and where are the rest of your men? Answer me. I have no wish to hurt you more than is strictly necessary."

"Sweet, David L. Gunnery Sergeant, United States Marine Corps." The rest of his reply was strangled off as al-Jaafri lifted his truncheon for another go.

* * *

0300 hours: Jerome crouched atop a small hillock five hundred meters from the Iraqi police compound. Castillo and their respective senior NCOs huddled nearby. Jerome swept powerful night-vision optics across the distant compound. The half-dozen buildings there were single story, concrete block and surrounded by a brick wall topped with razor wire. He saw a lone sentry stationed at the guard shack at the only gate into the place.

"Have one squad stay with my men, to perform a dynamic entry," Jerome whispered. "The rest of your people deploy in support. I want one squad here, and another here, to provide covering fire." He indicated two locations on his map for the Rangers to set up, the first atop a low rise to the west. The other was along the road leading into town, two hundred meters due north.

"Yes, sir." Castillo took a moment to regard his own map of the area. "What about blocking positions?"

"Set up an MG team here." He indicated a spot about three hundred meters down the road into Amarah. Any reinforcements from the city garrison would come from that direction. With luck the strike team would be in and out so quickly that the Iraqis would have no idea what hit them.

Minutes later the first Rangers began to move off into the night. Jerome noted the time once more: thirty minutes, he thought, until the last of Castillo's force would be in position.

* * *

Amina Jabouri watched as the last of the Americans crept into the darkness to begin their attack. She'd been stationed with a small force of soldiers at the road, a short way from the police station. The man she knew as Walter was nowhere to be seen.

She watched the soldiers now, deeper shadows that shifted against the night. There was no idle conversation of any kind. She felt lost and alone, buried in the darkness. Then, the glow of several sets of headlights came to her from the road, so bright it actually hurt her to gaze upon them.

She heard the American squad leader key his radio: "Wishbone Actual, Red Cap Seven. Contact report. Three, I say again, three Victors inbound your location."

* * *

Jerome answered the report with three clicks from his tactical set. He huddled in a drainage ditch fifty meters from the compound gate. His SEALs and the Rangers who made up the primary assault team crouched beside him. All waited in tense silence as the headlights of the approaching vehicles drew near.

* * *

"Lieutenant? The cars you asked for have arrived."

"Thank you." Zahra looked at the wall clock and saw that it was just after 0400. Orders had come via landline less than an hour before. He was to transfer both the American and Halabi to a dedicated interrogation facility in Baghdad as soon as possible. He'd already requested the services of a half-dozen National Policemen to serve as escorts for the drive north.

* * *

Jerome chose his best men for the approach. Chief Torres hung back, his rifle to one shoulder and aimed at the distant compound. Gehren was at Jerome's side, a suppressed MP-5 held tight. Jerome took point as the group edged closer to the lone Iraqi stationed at the entrance gate.

A light flared in his night-vision goggles. Jerome watched as the sentry put flame to the tip of a cigarette and inhaled deeply. The glow illuminated the policeman's blunt, hawk-nosed features and wrinkled uniform. Jerome peered over the sights of his Heckler & Koch submachine gun, settling his breathing, and took up the slack on the trigger. The squat little weapon chugged once, softly, like the airbrake on a Kenworth truck.

He saw the guy fall in a boneless tumble, and go still. Gehren was up and moving in a heartbeat, dragging the dead man out of the way.

Once Gehren was finished Jerome eased forward, his weapon held tight. The assault team was dashing through the gate and into the compound seconds later. Jerome heard a voice, questioning, followed by a shouted alarm. A Ranger aimed at the distant figure. His rifle stuttered, and the man spun back. Jerome knew the sound of those shots would carry for miles.

He ran on, legs piston-like across the hard-packed ground. His weapon was a leaden weight in his hands as he sped on toward the compound's main administrative building. Gehren and the others, he knew, would be tight on his heels.

* * *

Sweet lay on his cot, battered, bleeding, and alone. They'd already come for Halabi. Sweet had offered token resistance, and received a punch in the gut for his trouble. Now he sprawled lifelessly, clutching at his wounded leg, which seemed to throb dully with every beat of his heart.

It was then that he heard a weapon discharge. It was an assault rifle on full auto, one part of his exhausted mind noted. Staccato and all-too brief, the gunshots echoed far amidst the rainy night.

His first thought was they'd just executed someone, Halabi probably, but he dismissed the idea almost immediately. The Iraqis would kill them both, certainly, but not right away. Not without a thorough interrogation first. He was just trying to lever himself up to a sitting position when the crackle of more gunfire split the night. This time he recognized the sound without a doubt: the pop of M-16s mixed with the meaty rumble of a belt-fed M-60. He felt his pulse race as he rolled painfully to the floor and began to listen to the hallway outside for signs of rescue.

* * *

Jerome crouched behind one of the several police vehicles parked at the southern end of the compound. His men had already killed the Iraqis positioned there. At the moment they were trading potshots with police sentries at the entrance to the main administrative building.

He heard the fresh roar of gunfire from outside the compound. The balance of Castillo's Rangers had joined the fight, and now poured concentrated fire onto the various outbuildings scattered around the courtyard. Now and again the startling *CRACK* of an exploding grenade would sound, punctuated by more incoming small arms fire.

"Sergeant Rodriquez!"

A Ranger turned away from firing his weapon. "Sir?"

Jerome indicated the entrance to the administrative complex, where enemy muzzle flashes now flickered. "Clear that door, soldier."

"Roger that." Rodriquez dug the blocky shape of a disposable AT-4 rocket launcher from his pack. All stood clear as he extended the launch tube and settled the weapon on one shoulder.

"On the way!" The launcher discharged with a roaring *WHOOOSH*, followed by a great gout of thick, cloying smoke. The propellant motor ignited, carrying the 84mm rocket downrange. Jerome saw it impact the door to the distant building, still occupied by Iraqi gunmen. The resulting blast blotted all away before him, concealing the remains of the opening through a thick haze of filthy smoke and flame.

* * *

Lieutenant Qassim Zahra crouched in the darkness, struggling to fit a magazine into the assault rifle somebody had handed him. The lights had gone out seconds before, shortly after a deafening blast had rocked the building. His hands were slick with sweat. Policemen screamed to one another, and gunshots roared.

The Americans were here? Zahra threw down the rifle and cowered beside a desk, praying for salvation. He was just considering whether or not to try to find the door out of this place when there was yet another detonation, this one much louder and more close by.

He stood and raised his hands high. "Don't shoot! I surrender!"

* * *

Sudden, darting movement drew Jerome's attention as he entered the next room over. Acting on instinct, he pivoted right and felt the suppressed MP-5 go into recoil. The figure tottered and fell, ventilated through the torso and stomach by multiple hits. He realized only belatedly that the man had been trying to surrender.

There were more gunshots, followed by a smoke-seared silence. "Clear!" one of the Rangers shouted.

"Clear." Jerome buttoned out the partially spent magazine in his weapon before reaching for another.

* * *

Sweet huddled in one corner of his cell, listening to the furious clamor of gunfire. Occasionally he could hear men shouting to one another, frenzied and strident, near panic. Long minutes came and went, streaming by like burning tracers, before those sounds began to diminish, and taper off altogether. He heard a clatter as the door to the cell block was levered open, and heavy footsteps sounded on damp concrete.

His cell was the first in line. Sweet tensed as the key sounded in the lock and the door was thrown wide. The glow of a weapon-mounted flashlight blazed forth, and a stern voice ordered him to identify himself.

"Gunnery Sergeant Sweet, United States Marine Corps." The words came out as a hoarse rasp.

The man lowered his weapon, and held out a hand. "Good to see you, Gunny. Care for a ride home?"

The wind was cold as Sweet was carried outside, past a litter of bodies and the fires lit by the American assault. He guessed the men rescuing him were SEALs or Delta. All moved to secure the area and get the rescued POWs out as quickly as possible.

Someone hustled up a stretcher and ordered Sweet to get on. A corpsman gave him a shot, another course of painkillers probably, and the group moved out, jostling Sweet over the rough, uneven ground. He heard radio chatter, and the soft crunch of boots on wet, rocky soil.

"Sweet! You made it! You're alive!" Mohammed Halabi loped along beside him, wrapped now in borrowed Kevlar body armor.

"We made it, Colonel. We made it."

"Yes. Now you rest! They tell me helicopters are on the way to bring us out." Halabi moved on ahead into the gathering night.

* * *

The sky had begun to glow with the first hesitant vestiges of dawn. Sweet rested on the litter as a medic gave him an IV. The drugs left him loopy and disconnected. At first it seemed like some cruel dream when Amina sat by his side and took him by the hand.

"David, you're alive."

"So they tell me." He licked too-dry lips and tried to sit up. The Ranger medic forced him back down. "What happened to you? How did you get away?" he asked her.

"None of that is important." She wouldn't let go of his hand. He heard the thump of approaching choppers now, drawing close.

"Halabi lives as well." She had to lean close so he could hear her over the roar of jet turbines.

"I saw him. Are you coming with us?"

She said nothing in return. But those beautiful dark eyes told him everything. He squeezed her hand gently.

"I'll never be able to thank you enough," he said. It was getting very hard to stay awake.

"Go. Just go." She clung to his hand for one last moment.

A quartet of Rangers picked up the litter. He felt Amina's hand being pulled away, and she was gone, lost to the surrounding darkness. Sweet peered into the night and saw Halabi running toward one of two grounded Pave Low special-ops transport helicopters. Red station-keeping lights glimmered in the rain. The soldiers were moving forward as well, and beginning to climb aboard.

Suddenly the world tilted crazily, and seemed to vomit fire. Halabi and his two escorts had been about thirty meters ahead, leading the way through the grit stirred up by the rotors. Fire blotted away everything before him, followed by the slap of a great fist of heat and terror. One of the helos was burning. Sweet saw a man in desert BDUs cast off to one side. Most of his right leg was gone, with just a bloody stump remaining. A heartbeat later Sweet was facedown by the roadside, upended as the men carrying his litter hit the dirt.

"Medic! Oh my God! *Medic!!!*"

Sweet was trying to crawl forward even as the last echoes of the blast faded away. He knew instinctively what had happened even before he reached the wounded and the dying: incoming artillery fire, the Iraqis had gotten the range. He found Halabi on his back, staring up at the storm-clouded sky. The air smelled of burning avgas.

"Colonel? Don't move, all right? Help is on the way."

Halabi's right arm was gone at the elbow. Blood covered everything. Sweet looked down as Halabi reached out and grasped him weakly by the arm.

"You'll tell them, won't you? Tell them. About Abernathy, and Bed Check. Tell them . . ."

It was already too late by the time the medics arrived. The dead were tagged and zipped up in black body bags, and carted off on the surviving Pave Low. Sweet went along too, settled beside Halabi's remains and staring out the window at the vast, empty desert far below.

CHAPTER 20

MCAS Kaneohe Bay – Hawaii
(0009 hours – Tuesday, 26 February 1991)

The long wait was finally over. The ground component to Desert Storm had kicked off three days before, amidst a massive preparatory artillery barrage and air assault. Tens of thousands of American, British, French and other Coalition troops were on the move, with armored columns snaking for miles across the desolate Arabian Peninsula.

In the east the attack was led by Task Force Ripper, a composite unit encompassing elements of the 5th and 7th Marine Regiments. Supported on either flank by U.S., Saudi and Kuwaiti infantry, the task force had torn through the Iraqis screening the border like a Mameluke sword through wet tissue paper.

What had followed was something the talking heads were already referring to as the largest tank battle in Marine Corps history. The steel fist that was Task Force Ripper had slammed into the Iraqi units holding the al-Wafra and Umm Gudair oil fields, destroying them utterly. Now Coalition forces were driving on Kuwait City, with spearhead units already entering the outer suburbs. Iraqi forces were reported to be in full retreat.

It was a grand victory, the network pundits all said. A complete and total rout. And Jessica Seeley had gotten to see it all, live on CNN!

As she had suspected, Colonel McCurry had finally decided to relieve her for cause, and ship her back to the States. Upon arrival at Kaneohe Bay, she had been told by JAG to prepare for an Article 134 hearing. The expected charges: dereliction of duty, failure to obey a lawful order, and adultery. Seeley had assumed more charges would be coming forthwith.

Then everything had ground to a halt. There would be no courts martial, no UCMJ hearing. At first she had been unsure why the Corps' well-oiled, nigh-unstoppable wheels of justice could fail at such an opportune moment, but then a letter had arrived with one possible explanation.

The letter had been from 1st Lt. Moira Peay, USMC. Moira and Seeley had been roommates during her tour at Guantanamo Bay, and had remained close friends in the years since. Moira was in Saudi even now, assigned to an admin slot with Headquarters, 1st Marine Division:

2/8/91: Hey, kiddo. I guess there's no easy way to say this. We just got the final casualty reports from Khafji. David is listed as missing and probably KIA, along with four of the Marines who were on his helo. The only survivor we know of is a female PFC from H&S Company. The Iraqis have her listed as a POW.

Seeley sat and reread those damning words for what had to be the thousandth time. She was also very, very drunk. The base package store had been open earlier, so she had stocked up on tax-free Jose Cuervo and any other sundries she would need in the coming hours.

The bastards would never lynch a dead hero, she thought. She scrubbed tears from one cheek. The end of Moira's letter had suggested that David was being considered for a posthumous Bronze Star, a high honor in light of the war's relative brevity. Punishing her would only shed unwanted attention to what she and David had had between them.

She topped off her glass before settling in to watch the show. Arthur Kent blathered on about Saddam's chemical stockpile, blah-blah-blah, at some safe location far from the fighting. The prick. It took effort for her not to throw her glass at his smug, pretty boy face.

Seeley wondered if David's mother had been told yet. Probably the local recruiter had stopped by with the bad news, an ugly duty, but part of his responsibilities nonetheless. She wished she could have been there, even if the two women had never met.

She didn't even have a photo of him. Not one. They never dared keep anything that personal as proof of their illicit liaison, and now Seeley regretted it terribly. As she regretted a great many things.

She had looked up his mother's telephone number. The address, too, to his childhood home in Illinois. Seeley considered placing the call for what had to be the tenth time that night. What would the poor woman think? Certainly David had not told his family about her. Not the proud gunnery sergeant, from a long, colorful line of career military stretching all the way back to Antietam.

Arthur Kent continued to stare back at her, mocking. Sighing, she refilled her glass once more. The tequila, her best friend, her only friend, would hold her hand until morning and the sun rose to greet the new day.

* * *

Wednesday, 27 February: the highway to Basra was clogged with vehicles fleeing north. Staff Sergeant Bill Marino huddled atop a nearby ridge, peering through a set of high-power binoculars. The remainder of his Force Recon patrol was scattered nearby, weapons outboard in case of attack. The thump of heavy artillery still sounded to the north, in the direction of Iraq's only major seaport. He'd been watching the vehicles move north for nearly twenty minutes. There were hundreds of them: civilian cars, trucks, plus more than a few Russian-built cargo carriers, jeeps, and infantry fighting vehicles. Enough, he thought, to move an entire Iraqi infantry division.

His radioman handed Marino the SATCOM handset. He checked the grid coordinates on his map before asking Higher for fire support.

"Bravo Seven, Zulu Two-eight. Stand by." Marino huddled beneath his camouflage poncho and waited. Moments later the voice of someone in the First Marine Expeditionary Force fire support center came on the horn: "Bravo Seven, stand down. I say again, stand down. A general ceasefire is now in place. Stand by to receive further orders."

Fifteen minutes later Marino had those orders: stay hidden and watch the Iraqis as they fled north, away from the burning remains of Kuwait. It seemed the war was over. Marino had never gotten to fire his weapon in anger.

The first stragglers began to trickle in just before nightfall. At first there were twenty of them: lean, hungry young men, filthy and bedraggled and clad in the scraps of proper military attire. They surrendered the moment they stumbled upon one of his marines, throwing down their rifles, prostrating themselves, calling out for mercy. One young lieutenant actually kissed Marino's hand as he begged for something to eat. Marino gave out what he had and asked Higher for new instructions. He was told to send them to the rear, toward where other units were setting up EPW collection points.

His mission of forward reconnaissance rapidly became impossible to accomplish. Word spread of the presence of an American unit on the ridge. By dawn nearly eight hundred men had crossed into his AO, been disarmed and now sat in neat rows beneath the polluted, cloud-smeared sky. The senior Iraqi was a brigadier general. Marino accepted his surrender with all due ceremony, and called it in. Soon helos came with reinforcements, as well as more food and medicine.

Marino silently thanked God as the first marine riflemen began to spill from the grounded helos. Until their arrival, his team had been outnumbered by the Iraqis by more than two hundred to one.

The man in charge was a major. Marino was only too happy to hand over the entire mess to him. Four days later the men of Recon 2/4 found themselves on a helo headed back to base. With luck, Marino thought, showers and hot chow would be waiting for them there.

* * *

The Regency Palace Hotel – Amman, Jordan
(0900 hours – Thursday, 28 February 1991)

Michael Litke had been in the midst of doing his daily twenty-five when a pool attendant came looking for him.

"Mister Koehler? Your wife is looking for you, sir."

"Thank you, Artemio."

Litke climbed out of the water and grabbed his robe. There was no time for a shower, he thought. He found Elise Shilling waiting for him in the hotel restaurant.

"Sorry to interrupt, but we have confirmation. Halabi is dead. We head back this afternoon."

"I see." Litke signaled for a waiter and ordered orange juice and a fruit plate. "So now we're on cleanup detail?"

She smiled languidly. "Yes. Control has identified two targets, both in the Washington D.C. area. We should have details within the week."

"You seem inordinately pleased with yourself."

"I do not take to inaction as well as you. Better to be on the move, and doing something."

Litke nodded. "To each her own. Still, it was a nice little holiday."

"So it was." She caressed his hand as the waiter returned with Litke's order.

"There is something to add, however."

Litke sipped his juice. "Go on."

"Control has another possible target, location unknown. I get the impression it's a rush job, something unexpected in the original contract. They've authorized us to bring on extra personnel as required."

"Hmm." The cantaloupe was a bit gamy, he decided. "Dietrich and Peter are still in Marseilles. Add their teams to the mix and we'll have a total of thirteen men. Will that be enough to handle three separate targets?"

"It will have to do." She stood. "Call Dietrich and make sure they catch the first flight out."

"Of course." Litke watched her go before summoning a waiter to ask for an overseas telephone line. The call lasted less than seven minutes. Once he was finished, Litke joined Elise in their room. She had already packed his bags for him.

One hour later Wolf and Elsie Koehler, of Bern, Switzerland, checked out of the Regency and headed for the airport. Their flight to Toronto was scheduled for 1320 sharp.

CHAPTER 21

The Persian Gulf
(0955 hours – Friday, 1 March 1991)

David Sweet's final debriefing took place aboard the USS *New Orleans*, an amphibious assault ship in the Persian Gulf.

Sweet had been sequestered the moment he'd been brought aboard. Armed marines had taken over his security, and filed him away deep below decks. Soon thereafter the interviews began, and continued nonstop for the better part of a week. A deluge of counterintelligence types had come to see him. Humorless men from CIA, NSA, even the Defense Intelligence Agency, all had come and spoken to him, questioned him, asking him about Mohammed Halabi, and what he'd wanted to give the Agency that was so goddamn important.

His lead interrogators had been a trio of CIA field officers he'd been introduced to on his first day here. The first two, men named Detloff and Lattimore, seemed to be typical Agency bureaucrats: Ivy League prissy, soft.

But the man he knew as Vermeer seemed different. Sweet had heard of him before, mostly vague rumblings from guys on the SEAL Teams or with U.S. Army Special Forces. They called him the Painter, and said he was former Delta, one of those larger than life boogey men you hear about if you stay in special ops too long. At the moment the two were alone. Peter Vermeer regarded the file folder on the table before him. Sweet thought it looked like a copy of his military service record.

"I think it's time you were on your way, Gunny."

"Sir?" A twinge of pain lanced through his wounded thigh as Sweet shifted his weight without thinking. His meds were wearing off again, he thought. Thank God the bullet had missed the bone.

Vermeer opened the file and extracted a sheaf of papers. They were transfer orders, Sweet saw. His name was printed at the top.

"You're being reassigned." Vermeer smiled. "It's a clean slate. An honest-to-God fresh start. Your CO sent them over personally."

His new assignment would be a training slot with the Amphibious Reconnaissance School at Little Creek, Virginia. It was not a punishment, Sweet thought, but it also wasn't exactly a reward either. They were taking him out of Force Recon, if not in the way he'd first expected.

"I haven't been allowed to speak with anyone since I was rescued, sir. I'm talking about my family and the guys in my unit. I figure they're pretty worried about me."

"I'll see to it after we're done here," Vermeer promised. "I just want you to remember something for me."

"Sir?"

"You've had a sterling record until now. I'd like you to keep it that way."

It felt as if a sudden chill had swept through the compartment. "I beg your pardon?"

Vermeer lit a cigarette. "Everything you heard, everything you saw in Iraq is classified to the highest level. This operation is strictly black side, no exceptions. You say nothing to your mother, your pet hamster, your fucking parish priest. Have I made myself perfectly clear?"

"Yes, sir. Perfectly clear."

"Good. There's a helo leaving for al-Kharj in one hour. I want you on it. From there you should be able to catch a flight back to the States."

There could be no clearer dismissal, Sweet thought. He grabbed his crutches before making his way through the nearest knee knocker and out into the passageway. Blue sky scudded with high cirrus greeted him as he hobbled his way up on deck.

It felt good to have the clean wind on his face. He watched as a guided-missile cruiser came up on their port quarter, three or four miles out and making way at twenty knots or so.

A man in civilian attire stood smoking a cigarette at the rail. James Detloff was tall and heavyset, with round, cherubic features and flat brown eyes. He also looked kind of sickly,

Sweet thought, with a faint gray cast to his already sallow complexion.

"Mr. Detloff."

"Sergeant." For a moment the two men stood and watched the distant warship. Neither spoke. Detloff flicked his cigarette over the rail.

"I wouldn't take Pete Vermeer too seriously," he said. "He's just doing his job. Putting the fear of God into you, keeping you in line. Being an asshole comes naturally to some people, I guess."

"Things could have come out differently, sir. I know that."

"I suppose so." Detloff's expression was flat, unreadable. "Still, you did good, getting out of Iraq in one piece. Too bad it turned out the way it did."

"Yeah." The word was bitter against Sweet's tongue, like stale ash.

"The worst part is that Halabi died before he could tell us anything of value," Detloff was saying. "Those names he mumbled to you before he died? Worthless. It's old data, stuff from an operation that ran its course years ago. It's sad, really, considering all the trouble you went through to bring him out."

"I understand. Thank you, sir." Suddenly this wasn't the place Sweet wanted to be. As he left, however, he saw Detloff turn to look at him, and continue to regard Sweet with those dark, thoughtful eyes.

CHAPTER 22

Prince Sultan Airbase – al-Kharj, Saudi Arabia
(0505 hours – Saturday, 2 March 1991)

Sweet spent most of the night camped out on a chair inside the base's cramped dispersal area. His only companions had been a tattered paperback novel and an endless supply of bad coffee in those little Styrofoam cups they hand out at AA meetings.

Now he sat, looking out the window at the coming dawn. The winter rains had finally ended, bringing fierce sandstorms that choked the sky beneath clouds of crimson, stinging grit. In the distance he could see a lone C-141 transport taxiing onto the main runway, prepping for takeoff. His own space-available MAC flight was scheduled to depart at 0750, destination the Continental United States.

An airman turned on a nearby television. It was tuned to CNN. Sweet looked up, and saw burning Iraqi cities on the screen.

The Americans had just liberated oil-rich Kuwait, Sweet thought. Now the Iraqi people seemed to expect the same for themselves. Spontaneous uprisings had already flared up in both the Kurdish north and amongst the Shiite majority in the south. Amarah was one of the cities in flames. He thought of Amina, and wondered where she was now.

The door to the ready shack opened, and more than a dozen men in desert BDUs sauntered in. Most lugged duffle bags and unloaded M-16 rifles. The promised troop draw-downs had already begun. Time for everyone to come home, mission accomplished, aye aye, sir.

He pulled his crutches closer as a quartet of young soldiers from the 82nd Airborne settled in, speaking loudly amongst themselves. They stank of sweat and dust. Sweet was suddenly very keen to be on his way home.

He had called Mom the night before. She had been overjoyed to hear from him, of course. Sweet had asked her to call

Jessica and let her know he was all right. The fact that he'd been listed as missing and probably killed in action could not have sat well with either of them.

A man dressed in desert utilities and a rumpled boonie cap appeared before him. "Mind if I have a seat, old man?"

"Aw, shit. Bill!" Sweet grinned ear to ear as Bill Marino and the rest of the marines of Recon 2/4 pressed forward through the crowd.

"Good to see you." Sweet greeted his old teammates in turn. "What are you doing here? Did the colonel finally come to his senses and send you packing?"

"Something like that." Marino eyed Sweet's crutches. "Can we talk a minute?"

"Sure." Sullen heat washed across them both as they made their way into the dusty morning sunshine.

"They told us you were dead." Marino lit a cigarette. "It was confirmed all the way up to Division."

"You sound disappointed."

Marino snorted. "Not particularly. Just remember the two hundred bucks you owe me."

The two braced to attention and saluted as some Air Force brass wandered near.

"Good morning, sir. Ma'am." Sweet shifted his interest back to Marino. "Seriously, though. What are you doing here?"

Again his old friend shrugged. "McCurry cut us orders, TAD. I have no idea where we're going, or what we're gonna do once we get there. You know the drill. How about you?"

Sweet explained his spike of 'good fortune,' although not exactly how he had come by it. He asked Marino if he'd heard anything about Jessica.

"She's fine, from what I hear." Bill related everything that had happened back at Division since Sweet had gone missing the month before. "JAG was forced to drop the charges against her. You're both in the clear, Dave! Everyone in the company is wondering how you managed to pull it off."

Sweet considered how much more he should say. "I just wanted to thank you. You know, for coming to see Jess when you did. Mom tells me it helped her to know something about what happened to me. I guess it drove her nuts, thinking I was dead."

Marino blinked. "Your mom? What, they're on speaking terms already?"

"Yeah, I guess."

"Damn." Marino flicked his cigarette into a nearby butt can. "Looks like you're gonna be shopping for rings soon. Give me a call. I know a guy."

"Thanks, Bill. You're all heart."

"Staff Sergeant Marino!" A young marine by the name of Ahern stuck his head out of the ready shack window.

"Yeah?"

"Our bird's ready, Staff Sergeant. Fifteen minutes."

"Have Corporal Rice stage everybody's gear. I'll be there in five."

"Aye, Staff Sergeant."

The two said their goodbyes, secure in the knowledge they would almost surely meet again. Force Recon was just too small a portion of the special ops community for it to be any other way.

CHAPTER 23

Aboard USS *New Orleans* (LPH-11)
(1115 hours – Saturday, 2 March 1991)

Peter Vermeer had sat through the video of the Amarah rescue mission at least a dozen times. Seven U.S. military personnel were dead, with another nine critically injured. A multi-million dollar aircraft had been lost, and Mohammed Halabi was confirmed as one of the fallen. Yet it seemed to him that answers, for the moment at least, would be few and far between.

The screen, frosted in static, cleared on a blank screen. The date stamp read: 0350 ZULU 210291 / Amarah Iraq. Vermeer watched as the image steadied, showing a helo outlined in the night-vision pick-up. Dark forms scurried through the black, evacuating the extraction team's primary LZ. Vermeer had been on enough covert operations to know that everything had gone perfectly here, with no friendly fatalities, and the rescue team on the cusp of a successful withdrawal from Indian Country. Then, chaos and death: he saw the screen grow clouded by white frost, followed by an eruption of fire and burning wreckage. Moments later the tape ended, cut off as the camera operator ran forward to help with the wounded and the dying.

"You still down here, Pete? I thought you were packed and ready to go." Vermeer looked up to see Grant Lattimore standing at the hatch, carrying a light duffle.

"Sorry. I guess I'm just trying to make sense of it all." He clicked off the VCR. "Although I'm not really sure what I'm looking for, to be honest."

"You still think it was an internal explosion?" Lattimore watched as Vermeer ejected the tape and put it in a secure document bag.

"That's the only thing that makes sense to me, yeah."

"We've exhaustively interviewed the personnel involved," Lattimore said. "That includes Sergeant Sweet and the members of Jerome's SEAL team. At this juncture, none of them are sure what happened out there."

"Is there any chance the Iraqis simply got lucky, and hit the landing zone with artillery?" Vermeer asked.

"It was that, or something similar," Lattimore replied. "Look. There was a lot of unexploded ordinance in the area. Maybe it's as simple as someone stepping on an Iraqi toe-popper or tripping a stray bomblet that we put there ourselves."

"What about the surviving Pave Low?" Vermeer gathered up his satchel and other personal items before joining Lattimore in the passageway outside. "I assume you had someone sweep it after the Rangers made it back to Saudi territory?"

"They found nothing unusual." Lattimore shrugged. "If you're right, and there was a bomb planted aboard either chopper the people responsible are very good at covering their tracks."

Both men paused long enough to let a gaggle of sailors pass in the tight confines of the passageway. "That's why I contacted Admiral Mollar last night," Vermeer said, "and asked for an NSA forensics team to head out to the site and investigate. He still hasn't got back to me, though."

"That may not be a good idea, Pete. That helo went down deep in Iraqi territory. We don't have any troops in that area, even now. It'd be a major operation to get a team in there, even with the ceasefire in place."

"We have to try, Grant. You know that."

"It's your funeral."

"What about the file I asked you to get me?"

"Sorry, I forgot." Lattimore dug into his bag and extracted a folder bordered with Top Secret signage. "The DOD courier brought it in just this morning."

"Thanks." There was a Navy Sea King idling on the flight deck. He and Lattimore settled onboard, isolated by the throbbing turbines as the helicopter lifted off and headed west, toward the Saudi coast. Once they were safely airborne, Vermeer opened the file and began to read.

One of the names Gunny Sweet had brought back from Iraq had tugged at him, stirring some distant memory. It seemed to belong to Brigadier General Mitchell Abernathy, United States Army. The general had been another old Special Forces hand, one of the best of the crowd that came up with legendary operators like Dick Meadows and Bull Simons, all veterans of Vietnam. By the latter 1980s Abernathy had been a senior officer at SOCOM, and in charge of covert operations in Europe and the Middle East.

His death four years earlier had come as a tragic blow to the Special Forces community. He'd died in a helicopter crash, a pointless end hardly fitting a warrior of Abernathy's stature. Vermeer recalled the investigation into the accident, carried out by a dual U.S. Air Force/NTSB committee. No sign of foul play had ever been discovered.

Vermeer sat and regarded the photo included in the file. It was of an older man, age fifty or so, with wide, smiling features and tidy grey-brown hair. Nothing in the official record linked Abernathy with Operation Backgammon. At the time of his death he'd been attending a NATO Special Forces exercise in southern Europe. His personal Huey had crashed on takeoff, killing all seven men aboard. Another photo showed the wreckage, deep in a ravine somewhere in the Italian Alps.

Abernathy, the death of Halabi and Bed Check: was it all connected somehow? Or was he was seeing phantoms where none existed? Vermeer gritted his teeth as he felt the big Sikorsky bank gently to the west, toward landfall and the nearest military airfield. From there he and Lattimore would board yet another outbound flight, and continue their long journey home.

* * *

A little over thirty-six hours later, James Detloff caught a taxi in from Andrews Air Force Base. He'd been on a military flight for the last part of the trip back from Saudi. It was already dark when he got out and paid the driver. The Charter Arms .44 Special he carried was a comforting presence as he was walked up the path to his modest two-story brownstone on Eisenhower Avenue, just off the I-495 into Maryland.

"Jim?" It was a familiar voice, and yet it startled Detloff . He turned to see a man in a trench coat coming up the walk.

"Yes?"

"It's me, Ian Trucco."

"Colonel. Hello." Detloff let his hand fall away from the concealed revolver. "What do you want? It's late, and I just got home from a very long trip."

Trucco came more fully into the light. "Do you have a minute? It's kind of important."

"I'm pretty tired."

"This will just take a minute," Trucco repeated. "Come on. I'll buy the first round."

There was a neighborhood bar just a block away. The two settled in to a booth at the back and waited until the girl had come to take their order.

"What do you want, Colonel?"

"Nothing too juicy." Trucco toyed with his bottle, scribing wet circles on the table before him. "And nothing classified, either. It's just something from a few years ago, background for the story I'm writing."

"Why not go through the public information office at Langley? I'm sure they'd be happy to help you."

"I already tried that. They gave me the 'need to know' runaround, just like always."

Detloff lit a cigarette. "What makes you think I'm going to be any different?"

"Just take a look, all right?" Trucco pulled a tattered manila envelope from his pocket. "Somebody sent me this in the mail a couple of days ago. I was wondering if you'd give me your opinion."

Detloff took the envelope and removed the three photographs therein. One look and he was on his feet, ready to head for the door.

"Good night, Colonel." Detloff threw a ten dollar bill down on the table to pay his part of the tab. "Don't ever come to see me again."

"I thought Backgammon was old news, Jim. Why—"

But it was too late. Detloff was already halfway to the door before Trucco could gather up his coat to follow.

CHAPTER 24

San Diego, California
(1813 hours (PST) – Friday, 5 April 1991)

David Sweet spent his last night in California at the Ramada Inn located just a few blocks from the airport.

He'd already checked out of his prior duty station at Camp Pendleton. Boxes packed, gear forwarded to Norfolk, service records shipped on ahead. Sweet settled on the bed and checked out what was on cable. His flight was scheduled to depart at 0945 tomorrow.

Everything he needed for the next thirty days was in the olive drab sea bag on the floor by the bed. Besides civilian clothing, a few uniforms, and various personal things, Sweet had brought one item in particular, more precious in its own way than the blood that flowed through his veins. The girl at the jewelry store had helped him pick out a diamond engagement ring, one-half karat in a white gold setting. He'd bought it the week before, spending most of his back pay in the process. He hoped Jess would like it. He put it in the black velvet-lined box it had come in and hid it away in his carry-on.

There wasn't much on TV, just grainy video of the LAPD beating some poor guy with nightsticks. It seemed to be on all the channels. Soon Sweet grew bored and turned it off. Should he call Jess? He'd just talked to her a few hours ago, as part of their plans to meet on Sunday. Just the thought of seeing her again left him feeling anxious and excited.

She'd mailed him a bundle of photos, dozens of them, all taken recently. Pictures of her smiling, laughing, or of her in a string bikini, and holding up a calendar that showed the days remaining until they would see each other once more.

More than a few of them had her wearing nothing at all. He was just wishing she was there when an airliner outbound from the airport passed overhead. The dull-throated rumble of its engines set his teeth on edge. The memories swirled deep inside him, like Coalition air circling endlessly overhead.

It all came back to him in a flash: the dampness of the old farmhouse, the smell of overcooked lamb and unwashed bodies. The cold, and the fear. Amina's dark eyes, and the way she seemed to laugh at every little stupid thing he said.

He set Jessica's photos aside before shutting off the light. He sat in the darkness, and tried to clear his mind, to think of nothing beyond the moment. But the airliners continued their cacophony long into the night, and sleep, it seemed, would be a long time in coming.

* * *

Valley Mede, Maryland
(2207 hours (EST) – Friday, 5 April 1991)

The two men had waited in the parked Mercedes-Benz for what seemed like hours. Willi Krenz sighed and checked his watch for the fourth time in as many minutes.

"Willi, relax. They'll be here soon."

"Sorry, Herr Hauptmann." Michael Litke did not bother to remind Krenz that he no longer deserved his old rank.

They were in the parking lot of a shopping mall near the westbound I-144, in an upscale neighborhood just west of Baltimore. Their target lived in a tidy two-story colonial less than six kilometers away.

Litke's car phone rang. He answered, spoke tersely for a few moments, and hung up.

"That was Elise," he said. Willi turned the key in the ignition. "He's on the way."

Litke unzipped the satchel at his feet and withdrew the Kalashnikov AKS-74U secreted inside. The Russian assault rifle was neatly counterbalanced by its short barrel and compact folding stock. He locked a magazine in place and drew back the bolt.

His pulse raged between his ears, an angry torrent, as both men scanned the street for any sign of their approaching quarry.

Minutes passed. “There he is.” Willi gunned the engine and pulled out into traffic, maintaining a three- to four-car distance between the two vehicles.

“Careful, Willi.” Litke gripped his weapon tightly. “Don’t get too close.”

The target drove a 1978 Corvette Stingray, candy apple red and nicely restored. The glow of a passing streetlamp briefly illuminated the Maryland plate on the rear bumper.

“That’s him.” Litke recognized the tag number. He maintained a death-grip on the AK as Willi closed in and changed lanes. Soon they were directly behind the target vehicle.

“There he goes.” Litke looked out to see the freeway exit on their right. “I’ll take him at the next light.”

“*Ja.*” The Corvette’s taillights glimmered as its driver slowed to take his customary route toward home.

A stoplight turned crimson just ahead. Litke watched the Corvette slow and then come to a complete stop. It was picture perfect, he thought, signaling Willi to pull up alongside. He stepped into the humid night air.

Grant Lattimore looked up from behind the wheel as Litke drew nigh. His pupils widened as Litke leveled the assault rifle and pressed the trigger. The little weapon rattled and spat, ejecting spent casings into the street.

Glass shattered, and Lattimore danced grotesquely as a dozen 5.45mm projectiles tore into him. Then he was down and bleeding out through multiple wounds to his chest and stomach.

Litke pulled the pin on a white phosphorus grenade and tossed it inside. He was back in the Mercedes, rolling for the freeway entrance when the first white-hot flames erupted from inside the vehicle.

Krenz merged into the fast lane as Litke dialed his car phone once more. Moments later a familiar female voice answered on the other end of the line.

“This is Deborah.”

"I need to talk to Mr. Saunders."

"He's not here right now. May I take a message?"

"Never mind." Litke rang off and turned to Willi. "Go to Rendezvous Three."

* * *

The Puss 'N Boots Tavern was located in the suburb of Maryland City, west of Fort Meade. The place catered mostly to bored government employees or the occasional lost tourist.

Litke found Elise Shilling in a booth near the back. The frown on her face him told him something was wrong.

"What is it?"

"Team Four missed the target. Hans called in twenty minutes ago."

"Shit."

She lit a cigarette. "They're trying to pick him back up, but I doubt anything will come of it."

Litke fought down the ticklish feeling that played around the base of his spine. "What happened?"

"Detloff didn't show up for work today." She made an angry gesture. "He wasn't at home either. Hans thinks he may have skipped town last night, before his team could get into position."

"So someone tipped him off?"

"Your guess is as good as mine."

"What about his family?" Litke asked.

"He is unmarried, with no children. I've already contacted Control. He says to wait for further orders, and to prepare to hit our last target."

That last bit caught Litke's attention. "You finally have something on the final contract?"

"It doesn't matter." She shook her head. "We're not going. Our team has already closed one account, and spotted for another. We're too exposed, too likely to be identified by the authorities. So I've sent Dietrich's team instead."

* * *

Lambert International Airport – St. Louis, Missouri
(1300 hours (CST) – Sunday, 7 April 1991)

Ian Trucco sat at the airport bar, nursing his first gin and tonic of the day. The place was filled with soldiers in desert camouflage, most headed home after their long service in the Gulf.

He had been at his post for nearly fifteen minutes when the man he had been following all day emerged from the terminal's florist shop. Gunnery Sergeant David Sweet was tall and athletic, and walked with the innate casual confidence found in career NCOs the world over. Today he was clad in casual civilian attire, blue jeans and an old Pink Floyd concert T-shirt.

Upon reentering the terminal, Sweet made his way toward the Northwest Airlines ticket counter. Trucco left a tip for the waitress and followed. Minutes later he and Sweet arrived at the gate and settled in to wait. He checked the status board and noted the next scheduled flight: Northwest 1083 from Honolulu.

Thirty minutes later the plane arrived at the gate. Sweet stood and waited eagerly, or so it looked to Trucco.

Soon the passengers began to deplane. Sweet stood, seemingly agitated, until one young woman in particular appeared on the jet-way.

She was pretty, Trucco thought, perhaps even beautiful, with startling blue eyes and mid-length auburn hair. She was definitely not Sweet's ex-wife, Laura, with whom Trucco knew Sweet maintained an understandably strained relationship.

The woman saw him and the two embraced, tightly, desperately it seemed, as if they had not seen one another in a very long time.

Finally Sweet released the girl, and gave her the flowers he had bought. She laughed, and the two headed off, hand in hand, toward the baggage area. Trucco watched them go before falling in behind at a discrete distance.

CHAPTER 25

Belleville, Illinois
(0549 hours (CST) – Monday, 8 April 1991)

David Sweet lurched awake, his body slick with sweat. For a moment he lay paralyzed, tangled in the sheets as the last vestiges of the nightmare faded.

For a moment he forgot where he was. Again the sound of circling jets came to him, rumbling deep inside his skull. But it wasn't there, not really. Sometimes it felt as if the sound of those circling aircraft would be there, deep in his bones, for the rest of his life. In reality the hotel room was dark and quiet. Sweet got to his feet quietly, so as not to disturb Jessica. He went to the bathroom and snapped on the light.

His leg gave off a phantom throb. He was just reaching for the ibuprofen when a shadow fell across the bathroom mirror.

"David? Are you all right?"

He turned to see Jessica Seeley standing in the doorway. Her eyes were the most vivid blue he had ever seen.

"I didn't mean to wake you," he said.

"Is something wrong?"

"I'm fine." He chased the pills down with lukewarm tap water. "You should be in bed. It's not even zero-six hundred yet."

"I'm awake now." She took his hand. Her touch was warm and supple, like fine silk. "Come with me."

Jessica led him back to bed. She wore a baggy gray sweatshirt and nothing underneath. He pulled it over her head and flung it aside.

* * *

Much later, Sweet stood in front of the mirror and adjusted his tie. He wore gray slacks and a white dress shirt.

Jessica took the tie from his hands and worked it into a perfect Windsor knot.

"When did you buy this suit, David? For senior prom?"

"It's the only suit I own."

"I guess we go shopping tomorrow." She smacked his bottom. "Now quit hogging the mirror. We're gonna be late."

"I'm not the one who spent an hour on her hair." He made room for her at the sink. "Besides, my mom and dad aren't exactly known for their punctuality."

"I still don't know if I'm ready for this."

"You've talked to my mom on the phone a million times, Jess. This is no big deal."

"That's easy for you to say. I still feel a little nervous." She applied some eye shadow. "David?"

"Yeah?" He tugged on his suit coat.

"What are we going to do?"

"We're going to go have some wonderful seafood, and meet my parents. The rest is bullshit, Jess. For tonight at least."

"No, it's not."

He sighed. Sweet had hoped to get through the next few days without having to deal with this particular issue.

"Don't you think you're jumping the gun?" he asked.

"No." She applied red lipstick to go with the sheer black dress she was wearing. "I talked to my detailer over at Division. Right before I came to see you."

"And?"

"I've got orders." She looked him full in the eye. "McCurry cut them the minute he got back from the Gulf. They're shipping me out to Okinawa, for a slot with the Third FSSG."

She referred to the 3rd Field Service Support Group, Sweet knew, the 3rd Marine Division's component supply command. It was a gathering house for cooks, mechanics and other rear-echelon types when the division was not at war.

"Oh." A chill came across him. "What the hell are you supposed to do there?"

"Something with Public Affairs, or so I'm told. With you at Little Creek, we'll never see each other."

"It's not as bad as all that."

She stepped back from the mirror, examining herself from every angle. Sweet liked what he saw.

"I'm thinking about resigning my commission."

"No." It felt as if someone had punched him squarely in the gut. "You've worked too hard to make it this far, Jess. If anyone takes the fall, it'll be me."

"Enlisted men can't resign."

"I won't need to." His smile was tinged with very real regret. "I'm due for reenlistment this July, right? Maybe I should go ahead and update my résumé."

She took him by the hand. "No. You love the Corps. There's got to be another way."

"Not that I can see." He checked his watch. "Now come on, or we'll miss our reservations."

* * *

"Excuse me? David Sweet?"

Sweet and Jess halted just shy of the lobby entrance. Sweet turned to find himself looking into the clear slate-gray eyes of a man somewhere just past sixty years of age.

"Yes, sir?" he said. "Can I help you?"

"You might, son. You just might."

The face was somehow familiar, Sweet thought. The eyes, those weathered features, and the tired, world-weary smile that seemed to suggest a life full of hard-won experience. It dawned on him next that the guy had somehow known his name.

"Do I know you, sir?" Sweet asked.

The two men shook hands. "We've never met, no. My name is Ian Trucco. Maybe you've read some of my stuff."

"Yes, sir, of course."

The name, the face. It all came flooding back to him. Lieutenant Colonel Ian Trucco: former U.S. Army, veteran of both Korea and Vietnam, and now prominent freelance journalist. Trucco, Sweet recalled, was a darling of the political Right, and longtime opponent of pork-barrel spending, graft, corruption, and other types of business as usual in Washington D.C.

"David?" Sweet was startled out of his reverie by the sound of Jessica's voice. He made quick introductions, careful to avoid giving her full name or her place in the grand scheme of things.

Trucco smiled graciously as he took her hand. Then he seemed to put Jess out of his mind entirely. "Do you think we could have a word, Gunny?"

Sweet traded a glance with Jessica, judging her mood. "I'm a little busy right now."

"It'll only take a minute."

"Go on." She gave Sweet's hand a little squeeze. "I'll be in the car."

She headed outside. "So? What's this all about?" Sweet asked. Butterflies danced a jig deep inside his belly.

"Desert Storm. An operation known as Eager Sky."

Sweet's nameless fears lessened a bit. "Sorry, never heard of it."

"I'm not surprised." Trucco offered him a crooked smile. "Eager Sky was the military portion of the mission sent in to recover Mohammed Halabi. The CIA referred to it as Operation Wishbone."

Sweet felt his skin prickle. Nervous sweat lingered under his arms, and at the small of his back. "I can't help you."

"How about an Army one-star named Mitchell Abernathy?" Trucco pressed. "Or something known as Operation Backgammon?"

Sweet made ready to head for the door. "It was nice to meet you, sir."

"I understand if you don't think you can talk to me right now." Trucco reached out, snagged Sweet by the arm. His grip was like steel.

"Just take this, all right? In case you change your mind."

He held out a business card. Sweet took it against his better judgment.

"I have to go."

"Okay." Trucco let go, probably unaware of just how close he'd come to earning himself a busted nose. "But I'll be in town for a couple of days, all right? That's the number for my pager. Call it if you change your mind."

"Don't count on it, sir." Sweet had to fight down the urge to run for the door.

* * *

"There he is." Lothar Wisch sat tensely behind the wheel of their parked rental vehicle. "I don't recognize the man with him, though. Do you?"

"Just a second." Dietrich Hagen peered through the viewfinder of his 35mm camera and clicked the shutter. The telephoto lens caught every detail of the young man leaving the hotel lobby just behind Trucco. "I don't recognize him either. Check the file again."

Wisch did as he was told. There were a lot of photographs to go over. "No, nothing. The girl doesn't match either. Do you still want to go?"

Hagen eyed the flurry of rush hour traffic. "No. I don't like it, Lothar. This is something unexpected."

"So call it in."

Hagen picked up the phone and dialed a number he had long since memorized. He heard Elise Shilling pick up on the first ring.

"Yes?"

"This is Frank. We may have a problem."

Hagen briefly explained what he and Lothar had witnessed. Once he was finished there was a pause, and Hagen thought he heard Major Shilling conversing with someone just out of earshot.

"You have photographs of the man he was meeting with? Forward them to me. I'll see if I can have him identified."

"I understand. What about the Primary? Do we move as planned?"

Another pause. "Wait until I get back to you. I'd rather wait to see what Control has to say."

CHAPTER 26

Belleville
(0016 hours (CST) – Tuesday, 9 April 1991)

David Sweet and Jessica Seeley returned to their hotel a little after midnight. Sweet parked out front and the two entered via the main lobby, hand in hand.

"That was nice." Jess giggled and snuggled in close. She was still a little tipsy, Sweet decided. He'd suggested a glass or ten of white zinfandel to steady her nerves before going to meet his folks. He was happy to see she'd taken his advice to heart.

"I told you everything would be okay." He pressed the button for the third floor.

They entered the elevator, and ascended to the proper floor. "Yeah, you did." She seemed to sober then, mentally, if not physically. "So. Do you want to talk about it?"

He felt alarm bells clamoring deep inside his brain. "Talk about what?"

"You've been on edge ever since that man came to see us in the lobby. What was his name? Trucco? I take it you know him from somewhere."

"I've never actually met the man before, no."

"Does it have something to do with what happened in the Gulf?"

Icy fingers danced across his spine as Sweet unlocked their hotel room. This was the last thing he wanted to think about, especially tonight.

"I'm not supposed to talk about it." He took off his coat, undid his tie. She went into the bathroom and turned on the light.

"I'm not interested in anything classified," she told him. "Your helo got shot down, I know that much. Staff Sergeant Marino—Bill—told me about it. Did you know his team was first on the scene after you went missing?"

"No, I didn't." He shucked off his shoes, opened the mini-fridge. He took out a Michelob. Jess came out of the bathroom, clad in something silky.

"I'm fine, Jess. Really."

"I'm not so sure." They climbed into bed and turned out the light. For a time it was dark and quiet, her skin gradually warming against his. "You're not the only one who saw some shit over there, you know."

"What do you mean?"

He heard her voice tremble as she told him about helping to hold the line at Khafji. Artillery screaming in endlessly. Watching the Whiskey Cobras as they worked over an Iraqi column with TOW missiles and 2.75-inch rockets. The sickly-sweet stink of burned corpses, lingering death.

"Jesus." It was all he could think of to say. After she was finished, they lay for a bit, content in their mutual silence.

"Tell me what happened," she whispered. "Please."

"I met some people over there, you know?" Once he began the words came out in a rush. "While I was in hiding. They were Iraqi Shi'a, working against Saddam."

"Go on," she said.

"They helped me when I needed it. Took me in, hid me from the army and the police. If it weren't for them I'd be dead a hundred times over."

He told her about Halabi, from start to finish. Jessica listened intently, never interrupting. Once he was done she helped herself to a beer.

"So you think they're all dead?" she asked. He felt something, a flicker of guilt perhaps, sweep through him. He forced it down resolutely before moving on.

"From what I gather, yeah." Sweet drained his bottle before setting it on the nightstand. "I suppose some of them might still be alive. I wish there was a way to know for certain."

"Do you think Trucco might be able to find out?"

"He's a writer, Jess. At the very least he's investigating what Halabi knew that was so damn important."

She sat on the edge of the mattress, now just a silhouette against light from a partly drawn window.

"I'm willing to go see him if you are."

She killed her beer and let the bottle clatter to the floor. She was a bit of a slob, Sweet was discovering. He liked that about her: she was unpredictable, volatile, and eager to take risks, unlike far too many career-driven assholes in their mutual line of work.

"I'm not supposed to talk about it, remember?" He couldn't help but think of the Painter, and his final ultimatum aboard the *New Orleans*. "To anyone. We're both in enough trouble as it is."

"It's just a thought, love." She nuzzled in close and nipped at his ear. Sweet was only too happy to reply in kind, and for a time he was able to devote his energies to other matters.

* * *

Klara Schroeder sat in her rental sedan, a few pills cupped in one hand. She swallowed the Dexedrine, and chased it down with lukewarm coffee from a nearby fast-food place. Then she waited some more. It seemed like centuries since she'd gotten a good night's sleep.

She'd been parked outside the hotel for almost four hours. Schroeder could see that the lights in the room she was interested in had gone dark. Information on this new contract had come in with surprising alacrity, she thought. But Hagen was wrong nonetheless. Forcing her to shadow Sweet and the woman by herself was a mistake, a blatant tactical error.

They should have all been together on this one. Schroeder had seen Sweet's kind before. He was like one of Achilles' Myrmidons: stoic, solid, unpredictable. One operator, acting on her own, was all too likely to be noticed, and remarked upon. She'd have to be cautious from here on out.

Her car phone suddenly clamored for her attention. She answered it.

"Yes?"

"It's me." Dietrich's voice. "How are you holding up?"

"Fine." She stifled a yawn. "A little tired, I suppose. The medication you gave me helps."

"We're going to go ahead and move on Sweet. Can you put one of the special packages together by morning?"

"No problem." Schroeder lit a cigarette. "What size?"

"No more than a kilo, including the payload. Make it a shaped charge with a sticky back. I'll call you with exact instructions later."

"Right. Talk to you then." Klara rung off and turned her attention back to Sweet's distant room. She saw nothing, no light, no movement. She looked at her watch, and noted the time. Less than three hours remained before first light.

CHAPTER 27

Belleville
(1025 hours (CST) – Tuesday, 9 April 1991)

Jessica Seeley came awake slowly, indolently, and reached out to find something to cover herself. After a moment's work she found a blanket and plumped her pillow into a more comfortable position.

A painful stab of sunlight leaked into the room. Her mouth tasted like a dirty penny, and whenever she closed her eyelids it felt as if bits of raw grit grated across them.

"David?" She pawed his side of the bed. Nothing there. She looked up, saw that his wallet was gone. His car keys, too. It took her a long moment to get up, and stumble into the bathroom.

The toilet swirled, flushed. Where was he? She got back into bed, and found one of David's T-shirts on the floor. She climbed into it and got back under the covers. Sleep. That was what she wanted now. Sleep and some peace and quiet.

A key rattled in the door, stirring her back to full awareness. She sat up blurrily as David entered, juggling Styrofoam clamshells displaying the logo of a popular restaurant chain.

"Rise and shine, beautiful! Breakfast is served."

"Ugh. It smells like something died in here." She opened a clamshell to find a congealed mess consisting of pancakes, sausage, and scrambled eggs mixed with cheddar.

The very idea of food revolted her. "Did you happen to get some orange juice?"

"Way ahead of you." He handed her a large Styrofoam cup.

She drank deeply and found herself feeling just a little better.

"Try this." He handed over the painkillers he'd been taking. She swallowed a few, and sat and watched, in equal parts fascinated and repelled, as he wolfed down first his portion of breakfast, followed by most of hers as well.

"Waste not, want not," he told her, and grinned.

"You've got some on your chin." Seeley wiped at him with a napkin. "You're up bright and early," she said. "What's the occasion?"

"You said you wanted to take me shopping today. I just thought we'd get an early start. Besides, we have plans for tonight. I want to get everything else out of the way before then."

"What do you mean?" she said.

"You'll see."

* * *

1835 hours: Sweet and Jessica entered a spacious hotel lobby, dominated at the back by a massive, three-story waterfall complete with faux jungle vegetation and a tiered rock garden. The Monterrey West was one of the finest hotels in downtown St. Louis, the sort of place to hold a wedding reception, or even spend your honeymoon. Just a block from the Gateway Arch, the place was walking distance from a wide variety of the city's many attractions.

The ring was in his pocket. He patted it subconsciously as the pair entered through the door into the main lobby. Some sort of convention was underway, he saw. Something to do with the American Dental Association, according to the storyboard easel just inside the door. The chief porter smiled at them both and hoped they would enjoy their stay.

* * *

It had been relatively simple for Klara Schroeder to follow Sweet and the woman as they crossed the river into Missouri and headed downtown. Once at the Monterrey West she parked in the hotel's underground parking structure and took the elevator up to the lobby floor. She arrived just in time to see Sweet and the girl enter the hotel restaurant.

She carried a paper shopping bag at her side. As per Schroeder's request the hostess found her a seat in the back, near the bar. As she settled in she took a moment to regard Sweet and his date, seated now just a few short meters away.

* * *

Jess waited until the server had come and gone before leaning forward to whisper conspiratorially: "Are you going to tell me what this is all about? Or do I have to guess?"

He shrugged. "I just thought you'd like to go somewhere nice for a change."

"We ate with your parents last night, David. That was nice enough." She looked at the prices on the menu and grimaced. "I feel guilty, seeing you spend all this money on me."

"We're fine, honest." He grabbed a dinner roll and slathered it with butter. "Just sit back and enjoy yourself. Mom tells me the chicken parmesan is delicious here."

* * *

The package hidden in her shopping bag was deceptively small. Its outer shell was cardboard wrapped in electrician's tape, and about the size of a hardcover novel. Schroeder peeled away the adhesive backing and pressed the package into place beneath her table. She was careful to ensure that the shaped charge within (molded expertly from Czech plastic explosive) was aimed directly at Sweet and the girl. Its payload consisted of a half-kilo of #2 buckshot, intended to create a kill zone ten meters out from the primary blast point.

She keyed the arming switch and got to her feet. The tablecloth would hide the presence of the bomb long enough for her to be on her way. She made a point to nod pleasantly to her waitress as she made her way outside.

A quick glance to her rear assured her that both of her targets were still at their table, huddled over in private conversation.

* * *

The waitress came back, and they got down to ordering. Sweet ordered the twenty-ounce porterhouse with a baked potato, Jess the chicken fettuccine. He made a point to ask for the wine list, and ordered something expensive.

Jess watched as Sweet absentmindedly wolfed down another roll. "You look like you're a million miles away. Is everything all right?"

"I'm fine, really. I guess I just need to use the head."

"Okay." Jess watched as he stood and headed for the men's room.

Sweet's problem wasn't a needy bladder. Once in the men's room he splashed cold water on his face, toweled off. The ring was in his pocket. He took it out and regarded it in the garish glow cast by an overhead light.

* * *

The street in front of the hotel was at the nadir of the afternoon rush and very crowded. Dietrich Hagen had to circle the block once before edging in and parking just outside the main lobby. Moments later Klara hopped in and slammed the door shut behind her.

"All set?" Hagen asked.

"Go when you're ready."

Hagen pulled a small black box from his jacket and keyed a switch.

The world changed, abruptly, crazily. The lobby behind them vomited fire, and windowpanes shattered into millions of glittering shards. Hagen saw a woman with a baby stroller thrown into the street by a tidal wave of flame, broken masonry and other bits of unidentifiable debris. Both the woman and her child had been killed instantly.

He waited a moment longer, just as the plan dictated. Chaos reigned as people ran past, screaming for help. But Sweet and the girl never emerged. Just random patrons, hotel guests, most injured or badly burned. Quite a few had to be carried out.

Hagen felt his heart pounding, thundering like a stampeding herd. He put the car in gear and accelerated off into traffic. No one seemed to pay them any heed. Moments later he and Klara Schroeder merged onto the nearest highway headed east, intending to rejoin Lothar Wisch for the hit on the primary target.

* * *

Sweet got up off the men's room floor, gagging on a mixture of plaster dust and acrid smoke. It was dark, save for the feeble glow of a battery-powered emergency light.

A shadow appeared above him, blocking the light. "Help me, please! Somebody help me!"

Jessica. Sweet's only thought was to find her. He pushed the man aside, and made it to what remained of the restroom door. It had been splintered by the explosion. Someone lay on the floor outside, twitching from some vague nerve impulse. Sweet noticed distantly that the man, a waiter most likely, had been almost entirely eviscerated.

Beyond the doorway: a vague half-light illuminated by cavorting flames. The overhead sprinklers poured dirty water down upon the scene, limiting his vision and chilling him to the bone.

A girl staggered past him, clutching a shattered arm. One look told him it wasn't Jessica. He stepped past her, trying to remember where they'd been seated. Then he saw another man at his feet: one leg was gone completely, severed at the thigh.

Moments later he spied a woman huddled nearby. She lay beside a shattered table, her back to him. Jess! He ran to her, and gently rolled her onto her back. Fresh gore clotted in her auburn hair, masking her features. But the class ring at her finger, that blood-stained blouse. The smell of her perfume came to him despite the carnage.

"Aw, Jess. No." The words came out in a choking sob.

CHAPTER 28

St. Louis
(1910 hours (CST) – Tuesday, 9 April 1991)

David Sweet had no idea how long he sat there, holding her. Was it a few minutes? An hour? Then cops came, and a guy was gently prying Sweet away from Jessica, and telling him that everything was going to be all right. The cop led him out of the hotel lobby into thin, watery sunlight. The sky was bloody with the coming of dusk, filtered now by thick, cloying smoke and an acrid stench.

The pair was roughly pushed out of the way as a stream of paramedics dashed into the ruined building. A woman sat on the curb, rocking to and fro, sobbing. Her hair was matted with blood. The bubblegum flashers from a dozen or so emergency vehicles flickered up and down a street littered with broken glass. He noticed somebody had covered a tiny, still form in the street with a blanket. Dozens of people milled about the entrance to the Monterrey West as Sweet was led a nearby ambulance. Glass crackled underfoot. He was given a blanket and told to sit. More sirens split the night, with numerous ambulances and fire department vehicles arriving every minute.

He doubted anyone noticed when he got up to leave. The surrounding chaos, the milling crowds, all conspired to aid in his escape. Ten minutes later, he'd recovered his car and headed for the Poplar Street Bridge, eastbound toward the Illinois side of the river.

* * *

Sweet felt numb, disconnected, as if he were floating somewhere deep beneath the ocean. At first he'd driven completely on autopilot. The sun continued to sink steadily toward the horizon.

Minutes later he found the sign he was looking for, Exit 12 into Belleville. It was the neighborhood he had spent most of his childhood in, moderately priced split-level homes, the streets orderly and lined with oak and birch. He parked his mom's Caddy. The engine ticked as it cooled off, allowing him time to think.

Time to wonder how much of the blood on him belonged to Jessica.

Sweet found Wet Wipes in the glove compartment, and used them to clean up a bit. Next he climbed out and headed up the driveway. He still had a key, and unlocked the front door. The house was dark and quiet. He remembered that his folks would be at the Sanderson's down the street, playing cards. It was a Tuesday night ritual that dated back to his early childhood.

The hallway leading to the rear of the house was lined with family photographs. More than half the men pictured wore Marine dress blues. He stripped out of his blood-stained suit and cleaned up some more, scrubbing his skin until it was raw. Soon the local TV news came on. The lead story had to do with the bombing. The latest tally came to ten dead, twenty wounded, with another in critical condition. The police had not yet released the names of those killed, the reporter said. Sweet sat quietly and digested it all.

He found some of his stepfather's clothing, jeans and T-shirts mostly, that would fit him. He got dressed before heading for what had once been his old room. It was a guest room now, tastefully decorated with frilly lace and whatnot. Gone were the Led Zeppelin posters, varsity trophies and all the other crap a seventeen-year-old kid thinks is so important. The battered U.S. Army footlocker, however, was still at the back of the closet. The inside smelled of mothballs and memories long buried. The pistol was at the bottom, beneath Grandpa Phil's class-A uniform, complete with ribbons denoting his service in the European Theatre of Operations, circa 1945.

The weapon was a .45 Colt Government Model, nicely customized with high-profile sights and a Bar-Sto Match barrel. He slotted three magazines full of jacketed hollow-point ammunition, worked a round into the chamber and set the safety. The business card Ian Trucco had given him was still in his wallet.

He headed for the kitchen and picked up the phone. He left his number on Trucco's pager and waited. The television his mom kept in the kitchen told him the bombing downtown had already made it onto CNN.

The phone rang a few minutes later. Sweet picked up, answered. The .45 sat on the counter beside him.

"This is Ian Trucco, returning a page."

"I'm ready to talk, Colonel."

There was a pause. "What changed your mind?"

"Did you watch the news tonight?"

"That mess downtown? I saw it. Were you there?"

"Yeah." It took effort for Sweet to get the word out at all.

"You all right, Gunny?"

"Just tell me where you want to meet." A minute later he'd scribbled down the directions to Trucco's hotel. "I'll meet you there in twenty minutes."

Sweet hung up. He slipped the pistol into his waistband at the small of his back. Moments later he was back on the road, intent on keeping a very important date.

CHAPTER 29

Belleville
(1955 hours (CST) – Tuesday, 9 April 1991)

David Sweet arrived at the Holiday Inn just off North Belt West and found a place to park. Sweet remembered staying here years before. He'd asked Laura to marry him, what? Fourteen years ago? He'd been all of twenty then, bald and sweaty beneath his dress blues. Laura had beamed at him, accepted his ring. They'd been too poor to stay anywhere better. It seemed a bad omen to be here now.

He headed inside. A young woman stood behind the desk in the lobby. Sweet keyed the elevator and stepped inside. Minutes later the doors slid open on the second floor. Trucco had already given Sweet his room number. He knocked, and seconds passed before he heard the lock clatter open on the other side of the door.

"Come in." Ian Trucco was dressed in gray sweats. He stood for a moment and regarded Sweet by the glow of the muted television at the far end of the room.

"Jesus, Gunny. You look like hell. Can I get you something?"

"Aspirin, if you have it." His leg had started its phantom throbbing once more.

"Sure. Hold on." Trucco got a Coke from the fridge and handed Sweet some Tylenol. Sweet gobbled down the pills and swigged the soda, willing himself to take it easy.

He saw Trucco eyeing him doubtfully. "Your friend, the woman I met yesterday? Is she all right?"

Sweet felt the storm clouds begin to gather. "No sir, she's not."

"I'm sorry, Gunny. I really am."

"You said you wanted to talk, Colonel." Sweet eased himself into a chair by the window. "So go ahead, talk."

* * *

Klara Schroeder and Dietrich Hagen arrived in Belleville a little over an hour after the bombing. Lothar Wisch was already waiting for them at the target location.

"Any movement?" Hagen asked.

"He should still be in his room."

"Right, come with me." Hagen popped the trunk and handed out two black nylon utility bags. Schroeder took one, as did Lothar. She led the way into the hotel lobby, bag in hand. A suppressed 9mm pistol was held low at her side.

The girl behind the counter looked up with a smile on her lips. The nametag on her blazer read: Margaret. "Good evening. May I help you?"

Schroeder shoved the Glock into her face. "Into the back. Now."

"Oh God. Don't shoot. Please! Just don't shoot!"

"Be quiet." Schroeder and Hagen led the girl to the office behind the counter and shut the door. Lothar stayed at his post out front.

"I can't open the safe, all right?" The girl smelled as if she'd pissed herself. "I swear to God! The day manager has the combination, and won't be back until tomorrow."

Schroeder maneuvered Margaret into a seat away from the door. "I thought I told you to stay quiet," she said. The gun remained leveled at the girl's head. "Check the guest list."

"Right." Hagen bent over the computer on the manager's desk. "What's the password?"

Margaret gave it up readily enough. Moments later Hagen had opened the desired file. "He's in Room Two oh-seven. Let's go."

"Just a second." Schroeder fired once into the back of the girl's head. The sound of the spent casing tinkling across the floor made more noise than the gunshot itself.

* * *

"This is a picture of Mohammed Halabi, taken about six years ago." Trucco showed Sweet a photograph. "Do you recognize the man next to him?"

"Yes, sir. I do." Mohammed Halabi was in the desert somewhere, incongruous in pinstripe slacks and a long sleeve, button-down dress shirt. Several men in Republican Guard camouflage stood nearby, flat-eyed and expressionless.

The individual next to Halabi had gained quite a bit of weight in the intervening years. But Sweet would have known that face anywhere. Hell, he'd stake his life on it.

"His name is Detloff, Colonel. James Detloff. He was one of the men the Agency had debrief me in the Gulf."

"I see." Trucco swept the photo back into his valise and snapped it shut. "Gunny, I've been told your aircraft was shot down in Iraq, and you were captured. During this time you met with a man by the name of Mohammed Halabi. He used to be one of Saddam's finest. But that's all changed, or so I'm told."

"Yes, sir. It's true, all of it."

Trucco's eyes burned at Sweet's admission, as if lit from behind by some strange inner fire. "Did he ever talk to you about anything classified? Something about an operation called Backgammon, or perhaps Bed Check?"

Sweet briefly outlined everything that had happened to him during the time he had been in southern Iraq. Fuck Peter Vermeer, he thought, and fuck the UCMJ. "I saw him die. Our helo got hit during the extraction. A lot of good men were killed."

Trucco lit a cigarette. "I heard about that, too."

"Halabi was dying," Sweet said. "Bleeding out bad. But he did say something, something about someone named Abernathy. And he did mention the phrase 'Bed Check.' "

"What exactly did he say?" Trucco pressed.

"Not much." A great weariness settled over Sweet like a shroud. "I'm sorry, sir, but he died before he could say anything more. What's this all about, anyway?"

* * *

Klara changed into a spare hostess jacket she found in the office and took Margaret's place at the front desk. Hagen took a moment to strip out the tapes from the hotel security system. Next he and Lothar summoned the elevator and headed up to the second floor. Moments later they were outside Room 207. Both paused long enough to bend over the heavy satchel that Hagen had brought. Hagen withdrew the Kalashnikov secreted inside. The muzzle of the weapon was crowned by a bulky sound suppressor.

Lothar readied his pistol and nodded. Hagen withdrew the universal passkey Klara had found at the front desk. It clicked in place, and Hagen was shouldering the door aside and rushing in, his weapon braced tight and ready to fire.

* * *

"It's complicated, Gunny. But I'll tell you what I can. It seems—"

Sounds came to Sweet then: a click as a key was fitted in a lock, the rush of soft-soled shoes on cheap carpet. He was digging for his pistol even as the door came crashing inward.

"Down! Get down!" Sweet yelled.

There were two of them, with one man clenching a suppressed AK. Time seemed to slow to an infinitesimal crawl. The .45 tracked up as if by a will of its own, recoiling, spitting hot brass. The shots sounded so closely together they blended into one. Sweet saw his rounds hit cleanly, center mass.

The rifleman tumbled aside, trailing blood. Sweet pivoted right, squeezed off another double-tap. He saw the second man jerk solidly as he was hit. Sweet continued to fire, pumping off rounds until the slide locked back on an empty chamber. He palmed a fresh magazine home and advanced, ready to continue the fight.

He found the second guy sprawled in the hallway outside. A round had torn into his throat, sending bright arterial blood spraying. Sweet recovered the man's pistol before kneeling at his side.

He was blond, pale, with long features and startling blue eyes. The Aryan race in its purest form, Sweet supposed. He was fading away rapidly: bleeding out, dying.

But not quickly enough, Sweet thought. He stroked the trigger one last time, and watched the blood and bone chips fly.

"Jesus." Trucco stood in the door, his face ashen. A distant babble of excited voices came to him then. Sweet knew the other guests would have heard the gunfire.

He ducked back inside the room. "Come on. We're leaving."

"Right, hold on." Trucco paused long enough to recover the travel-stained valise Sweet had seen earlier. Moments later the two men were on the run, headed for the stairway entrance at the far end of the hallway.

* * *

Klara Schroeder stood in stunned silence as one last, muffled gunshot sounded from somewhere above her. Something had gone wrong, she thought. She gripped her weapon and waited, watching the fire door she prayed Lothar and Dietrich would emerge from at any moment. After what seemed an interminable wait the door opened slowly, two men emerging.

Her heart thundered anew. It was Trucco, alive and unharmed. He looked pale, Schroeder thought, nervous. He clenched one of the team's suppressed 9mm pistols. Beside him: David Sweet, seemingly back from the dead. Schroeder dared not move, or act in any way that would tip her hand. Both men hurried past, armed and scanning the lobby for any sign of danger.

Seconds later the two had fled into the night. Her duty was clear. Schroeder took up her bag and tailed them, the pistol held low at her side. As she moved, the distant screams of hotel patrons sounded behind her, strident and in a near state of panic.

CHAPTER 30

McLean, Virginia
(2355 hours (EST) – Tuesday, 9 April 1991)

It seemed as if Peter Vermeer had only just turned in for the night. Groaning, he rolled over and reached for the ringing telephone.

"Hello?"

"Sorry to wake you, Peter. But this is important." Nicholas Farraday sounded tired, Vermeer thought.

"Hold on." He fumbled with the sophisticated encryption device on his bedside nightstand. After a moment a high-pitched squeal sounded in his ear.

"Go ahead."

"Someone tried to kill Sergeant Sweet earlier tonight. Initial reports suggest Shilling and her team are responsible."

"What happened?"

"Apparently he was meeting with someone at a restaurant in downtown St. Louis. You remember the marine captain he's been seeing, the one who got him in trouble in the first place? We think she was there, too. The bastards bombed the place during the dinner rush."

"Jesus." He grabbed the remote and turned on the TV, keeping the sound off so as not to wake Barbara. CNN was running a report on it now. "What about casualties?"

"The woman, a Captain Seeley, has been confirmed as one of the dead. Other reports place the death count at an even dozen or more."

"Anything else I should know?"

"We believe Ian Trucco is involved." Vermeer knew the name all too well. "There was a firefight at Trucco's hotel shortly after the bombing. Witnesses say a man matching Sweet's description was at the scene, and shot several people."

"Why would Sweet meet with Trucco?" Vermeer asked.

"No one seems to know. The FBI thinks Sweet killed two of Shilling's people, and took off for parts unknown. You need to find him ASAP."

"I understand." Vermeer felt as if his mind were reeling.

"I've already spoken to Admiral Mollar. The team we used for Wishbone is already on its way, pending final mission orders. They'll be under your direct command."

"Jerome and his men?" He absentmindedly scratched one cheek. "What about Posse Comitatus, Nick? I'd rather not break the law if I can help it." Military personnel, he knew, were normally prohibited from engaging in counterintelligence operations on U.S. soil.

"The President has already signed an Executive Order allowing us to proceed," Farraday countered. "As long as you keep it low-key there shouldn't be any problems."

"I'm on my way now."

"Don't bother." Vermeer heard Farraday shuffling papers of some kind at the other end of the line. "Jerome will be setting up shop at Scott Air Force Base in Illinois. I'm sending a car to take you to the airport. How soon can you be ready?"

He checked his watch. "Fifteen minutes."

"They'll be there in thirty."

"I'll let you know once I'm in place." Vermeer hung up the phone. His wife barely stirred as he got out of bed. After some consideration he slipped into his bathrobe and padded quietly downstairs.

There was another secure scrambler on the desk in his office. He picked up, activated the device, and dialed the number to a telephone in Langley, Virginia. The man on the other end picked up almost immediately.

"Yes?"

"It's me. He made the call, just like you said."

"You're doing the right thing, Peter."

"Yes, sir."

"When do you leave?"

"Twenty minutes. We're deploying to Scott, with a possible ops area somewhere near St. Louis."

"Keep me informed."

Vermeer hung up once more and stood, thinking. Barbara kept a bag packed for just such a contingency. He found it in the hall closet before heading back upstairs to change.

"Peter?" Barbara Vermeer sat up in bed, peering at him groggily.

"It's just work, honey. Go back to sleep." He saw headlights glow from the driveway outside.

"When will you be back?"

"I'm not sure. I'll call you when I can."

"All right." She snuggled under the covers, already drifting off to sleep. "Be careful."

"Love you." He closed the bedroom door and went downstairs. Minutes later he was on the road, headed for the airport and what he supposed would be a very uncertain future.

* * *

St. Louis
(0700 hours (CST) – Wednesday, 10 April 1991)

The flight in from Baltimore was crowded, near capacity. Michael Litke sat, jostled on either side by teenage soldiers as the American Airlines flight pulled into the terminal.

He couldn't stop thinking about Dietrich and Lothar. Two more of his men, both longtime comrades, were dead on what should have been a textbook-simple operation. He knew anger was dangerous at a time like this, making every decision he made suspect. But he could not help how he felt.

"You're sulking, Michael."

"Sorry." Litke climbed to his feet, handed Elise Shilling her carry-on bag. "Come on. August is supposed to meet us inside the terminal."

Willi Krenz joined them, and together the trio made their way through baggage claim and over to the rental car counter. There they found August Lange, the senior member of Team Five.

"What do we know, August?" Litke asked.

Lange was tall, fit, with piercing eyes and sharply chiseled features. He rarely smiled at the best of times, but today his expression was stark, guarded, as if beset with storm clouds.

"Klara is trailing them now," Lange replied. "As of her last report they had stopped in a small town, here." He pointed to a spot on the roadmap the rental agent had provided.

"They haven't gone very far, have they?" Litke examined the map, and saw immediately that there was very little between St. Louis and south-central Missouri, save anonymous small towns, rest stops, and the Mark Twain National Forest.

"They don't seem to be in any great hurry, no." Lange lit a cigarette. "I've checked his file, Herr Hauptmann. There is no obvious connection between Sweet and the area in question. Perhaps they are wandering aimlessly, unsure what to do next."

"Perhaps." Litke watched as Willi helped load their luggage into the trunk of a rental sedan. "For now we assume he is intent on going to ground." He checked the map once more. "We'll stage here, in Sullivan, and wait for Klara's next report."

Willi took the wheel as the four climbed into the car. Fresh raindrops tracked across the windshield as he pulled out into morning traffic.

"What about equipment?" Elise asked.

"All staged, and ready to be transported," Lange said. "I have Klaus Reinhardt standing by, ready to move into position once you give the word."

"Tell him not to bring the heavy weapons," Litke replied. "I want small arms only. This operation is already far too high-profile for my taste."

"Got it."

Litke turned to look out the window at passing traffic, his thoughts dark and turbulent. David Sweet: the name tickled at his thoughts, stirring the anger he had experience earlier. But despite his training and abilities, Sweet was no boogey man, no devil in human form. He was but a man, and a man could be killed. But they would have to be cautious from here on out. Litke and his team had lost their most precious asset, the element of surprise. And, he knew, the going from here on in would be much more difficult as a result.

CHAPTER 31

Rolla, Missouri
(1045 hours (CST) – Wednesday, 10 April 1991)

"Let me see that one, there." David Sweet pointed to a rifle set behind the counter of the dimly lit gun store.

"The Garand?"

"Yes, sir, that's the one." The store owner handed over the rifle in question: the U.S. Rifle, Caliber .30, M-1. Familiar to generations of American servicemen, the M-1 had served as the standard infantry weapon from World War II and beyond. It was heavier than Sweet remembered, and lovingly crafted from phosphate-gray steel and oiled walnut. His father had had one once, a DCM-surplus rifle he'd picked up in the 1960s. Sweet had inherited it when Dad didn't come home from Vietnam. To his eternal shame, he'd hocked the damn thing to help pay for his first car back in high school.

Sweet locked back the bolt and peered inside the chamber. The operating rod looked good, with no obvious damage from high-pressure loads. The bore looked clean and bright, and the trigger broke at an even eight pounds or so. He handed it over to Colonel Trucco before asking the owner for the one that had been beside it in the rack.

"You boys sure know your weapons." He handed over the second Garand. Sweet checked it, and decided it too would do fine.

"I'll take them both." Sweet handed over his driver's license so the guy could start the ATF paperwork. "We'll need ammo, too."

"You're in luck." The man began to copy down Sweet's information. "I just got a supply of surplus Oh-Six ammunition. It's mil-spec, non-corrosive. Originally from Greece, I think. I'll give it to you for fifty a case."

Sweet knew the guy was robbing him blind, but decided not to make an issue of it. Fifteen minutes later he and Trucco were loading the rifles and the other items they had purchased into the trunk of Sweet's vehicle.

"They'll trace us through my credit card, Gunny. You must know that."

Sweet climbed behind the wheel. "We'll just have to risk it. Luckily I know somewhere we can hide for a while."

He realized he hadn't had anything substantial to eat since the day before. After a brief discussion, the pair headed off for a local mom-and-pop diner. Once inside they took a booth near the back and ordered breakfast.

"I think it's high time we talked about a few things, Colonel. Like the picture you showed me, the one of Detloff and Halabi. Let's start there."

Trucco stared hard at Sweet for a long moment, as if considering exactly where to begin. "It was a black op, Gunny. Very covert, very Need to Know, and not something most people in the intelligence community would be comfortable discussing in public. Until recently I had nothing official. Mostly hearsay that's been bandied about for years, stuff the conspiracy nuts like to rave about in dark corners.

"It was all part of Backgammon, the official U.S. effort to assist Saddam during his war with Iran. The story goes that a separate, unofficial part of the operation, codename Bed Check, was initiated sometime in the early 1980s.

"Saddam was our buddy, right, our good friend? To keep him happy, and to help counter the Iranians it was decided to offer the Mukhabarat intel from top-notch CIA sources, but the men involved went one step further. Some say the Agency began to coordinate direct action missions outside of Iraq, mostly against anti-Saddam figures living in Europe or elsewhere in the Middle East. Most of those killed belonged to al-Dawa, a Shiite political group listed in the U.S. as a terrorist organization."

"I've heard of them." Sweet sipped his coffee and thought of Amina.

Trucco paused a moment to gather his thoughts. "Most of the assassinations would have been carried out by American military personnel, Navy SEALs or U.S. Army Delta. I doubt the troops involved ever knew the exact identity of any given target. It would be better to keep them in the dark, obviously, so as to keep the covert nature of Bed Check secure."

"I would have thought Saddam had his own people for that kind of thing."

The girl came with their order, and Trucco waited until she was gone before continuing. "Sure, Saddam has assassins of his own. But our people are better. The Mukhabarat isn't exactly known for its long reach, or its ability to act either covertly or with undue professionalism. They're thumb-breakers, Gunny. Nothing more."

"There was another name Halabi mentioned." Sweet poured syrup over his hotcakes before digging in. "Abernathy. No one said much to me when I mentioned it during my debrief, but it seemed to be a name they recognized. Is it important?"

"That, I'm not sure of." Trucco stirred the eggs on his plate. "The name is familiar. I knew a Mitch Abernathy, and served under him in Vietnam. He was Special Forces, and ran the European section of SOCOM a few years back."

"Where is he now?"

"Dead." Trucco sighed. "He was killed in a chopper crash in Italy about four years ago."

"And what connection would he have had to all this?"

Trucco grunted. "None, as far as I can see."

"Hmm." Sweet looked outside and saw a pair of state police cruisers ease into the parking lot. The two cops climbed out of their cars and headed in to eat. One of them had a folded newspaper under one arm.

"There is one thing that seems obvious to me," Sweet said. "No one in the government is interested in any of this becoming public knowledge. I doubt we'll be well served by going to the authorities right now."

"No kidding." Trucco stole a glance at the two policemen. "There is one thing you should be aware of, however."

"Oh?"

"The photograph I showed you, the notes? All of it is classified, stuff from the NSA archives. Somebody mailed it to me a couple of weeks ago, no note, no explanation. I'll be damned if I can explain it."

There was little more Sweet could say to that. The two paid the bill and headed out into the brisk morning sunshine. Minutes later they merged onto the I-44 interchange, and headed west, toward their next scheduled stop.

CHAPTER 32

Dixon, Missouri
(1425 hours (CST) – Wednesday, 10 April 1991)

The house was set back from the road, deep in the piney woods. It was an old, abandoned wreck of a place, long since its prime, its white-painted façade faded with seedy neglect. Seeing it now reminded David Sweet of a cadaver left too long in the sun. He had not been here in many years, and was gratified to see it was still here, still unoccupied.

"What is this place?" Ian Trucco asked. The two men had climbed out of the Cadillac and stood, regarding the building in the stark yellow light of middle afternoon.

"It belonged to a friend of mine." Sweet popped the trunk and began handing out the supplies stored within. "It was his grandfather's originally. We used to hunt and fish here when we were kids. Grandpa Vic died what, fifteen years ago? I'm guessing the place has been abandoned since then."

"Your friend owns it?" Trucco rubbed his jaw and surveyed the place with a baleful eye. "You're sure no one will think to look for us here?"

"As sure as I can be. I haven't talked to John Weidinger in years, Colonel. I doubt anyone comes here much. We should be fine."

They had bought the things they would need at a hardware store in town: sleeping bags, spare clothing, a Coleman stove, road flares and fishing line, plus more, all packaged in a quartet of cardboard boxes. Sweet staged the gear in the dilapidated living room before going back out to collect the rifles and other items they had brought.

"We need to zero the rifles," Sweet said. "There's a place to shoot around back. We used to stage targets to three hundred yards when I was a kid. It should be far enough for what I intend to do." The locals shot out here all the time, Sweet knew, hunting rabbits and the like. He doubted anyone would notice a few extra gunshots.

Trucco picked up a rifle. "I'll get on it right away."

* * *

Night came rapidly to the Ozarks, stealing over the land with swift velvet fingers. Sweet sat and worked beside a kerosene lantern, the atmosphere within the house heavy with swirling gnats and mosquitoes. He'd bought two sets of Dickies coveralls, a staple gun, and some burlap sacking. He now cut the burlap into strips before stapling it to the coveralls in an attempt to create a sort of half-ass ghillie suit.

"Not bad, Gunny. Not bad at all." Trucco sat before the Coleman, warming a tin of pork and beans. Both men worked with loaded rifles and sidearms within easy reach.

Sweet held one of the ghillies up to the lamplight and examined it minutely. "They should get the job done." He stood and took up a flashlight. "Why don't you go suit up? I'll make sure the tripwires we set up earlier are still good to go."

"Hold on a second."

Sweet held fast. "Sir?"

"Take this." Trucco held out a packet containing the documents he had shown Sweet earlier. "Keep it safe, all right? Just in case."

* * *

Michael Litke stood on the hotel balcony, smoking a cigarette. The lights from the nearby freeway glowed brightly against the night, moving quickly.

"Michael?" He was almost surprised to find Elise Shilling standing beside him, her eyes eager.

"Yes?"

"Klara's back." Litke stubbed out his smoke before heading inside. There he found the remaining members of his team, arrayed casually around the room he and Elise shared. Klara Schroeder stood beside a large-scale map of the area.

"They've gone to ground, Herr Hauptmann," Schroeder began. She pointed to a spot on the map just off the local interstate. Litke listened impatiently as she gave the remainder of her contact report. Dixon, Missouri: population 750, with a standing police force of three fulltime deputies. It was a largely rural community, widely spread out and remote. Nearly fifteen miles of winding country roads lay between the town and the I-44 interstate.

"Sweet and Trucco are located here, at an abandoned farm just off rural Junction three." Schroeder indicated yet another spot on the map. "They spent most of the day inside, as if settling in for a long stay. I left Sergeant Fanger in place to keep them under observation."

"What about weapons?" Litke asked.

"We heard rifle-fire earlier in the day. They have small arms, Herr Hauptmann. Hunting rifles, perhaps? Beyond that I cannot be certain."

Litke lit another cigarette. "Thank you. That will be all." After most of the others had left he stood for a time, smoking and studying the map before him.

"What are you thinking?" Elise sat on the bed.

"Sweet probably thinks he's being clever." He shrugged. "They may suspect we've followed them, and set an ambush. It's what I'd do."

"You've giving them too much credit. Sweet is just one man, and Trucco is long past his prime. It should be easy going from here on in."

"Don't be overconfident, Elise. It doesn't suit you."

"When do you think we should move?"

"Soon." Litke checked his watch. "Tell the others. I want to be on-site and ready to go by zero-two hundred."

* * *

St. Louis, 2200 hours: Peter Vermeer stood and regarded the young woman on the hospital bed before him. The name on her chart read Nancy Marie Stopa, age 28. She had once been young and pretty, but now her skin was waxy and haggard, almost translucent. The scent of hospital antiseptic and feces filled the room with a heady stink.

Vermeer had watched on television as bodies were carried out of the bombed-out restaurant. The tally so far: eleven dead, twenty-two wounded, with three still missing. He had also been told ATF investigators didn't know exactly what kind of device had been used, not yet, although the lead forensic analyst suspected that the main ingredient had been a variant of Semtex-A. Any seasoned operator would know it well, he thought. Semtex was a Czech-made, high-grade plastic explosive, and readily available on the international arms market. As a result it was found in the arsenals of nearly every terrorist, criminal and mercenary organization the world over.

He would find out nothing more here. But he still needed answers. Perhaps the girl would be able to talk to him later. Turning, he headed into the hallway. A lifetime diet of bad coffee and too many cobbled-together meals was finally starting to catch up with him.

He found a washroom a few steps from the ICU and entered. It was dark and blissfully unoccupied. He was just washing up when the door opened and a familiar figure walked in.

"Yes, Lieutenant?"

Walter Jerome looked out of place in civilian attire. "Someone from the Bureau is looking for you, sir."

They found the man in question in the hospital cafeteria, taking coffee with several of the FBI agents assigned to the case. Vermeer joined them whilst Jerome stood respectfully distant.

"Mister Vermeer." Special Agent Timothy Bozak was clearly not interested in seeing CIA involvement in what should have been a law enforcement matter. He motioned for Vermeer to join him at a nearby table.

"We got a hit on Trucco's MasterCard. It was used this afternoon, in a little town here, along the I-Forty-four interchange."

Another agent provided a roadmap of the surrounding area. Vermeer watched as Bozak indicated a town eighty miles southwest of St. Louis.

"Are your people on the move?" Vermeer asked.

"I have ten special agents and some people from the Federal Marshals en route even as we speak," Bozak replied. "There's a National Guard helo on its way to take us out that way as well. We should be in the air in less than thirty minutes."

"Outstanding." Vermeer got to his feet. "We'll meet you at the heliport in twenty."

Vermeer rejoined Jerome at the entrance to the cafeteria, his expression grim.

"Get the team together, Lieutenant. Full kit. We may have Sweet in the bag sooner than I thought."

CHAPTER 33

Dixon
(0159 hours (CST) – Thursday, 11 April 1991)

David Sweet crept through the darkness as the wind stirred at the tree branches overhead, hinting at a coming storm. Soon he came upon a steep fold in the land, covered by brush, and lined to the west by a thick stand of heavy foliage. From here he could just make out the house, lit within by the kerosene lanterns he'd procured in town. He could also see the dark curve of the road in from the highway, shadowed now, and screened by more heavy brush. There Colonel Trucco had set up his own hide, one hundred seventy-five meters away.

This was his third circuit of the established perimeter, and nothing seemed amiss. Occasionally headlights could be seen, passing by on the highway, but that was it. He was just beginning to consider making another go when there was a sudden flare of headlights as a vehicle turned off the main road, angling to the west. Sweet froze in place instantly as the light washed over him. The vehicle came to a complete halt: Sweet saw more movement, followed by voices. A car door slammed, followed by the gentle rustle of heavy boots against dew-wet grass.

* * *

"There they are," Elise Shilling said.

Michael Litke grunted an affirmative. Their headlights illuminated the U-Haul truck Klaus Reinhardt had used to ferry the heavy equipment in from St. Louis. He could see the other members of the team standing by the roadside, waiting. He pulled in behind the truck and shut off the engine, plunging the surrounding forest into absolute darkness.

Litke climbed into the open to find that the night air was cool and damp, as if expectant of rain. He moved around to the rear of the U-Haul to find Willi Krenz already in place, handing out weapons. Litke took an AKS-74U and its attendant bandoleer of ammunition before following Elise to the other side of the road, where August Lange and his team now waited.

"Standard team assignments," he told Lange. "Go now."

Litke had a total of eight people available, including Willi and Elise. He elected to leave Reinhardt behind to watch the vehicles and moved out, splitting the group into two separate detachments. All wore night-vision goggles and slinked through the forest as easily as a cloud passes across the face of the moon. Within moments the surrounding night had swallowed them completely. For several long minutes they swept forward, easing carefully from cover to cover, testing the night for any hint of danger. Abruptly Litke signaled a halt, and crouched at the edge of a brush-strewn trail. Elise and Willi huddled behind him, waiting.

He'd sensed movement, some minor stirring of the trees ahead. He brought his weapon to one shoulder and took off the safety. Willi eased forward to crouch at his side. The branches ahead rustled once more, and a low, dark shape ambled forward.

The doe's eyes were livid against the night. Litke released the pent up breath he was holding before lowering his weapon. He waited a tic, testing the night, before motioning for the others to follow. Minutes later the edge of the tree line came into view: glimmers of light showed through the sparse brush ahead, magnified thousands of times in the glare of his NV goggles.

Now Litke rose to a crouch, intent on moving forward to take up a good firing position. Instead he felt something, a tripwire perhaps, dig into his pant leg. He hit the ground, hard, fully expecting a dull roar, the flash and blast of a grenade. Instead a bright, sputtering red light engulfed him, blinding him, and washing out his night-vision gear.

* * *

Ian Trucco watched as the flare hissed to life just fifty yards away. Moments later he spied flitting shadows darting from the tree line parallel to the old house.

Somebody called out in a language he did not understand. There was more than enough light for him to target them, one by one. Trucco snuggled the M-1 against one shoulder and centered his sights on the closest figure, bracketed now against the glow of the burning flare.

The Garand was a heavy, comforting presence in his hands, like an old friend he had not seen in far too long. For the briefest of seconds it felt as if he was back in Korea, stranded just miles from the frozen Yalu. Then he took up the slack on the trigger, and felt the rifle go into recoil against him.

* * *

The first shots sounded the moment Litke signaled for his people to pull back, away from the light of the flare. A heavy .30 slug snapped past his right ear and perforated the tree beside him, cutting him with splinters.

"Down!"

Auto-fire tore the night. Litke watched as his people fired into the trees to his immediate right. He scrambled for cover, moving away from the flare as incoming gunshots spattered all around him. To make matters worse his night-vision gear had been burned out by Sweet's trap, partially blinding him. Litke knew he had to keep on the move. To stay in one place was to die. He scrambled to one knee and turned to Willi, who crouched a few feet away.

"Covering fire!" Willi dutifully raised his assault rifle and began shooting. A heartbeat later Litke was on his feet, dashing forward.

Once he was away from the flare it became too dark for him to see clearly. Branches whipped him across the face and tore at his clothing as he blundered into the surrounding foliage. He thought he could hear Elise and Willi close behind. Then he heard more gunfire, and the dull crack of a fragmentation grenade.

Litke paused, crouching, and waited impatiently for his vision to clear. Motes of light still danced before his eyes. After a moment he squinted forward, and saw the dull crimson flash of an outgoing muzzle-flare. Litke dug a grenade from his webbing, pulled the pin. He tossed it overhand, and hit the grass seconds before a dull roar shook the earth beneath him, spraying dirt and shredded foliage far and wide.

Within moments Litke was up and moving with several of his teammates in tight behind him. His heart pounded as the trio broke cover and charged the place where he thought he had detected the enemy gunman. The road flare illuminated the scene but dimly, exposing churned earth, torn foliage. A lone body sprawled amidst it all: even with that uneven light, Litke could just make out the mangled, blood-smeared features of Ian Trucco.

* * *

Sweet spotted an indistinct shape moving through the shadows, backlit by the glow of the sputtering road flare. He fired once and saw the guy go down. Now he squinted through his sights and squeezed off round after round, quickly, methodically, as if he were on the Known Distance course at Camp Pendleton, shooting for re-qualification. One shot, one kill. Repeat as necessary. It took him a little over ten seconds to burn through his first magazine of GI-surplus ball.

He dug a fresh eight-shot clip from his pocket and slapped it in place, and felt a sudden pinch as the bolt slammed his thumb out of the way. Then he was up and moving, staying low and seeking fresh cover as yet more incoming fire crackled all around him.

* * *

The back of Klara Schroeder's head had been blown apart. Bits of gray matter glistened on dew-wet foliage.

Litke crouched beside her, peering into the night. He had not seen where this fresh flurry of gunfire had come from.

"White phosphorous grenades. Now!"

"Yes, Herr Hauptmann." Litke heard several of his men rummaging through their field gear. Already the road flare had begun to sputter and die, leaving the forest shrouded in fresh darkness. Moments later he heard the click of safety spoons popping free, followed by a soft thump as grenades were loosed toward the distant gunman.

Litke looked away just in time. There was a flash, a roar, and a sickly wave of heat was washing over them, burning brightly and consuming all before it like some burning, hungry maw. The fire prickled at him, seeming to sear his flesh, and making it difficult for him to catch his breath.

"Michael! We need to go, now."

Elise stood over him, her features smudged with filth and grime. Her eyes were wild as she clenched her AK and surveyed the flame-shrouded wilderness.

"Go, Elise. We'll be right behind you." Then, turning to Willi: "Get the others and follow me. We're leaving."

CHAPTER 34

Dixon
(0944 hours (CST) – Thursday, 11 April 1991)

Frank Northacker had been the sheriff of Pulaski County for the past five years. During his tenure he had seen just about everything. Farm machinery decapitations, automobile accidents, methamphetamine overdoses, you name it.

But military-style firefights weren't part of his usual routine. For hours now the old farm just off Rural Route Three had been swarming with FBI, ATF and the state and local police. Now Northacker stood beside his patrol car and watched as an Army helicopter descended out of the rain-swept morning sky. The distinctive throb of the UH-60 Blackhawk's engines washed over him, tearing at his clothing, assaulting his senses.

He supposed the chopper was out of nearby Fort Leonard Wood. The big Sikorsky settled in, rotors spinning, and Northacker moved forward as its side door opened. Several men in civilian attire climbed out and began to approach.

They were all young and fit, and largely military in appearance. They had short hair, too, not quite GI regular, with military-theme tattoos visible on the occasional forearm or bicep. Northacker knew the aviation detachment over at Fort Wood had been providing the FBI with additional air transport since the terrorist bombing in St. Louis. Maybe they were Army CID, he thought with a mental shrug. Something told him not to ask too many questions.

* * *

Peter Vermeer stood for a moment and surveyed a scene of quiet devastation. The fire had engulfed both the old farmhouse and much of the surrounding forest. Only the coming rainstorm and the diligent efforts of the county fire department had kept the blaze from spreading farther. Still, the damage was considerable: from where he stood. Vermeer could see that the old house was a total loss. The remains of a late-model Cadillac sedan were parked besides the main building, burned down to bare metal and melted automotive glass.

"We have two bodies, bagged and tagged." Special Agent Tim Bozak stood, puffing away on a cigarette. "Both were burned pretty bad, of course. But the evidence techs did find something to ID one of them."

Bozak held out a plastic evidence baggie. Vermeer took it gingerly and examined what was inside: a charred U.S. Army dog tag. Ian Trucco's name, blood type and Korean War-era serial number were clearly marked thereon.

"Anything else?"

"A lot of spent brass." Bozak shrugged. "The lab guys are examining everything now, Mr. Vermeer. We'll know more in a few days."

"What started the fire?" Walter Jerome stood nearby, his slender frame hunched against the chill breeze.

"We're not sure yet. Why?"

"I was just wondering, sir. Thank you."

Bozak stubbed out his smoke and tossed the butt. "We just got word from the State Police: they're sending in dog teams to search the surrounding woods. If Sweet is still alive, we'll find him."

"Walter." Vermeer lit a cigarette of his own as Bozak moved off to confer one of his fellow agents.

"Yes, sir?"

"Get with someone and bum a ride into town. We'll need rental cars and a place to sleep. Nothing on base, mind you. Try to get something comfortable at a good local hotel. After that we wait and see what Special Agent Bozak and his team comes up with."

* * *

1825 hours: It had rained for most of the day. Now David Sweet crouched low, huddled in the lee of a moss-covered tree trunk. The purr of helicopter turbines sounded far overhead, setting his teeth on edge.

He'd heard dogs earlier, and knew he had to keep moving. Sweet peered skyward, and saw a flash of white against the clouds above: it was a police helicopter, performing a low altitude recon of the area. This was a different wrinkle altogether. In Iraq he hadn't had to worry about enemy aircraft at all. He waited patiently, never moving a muscle, until the airborne beast had moved on, and near silence returned to the forest around him.

A construction site bordered his hiding place, nearly abandoned now with the steady approach of night. Shadows lengthened, and darkness grew as Sweet watched the last of the workers close up shop and head home. Satisfied that he was truly alone, he stripped out of his impromptu ghillie suit. With no small regret he set aside his rifle and took up the small knapsack he'd saved from the farm. Inside were his pistol, what little money he still had, and the mysterious documents Ian Trucco had given him just hours before.

He paused a moment to survey the now-silent construction site. A sign by the road proclaimed the property to be the location of a new Quik-Save convenience store. He skirted the place, following the fence line until it led him to a two lane, blacktop road that bisected the forest, running east to west.

The old wound in his thigh burned dully, like rusty steel deep in the bone. He saw bright neon glimmer from just across the road. There a large sign flashed, boasting GIRLS GIRLS GIRLS, and DANCERS START AT 11 AM. The strip club building was long and drab, like a derelict aircraft hangar. Sweet could see young soldiers in civilian attire filing in and out of the place, fresh from the desert and eager for some action. He waited for the traffic to clear and darted across the road, staying in the shadows. A pair of police cruisers had been parked nearby, with men inside watching the festivities.

Moments later he plunged into the tree line, moving quickly. More artificial light shined to his left, away from the road. Skirting closer, he saw what appeared to be low, dark shapes huddled in a large clearing: a trailer park or camping ground, its occupants now hunkered down for the night. Loud voices came to him momentarily, followed by the slam of a car door. Sweet moved on, and left the lights of civilization far behind.

He came upon yet another line of fencing an hour later. This one was taller, and topped with barbwire. A battered metal sign, dimly visible by the light from passing headlights on a road just on the other side, told him thus:

U.S. ARMY INSTALLATION – NO TRESSPASSING – THE USE OF DEADLY FORCE IS AUTHORIZED

The vehicles passing by in column were military Humvees. He waited until the road grew dark once more. Then he took off his jacket and began to clamber up and over the perimeter fence. He draped the jacket over the barbwire, and gingerly surmounted this obstacle as well, tearing his pants in the process. Within seconds he was loping across the road, and moving quickly into the verge at the far end of the fence line.

Sweet had never been to Fort Wood before, but suspected the place would be laid out in a familiar pattern, similar to U.S. installations the world over. Taking a moment to reorient himself, he soon set off, moving deeper into the woods that cloaked the sprawling military facility.

* * *

He found the area he was looking for a little over an hour later. It too was brightly lit, with multi-story BEQs set back from the nearest road. A large parking lot was visible nearby, crowded now with dozens of automobiles. A sign at the entrance to the car park told him the area was home to the Army's 1138th Transport Battalion.

Men could be seen on the catwalks of the nearest barrack, smoking and speaking quietly amongst themselves. Snippets of

Nirvana and 2 Live Crew came to him dimly, carried on the wind. Sweet took a seat at a nearby picnic table. Occasionally teenage soldiers would pass him by, and nod politely.

It was just after 2300 hours when Sweet spotted a man who seemed to meet his criteria. He'd just come in from someplace, and parked his vehicle in the battalion lot. A sergeant E5, the guy was dressed in neatly starched BDUs and spit-shined boots. He stopped at the soda machine out front before heading for his room, which was located on the first floor.

Sweet took up his bag and followed. By now there was no one else in sight, save for the duty NCO, stationed in a small office at the front of the building. From his post the man had no way of seeing Sweet or the person he was now stalking.

Sweet walked up to the man's door and knocked. It opened, exposing a young kid, perhaps twenty-five or so, with mild blue eyes and sandy, short-cut blond hair. He and Sweet could have been brothers.

The kid's eyes seemed open and friendly. "Yes?"

Sweet produced his .45. "Inside, now."

"Jesus." The sergeant put his hands up and backed inside. Sweet followed and locked the door behind him. The room beyond was GI-standard, unremarkable. The kid's unopened Dr. Pepper sat on a nearby writing desk.

"What is this? What do you want?"

"Shut up and sit down," Sweet said. "Do as you're told and you won't be hurt. I need to borrow a few things, that's all."

The sergeant had the good sense not to resist. Sweet tied his hands and feet with strips of cloth taken from an olive drab T-shirt, and settled in to take what he needed. A gag in the guy's mouth assured he wouldn't be calling for help.

Soon Sweet had collected a set of starched BDUs, combat boots, and some civilian attire to replace what he'd lost in the fire. The kid had a grand total of $57.23 in his wallet. Sweet took this, too. He washed up a bit in the sink, shaved, and changed into the uniform. The boots were a bit large, but otherwise everything seemed to fit just fine. In the dark no one would be able to tell he wasn't what he appeared to be.

He made a quick check of the room to make sure he hadn't forgotten anything, and knelt at the bound soldier's side.

"I'm sorry about this, all right? It can't be helped. Once I'm away from here, I'll stop and call someone to come and untie you."

* * *

The sergeant's careworn Toyota Celica was still in the parking lot. Sweet climbed in, tried the engine, and drove away casually, as if he didn't have a care in the world. Again no one seemed to pay any attention to him. He drove on, heading for the main gate, and kept his speedometer hovering at just below the speed limit.

Ten minutes later he spied the seductive glow of neon on the near horizon. As he had expected there were MPs checking IDs on the road in. But no one bothered with vehicles on the way *out*. Sweet sped up a bit as he crossed over the invisible dividing line between the civilian world and the military, the road to either side brightly lit against the night. To his eye St. Robert was a typical military town, crowded with pawnshops, drycleaners, fast-food joints and lurid titty bars. Sweet had visited countless places just like it over the years, and saw little to take notice of now.

Save for the bright line of brake-lights glimmering on the roadway ahead.

It was a police checkpoint. Sweet felt perspiration break out on his exposed skin as he slowed to a stop behind the car ahead. His heart hammered inside his chest: he'd known this could happen, sure, but being in the here and now was something else entirely.

It took time for them to check the cars ahead of him in line. He watched as a freshening drizzle tracked across his windshield, the wipers throbbing. The police flashers glimmered against the water, tinting the inside of the car in garish shades of red and blue. He tightened his grip on the steering wheel and toyed with the idea of removing the pistol from the bag on the seat beside him.

Now it was his turn at bat. He lowered the driver's side window and tried to smile. The heavyset state trooper wore a rain slicker and had his Smokey the Bear hat covered in plastic. Sweet noticed distantly that he had a wad of Copenhagen between his cheek and gum.

"Good evening. Driver's license and registration, please."

Sweet handed it all over. "What's going on?"

The cop didn't answer at first. Instead he stood, regarding Sweet's purloined military ID, license, and insurance info by the glow of a heavy duty flashlight. Another trooper stood nearby, cradling a 12-bore Remington in the crook of one arm.

"This is your vehicle?"

"Yes, sir. It is." Sweet carefully watched the man's eyes. They were no longer so congenial.

"You need to step out of the car, son. Now." Sweet watched as the second cop leveled his shotgun. Others moved in as well. He raised his hands in surrender, and stepped into the rain. Within minutes he had been frisked, cuffed and settled in at the rear of a nearby police cruiser. The rain continued to pour down, unending, as Sweet was driven off, back toward the military facility he had so recently departed from.

CHAPTER 35

Fort Leonard Wood, Missouri
(0651 hours (CST) – Friday, 12 April 1991)

David Sweet stood, a pistol clenched in one hand.

The young Iraqi soldier knelt before him, begging for his life. Blood and bits of gray matter clung to his face. Sweet lifted the Browning and fired, and part of the kid's skull lifted off in an explosion of crimson gore.

Except his victim wasn't who he'd first thought. Jess looked at him, part of her face a ruin of bone and exposed tissue. Her one remaining eye bore into his. Why, David? Why did you do this to me?

Sweet did not answer. Instead he lifted the pistol once more, placed it to his temple, and began to take up the slack on the trigger.

* * *

Sweet opened his eyes and breathed deeply.

His cell in the base stockade was dingy and gray. He was alone, and still clad in the uniform he had been wearing the night before. He sat up, breathing heavily, and tried to calm himself. He remembered now that the MPs had taken his personal things when they'd brought him in. Jess's ring was gone, too. He wondered whether he'd ever see it again.

Jessica. A dull ache begun to grow inside his chest, a frantic scrabbling that tore at his heart with tiny, grasping fingers. He was still sitting there, staring blankly at the far wall when there was the rattle of a key in his cell door. The MPs entered and ordered him to his feet. He waited mutely as he was handcuffed and led into a long hallway. The quartet filed down a steep stairwell, past a suite of offices and into a cramped meeting room. The place smelled of aerosol disinfectant. The lead sergeant removed his handcuffs and told him to sit.

Sweet did as he was told. He saw no reason to resist. The guards waited a few minutes, ignoring him completely. Then the door opened and a pair of very familiar figures entered.

"That will be all, Sergeant. You and your men can wait outside."

Peter Vermeer was clad in rumpled khaki slacks and a nylon windbreaker. Sweet sat in silence as the guards departed, and got a good look at the man accompanying Vermeer. He was a tall guy, with hard features and piercing green eyes. After some consideration Sweet remembered seeing him in the desert the night Halabi was killed.

Vermeer took a seat across from Sweet. "You going to behave yourself, Gunny?"

Sweet eyed Vermeer's partner. "Do I have a choice?"

There was a pause. "Walter."

"Yes, sir?"

"Wait outside. I'll call if I need you."

Once they were alone Vermeer pulled a sheaf of papers from his briefcase. Sweet saw that they were the classified documents Trucco had shown him earlier.

"You know what this is?"

"You tell me."

"We recovered these papers when you were arrested last night. I'm going to assume Colonel Trucco told you everything he knew, about Operation Backgammon, Bed Check and Mohammed Halabi. The notes he took down are all here.

"But the question I have for you has to do with something else entirely." Vermeer leaned close. "Where did Trucco get it all? This is primo stuff, mind you. Top intel straight from the archives at Langley and the National Security Agency. I don't suppose you know how it came to be in his possession?"

Sweet met Vermeer stare for stare. "Someone sent them to Colonel Trucco in the mail. He didn't know from where, exactly."

"Okay." Vermeer nodded. "We both know you're no fool, Gunny, so I won't treat you like one. Someone appears to be killing people involved with the operation to bring Mohammad Halabi out of Iraq. You're not the only one they've targeted."

"I'm listening."

Vermeer kept his explanation quick and to the point. There were others who had been killed, he told Sweet, other than Jessica and Ian Trucco. Grant Lattimore was one, shot down on his way home from Langley just one week before.

"Another of our people has gone missing as well," Vermeer went on. "You remember Jim Detloff? He helped debrief you back on the *New Orleans*."

Sweet thought back to the brief conversation he'd had with the man. It seemed years ago now.

"I remember."

"Detloff has been missing since the night Grant Lattimore was killed. It's possible he's dead, too. But now I'm beginning to think he's gone to ground instead. And some of the things that have happened since we pulled you out of Iraq don't add up."

"How so?" Sweet asked.

"I helped arrange for a crash investigations team to be sent into Iraq shortly after the ceasefire in March. They went over the remains of the helicopter we lost with a fine-tooth comb. The results haven't been made public, of course, but now we know more than we did before."

A hard, cold feeling had settled in the pit of Sweet's stomach. "How so?"

"It's unlikely that helo was hit by enemy fire," Vermeer said. "The evidence techs think it was an internal explosion, probably a demo charge placed shortly before takeoff. Whoever detonated it must have waited until the rescue team was about to board before hitting the switch."

"Are you saying it was an inside job?"

"That's one possibility, yeah." Vermeer sighed. "The charge was made out of Semtex, pretty common stuff worldwide. We don't use it, of course, nor do most of our allies. But it seems the explosive residue found on the helo matches up with the demo that was used in St. Louis three days ago. According to my contacts with the FBI, the two are an exact chemical match."

Sweet felt the darkness growing within him anew. "What the hell is going on, sir?"

"That's what I'm here to find out. We know the men who tried to kill you are German, part of a former Stasi outfit that's managed to hang together since the Berlin Wall came down. I used to think they worked for Saddam, but now I'm not so sure. They're professionals, Gunny. Stone cold killers. You're lucky to be alive."

Sweet didn't feel particularly lucky at the moment. "That doesn't tell us who they're working for now."

"No, it doesn't. But it turns out you just may have given us a clue where to look next."

Vermeer pulled another file folder out of his briefcase. He showed it to Sweet, who recognized it as a military service record.

"This is the personnel jacket of Brigadier General Mitchell Abernathy, United States Army. He died back in 1987, during a routine helicopter flight in Italy. At the time he was the commanding officer of all U.S. Special Forces operations in Europe."

Sweet thought things over for a moment. "Trucco mentioned him, too. But he didn't know what connection the general may have had with our current situation."

"That may be the case. Personally, I believe Detloff is the key to it all. But I don't think he's dead. Not yet. So we need to find him, ASAP."

"I see." Sweet leaned back in his chair, suddenly spent. "So. What happens to me now?"

"You have a choice. You can come with us, and help stop the bastards who killed your girl."

"And if I say no?"

"You go into protective custody. No harm, no foul, okay? We have a safe house in Bethesda that I can have up and running in less than two hours."

"I see." Sweet sat back to consider what Vermeer had told him. "Forget the safe house, Mr. Vermeer. I'm with you all the way."

CHAPTER 36

Bolling Air Force Base – Washington D.C.
(1430 hours (EST) – Friday, 12 April 1991)

A message was waiting for Peter Vermeer when his flight touched down, forwarded thru Langley via the Soviet Embassy in Washington D.C. He ordered the others to sit tight while he went about scrounging up a car from the base motor pool, and drove onto the Anacosta Freeway, toward the I-395 north into the D.C. metropolitan area.

He steered the little Dodge Aries through the city proper, past the Washington Navy Yard, through Dupont Circle and into the northern suburbs, toward one of the highest points in the entire area. Soon he was putt-putting up a long, winding drive, onto a roundabout that fed onto the Soviet Embassy Annex at Mt. Alto, just off Wisconsin Avenue.

It seemed he was expected. Guards at the gate directed him to visitors' parking, where he left the car and headed on through security to the Annex's inner compound. There he stood for a moment, gazing at the grounds of what would soon be the new Soviet Embassy. It was an ugly, utilitarian structure, more a concrete blockhouse in occupied Normandy than the proud Embassy of a world superpower. Radio-intercept aerials and antennas sprung from the roof like strands of an old miser's stringy hair. He looked up and stared at the blood-red Soviet ensign as it fluttered against a stiff morning breeze. That same wind swept in from the Potomac as he stood and waited. Nearly twenty minutes passed before the man who had summoned him made an appearance, walking unsteadily from the main building's southernmost entrance.

There was little, Vermeer thought, about Colonel Lev Vasilyevich Stolyarov to impress the casual observer. The veteran Soviet operative was sallow and cadaverous in both visage and demeanor, like a cardstock undertaker from any random Sergio Leone picture you'd care to mention.

"Hello, Peter."

"Colonel." Vermeer could not help but notice the teakwood cane the older man carried. Stolyarov walked with an intense limp, a legacy, his Agency profile suggested, of wounds he had picked up during the battle for Stalingrad back in 1943.

The two men shook hands. "Thank you for coming so promptly."

"To what do I owe the honor?" Vermeer asked.

"It's this business with your man Detloff." Stolyarov handed over a thick manila envelope. "You are aware that I was once the operations officer for the unit known as Project Seven-four? Yes? They were good people once, good operatives. I trained them myself."

"You did too good a job."

"That is why it shames me to see what they have become."

Vermeer nodded. "I'm told they're working for the Iraqis now."

Was that the ghost of a smile that crept across Stolyarov's too-thin lips? "It is disgusting! Men of their caliber, working as common thugs? That is why the Secretary-General has authorized me to speak with you."

Vermeer lit a cigarette. "Go on."

"You understand we had nothing to do with this, yes? We are not involved! Not directly, at any rate. Indeed, your man Detloff came to our Cultural Attaché in Amman and stated his intention to defect."

Vermeer felt his pulse quicken slightly. "When did this happen?"

"Three days ago." Stolyarov shrugged. "Obviously we refused him. So he went to the Iraqis instead. You've heard of the senior man in the Mukhabarat's Section Seventeen?"

Vermeer took a moment to recall the name. "Hasim Awad, right? Formerly with the Iraqi air force?"

"The same. Our latest information suggests he's running Detloff's recruitment effort. The last we heard he was still in Amman, meeting regularly at the Iraqi consulate there."

"I see."

"Everything you need to end this is contained in that packet, Peter. Dates, locations, even a probable meet-site for Detloff's transference to Iraq." He smiled once more. "I will have to trust you not to let our friends in Baghdad know where the information came from."

"That goes without saying." Vermeer stubbed out his cigarette. "Thank you, sir."

"We do not take this action lightly, you understand." Stolyarov seemed to sag. "This is an ugly business. I think you'd agree that such violence is not in our mutual interest."

Vermeer could not have agreed more. The works of Ian Fleming aside, intelligence operatives rarely kill one another. Oh, the occasional local proxy might be sacrificed, but never an out-and-out member of the other side's intelligence apparatus. Such unneeded carnage would only serve to make it that much harder for organizations like the KGB and the CIA to do their jobs.

"Thank you again, sir. Is there anything else I should know?"

"Probably." The Russian turned as if to leave. "But I can't think of anything at the moment. "*Dosvidaniya*, Peter."

"Goodbye." Vermeer turned and headed back to his car. Once he was safely inside it took every ounce of self-control he possessed not to rip open the letter right then and there.

CHAPTER 37

Bolling AFB
(1527 hours (EST) – Friday, 12 April 1991)

Peter Vermeer returned to the base at mid-afternoon. He saw that Walter Jerome and his SEALs were waiting by the freshly refueled C-20 executive jet, ready to go at a moment's notice.

He climbed out of the car. "Where to now?" Jerome wanted to know.

"Back to KKMC." Vermeer climbed aboard the military-flagged Gulfstream-III. Lieutenant Jerome could only follow with a puzzled expression on his face, buffeted by the roar of the executive jet's engines.

The rest of the group boarded and found seats. David Sweet was seated quietly at the rear of the cabin. Jerome watched as Vermeer took a moment to speak with the pilot, an Air Force major.

"So. What's in Saudi?" the lieutenant asked.

Vermeer settled in as they reached the main runway and began their final preps for takeoff. "Our boy Detloff."

Jerome looked up, seemingly startled at this revelation. "We have a location? When did this happen?"

"It's a long story. You'll be briefed later, along with the rest of the team." He found a blanket and closed his eyes for a nap. "Wake me in a little while, all right? I'll need to make a phone call."

* * *

Two hours later Vermeer bounced a signal off a military communications satellite, direct to Nicholas Farraday's office at Langley. It took Vermeer nearly thirty minutes to spell out everything Lev Stolyarov had told him. Farraday seemed grimly stoic about the entire thing, including Vermeer's plan to deal with it.

"What do you intend to do with Sweet?" Farraday asked. "I was expecting you to drop him off with our people before you left."

"I think the gunny will be more useful to us in Saudi Arabia." He shifted the handset to a more comfortable position, and gazed out the window. "He's been on the ground there before, and knows the lay of the land. Besides, I'll feel better if he's close by, where I can keep an eye on him."

"You should have checked with me first."

"There wasn't time." Vermeer watched as Chief Torres and his men settled in for an impromptu game of spades. "Things are starting to move pretty quickly now."

"We'll talk more about this later." But Farraday seemed taut, on edge, as he changed topics. "Do you think you can find Detloff?"

"If Stolyarov was playing straight with me, yes. I just hope Shilling's people don't get wind of our intentions somehow. Sometimes it seems as if they've been ahead of us every step of the way."

"I'll give Norm Mollar a call. He'll make sure you have all the operational security on site you could possibly need."

"Thanks. I'll check in once we're on the ground."

They said their goodbyes, and Vermeer hung up. He saw that the card game was in full swing. After a moment's thought he decided to go and see if they would let him sit in on a round.

* * *

British Airways flight 7071, bound for London
(2020 hours (CST) – Friday, 12 April 1991)

Michael Litke waited tensely as the Boeing 747 pulled away from the St. Louis terminal. Elise Shilling sat at his side, pretending to read a fashion magazine.

Only ten out of the original fifteen members of Objekt-74 had made it this far. As a result Litke had been forced to reshuffle team assignments to cover the losses: he'd completely disbanded Teams Two and Five, and folded Hans Eberbach, Leo Bieserfeld and Klaus Reinhardt into what was left of Team Three.

"What about the extra equipment we asked for?"

"It's already en route." She licked one finger and turned the page. "Control is handling everything personally, Michael. Stop sounding like an old woman."

"What about transport out of the city?" he asked. "It's more than three hundred and fifty kilometers from Amman to Detloff's supposed meet-site, and all across rather inhospitable terrain."

She paused as the plane halted on the runway, nestled in behind the next aircraft in queue for takeoff. "There will be four long-wheelbase Land Rovers waiting for us at the airport."

"Weapons?"

"A local fellow is seeing to it." She shrugged. "I gather he's involved with the PLO somehow. I suppose it's someone Control scrounged up at the last moment."

"More witnesses, Elise?" Litke sighed.

"It can't be helped." Now it was her turn to sigh as they felt the 747 finally accelerate to takeoff speed. "Just let it go. We'll take things as they come."

"Hmm." He checked his watch. There was something like nine hours remaining before they landed. Maybe now he would finally be able to get some sleep.

CHAPTER 38

King Khalid Military City
(1825 hours – Monday, 15 April 1991)

David Sweet stood in the hangar office and stared out into the reddish haze of late afternoon. The horizon to the west was cluttered with the beginnings of a brutal spring sandstorm, leaving the sky tainted and churlish despite the steady approach of twilight.

He pulled Jessica's ring from his pocket, and watched it gleam in the light cast by the overheads, shimmering brilliantly.

"No one's forcing you to be in on this one, Gunny."

He turned to find Lieutenant Jerome standing in the doorway, clad in rumpled cammies. His deuce gear was festooned with spare magazines, grenades and a Recon Tanto fighting knife.

"I need to go, Lieutenant. This is personal for me." Sweet put the ring away.

"Maybe that's why you need to stay behind."

"Vermeer says to put me in a cell, or give me a parachute, Mr. Jerome. I'm going."

The lieutenant shook his head, apparently nonplussed. "Have it your way. There's a pre-jump briefing in fifteen minutes. Be there."

* * *

The air in the underground briefing room was brutally cold after the swelter outside. Sweet felt the sweat drying on salt-slick skin as he and the SEALs settled in. The walls around them were drab concrete, green-painted, and eerily claustrophobic.

"Attention on deck!"

Sweet and the others automatically snapped to as the briefing team entered the room. He was surprised somebody had bothered with the formality until he saw the senior man was a two-star admiral in desert utilities. He could not help but notice the SEAL trident emblazoned over his left breast pocket.

"At ease."

It was an U.S. Army Special Forces officer who had spoken. He stood at the podium, next to a female naval officer in khakis, and then cleared his throat.

"Can everyone hear me in the back?"

Murmurs, grunted assents. "Good afternoon. As of this moment you are on final mission prep. No calls off post, no contact with the world outside. Clear?"

A stirring, followed by assumed agreement. "My name is Lt. Colonel Kiley and I'll be your briefing officer. This is your pre-mission brief. The operation codename is 'Sandpiper.' Lieutenant Nguyen?"

The woman uncovered the storyboard easel at the head of the room. Sweet saw the 1:50,000 map of western Iraq underneath, highlighting the area near the Jordanian border.

"Good evening." She looked barely old enough to try out for the local cheerleading squad, Sweet thought. "This mission has priority. On order your team will insert via HALO into LZ Canoe. The secondary landing zone is designated as LZ Camera."

Sweet took notes as Nguyen indicated two points on the map, both located within fifty klicks of Iraq's border with Jordan.

"Once on the deck the team will rendezvous at Rally Point November, where transport has been pre-positioned." She indicated another point on the map, RP-November.

She continued with the rest of the mission outline. Once Sweet and the SEALs had mated up with their transport they were to cross the Jordanian frontier. There they were to link up with their backup team, codename Banjo, before heading on to a spot in the desert just a few kilometers east of a town by the name of Ar Ruwayshid.

Next an Air Force meteorological specialist took the podium. He reported clear skies, the weather hot and dry, with occasional sandstorms expected over much of the ops area. Sweet took it all down as Nguyen returned to her place before them, describing radio frequencies, available ground and air support, and routes of egress for the coming mission.

It was here that Peter Vermeer took over. He didn't bother to introduce himself, and instead asked that Kiley, Lt. Nguyen and the other, non-essential members of the S-3 team leave the room for the duration of the briefing.

Sweet saw that the admiral stayed behind, smoking a cigarette and standing silently in a corner.

Vermeer cleared his throat before beginning. "As you may have suspected, we've gotten a lucky break. James Detloff was spotted in Amman no less than six days ago."

A picture went up on the big screen. It was a long-range shot, Sweet decided, taken via telephoto lens. It showed Detloff standing on a dusty street corner complete with road signs in Arabic, next to a middle-aged man in sweat-matted civilian attire.

Vermeer gestured to the photo. "Here he is, meeting with his primary contact in the Mukhabarat. The guy's name is Awad. He's Iraqi air force, or used to be at least. Now he's their number one guy in counterintelligence operations, especially on foreign soil."

He clicked the projector once more, changing the item to show a map of the Iraq/Jordanian border.

"Once at the meet-site, you and Ops Team Banjo will set up and wait for the Iraqis to arrive. We believe enemy strength will be in the neighborhood of two to four men. No more. They're not trying to draw attention to themselves."

Vermeer clicked off the slide projector. "Lieutenant Nguyen said this mission has priority, gentlemen. I want you to remember that, and remember it is vital you recover Detloff alive, and mostly in one piece. The man is a traitor, yes, but he has information we need."

He turned to the admiral. "Is there anything else, sir?"

"Yes, Peter. Thank you." The guy stepped forward, stubbed out his smoke. Sweet saw that his name, Mollar, was stenciled on the front of his utilities.

"All right, men. I'm not going to waste your time with some bullshit pep talk." He offered them a brief, wry smile. "Just remember what Mr. Vermeer said: it is of vital consequence that this man be brought into U.S. custody. A number of American citizens have died because of his actions. That alone is enough for him to be brought to justice."

Admiral Mollar seemed to look Sweet's way for a moment, his expression unreadable. "That will be all. Carry on."

* * *

2150 hours: Sweet followed the SEALs out into the night. Like the rest of Jerome's team, Sweet was dressed in U.S.-pattern desert camouflage, similar to uniforms the Jordanian military used. In a pinch, and at a distance, it was hoped the team would be mistaken for a contingent of local infantry.

He was also kitted out for war: strapped upside-down to his side was an M-16 rifle, fitted with a single-shot, 40mm grenade launcher beneath the barrel. A 9mm service Beretta was holstered beneath his left armpit. A heavy ALICE pack, containing field equipment and supplies, was suspended from his belt, while at his back was an MC3 free-fall parachute, similar to civilian sport models that allow a jumper to steer himself in flight.

The group strode through the dark until the huge outline of a four-engine, turboprop transport appeared ahead. Sweet recognized it as an U.S. Air Force MC-130H Combat Talon, the Special Operations version of the venerable Hercules transport. Its props were already turning over for takeoff.

The five-man detail trooped up the Talon's loading ramp and into its cavernous interior. As they took their seats the jumpmaster closed the rear hatch, sealing them away behind red-tinted darkness. Sweet felt the bird give a sudden lurch as the pilot started to taxi.

There was a bump, a shudder, and Sweet felt the MC-130's big tires cross onto the main runway. He looked up, and saw the other jumpers seeming to wait patiently, their features masked, insect-like.

He could still recognize each man, however: Lt. Jerome, Chief Torres. And the other SEAL team members: Boatswain's Mate Louis Gehren and Gunner's Mate Lester Griggs, who sat cradling the team's big M-60 'Echo' general purpose machinegun.

There was the whine of hydraulics as the pilot set his flaps for takeoff. Sweet noticed Lieutenant Jerome was sitting across the isle, regarding him silently. The roar of the engines increased to takeoff speed, and Sweet felt the big Combat Talon roar down the runway, struggling to climb above the haphazard clutter of sandstorms that cloaked much of the Arabian Peninsula.

Sweet checked his watch. Less than fifty minutes remained until they were due at the drop zone. He settled in to wait, hands folded across his reserve parachute. He willed himself to absolute stillness. It was a picture of tranquility that did not match the roiling emotions he felt building inside.

* * *

Amman, 2230 hours:

"Everything you asked for is here, and more."

Their contact was known as Malik. He was a dark, reedy little fellow who stank of coffee and cheap tobacco. Michael Litke told the man to wait outside. He then had Willi and the others empty the large metal shipping container so they could more readily examine its contents.

The inside of the box smelled of petroleum and hot metal. Willi tore open the largest of the wooden crates inside to discover a dozen oblong shapes, each packaged for long-term storage. At Litke's direction Willi tore away the protective paper, exposing a dozen Israeli Galil assault rifles. He picked one up, racked the bolt and peered into the chamber. A greasy film gleamed back at him. And as Malik had said, there was more: plenty of 5.56mm ammunition for the rifles, a pair of FN "Minimi" light machineguns, grenades, and a Soviet "Igla-1" man-portable surface-to-air missile launcher, capable of destroying low-flying aircraft out to a range of more than five kilometers.

August Lange came over to speak with Litke. "We'll have to soak the rifles in petrol to get the preservative coating off, Herr Hauptmann. It could take a few hours."

"Get to work. I want to be on the road as soon as possible."

CHAPTER 39

Somewhere over western Iraq
(2302 hours – Monday, 15 April 1991)

"Five minutes!" The jumpmaster had to shout to be heard over the snarl of the MC-130's engines.

David Sweet climbed to his feet, burdened by the weight of his parachute, field gear, and weapons. He watched as Jerome and his SEALs did the same.

He carefully checked his oxygen line for signs of damage or blockage. He then fitted it to his chest bottle and turned the knob. The resultant air tasted like stale rubber.

"Stand by. Two minutes." The group paired up for the buddy system, patting down gear, checking parachutes. He was seconded to Petty Officer Gehren, who went over Sweet's gear with a professional's eye for detail. Cold air spilled into the Combat Talon as the massive rear hatch opened, rudely admitting moonlight and the increased roar of the turbofans.

"Stand in the door!" Sweet looked up, saw the red light. On green they would go.

The light clicked over to emerald. "Go! Go! Go!" Sweet watched as, one by one, the SEALs shuffled forward, buffeted by the wind, and stepped off the ramp into absolute blackness. He followed them out, feeling the wind rip at his clothing, his equipment, and threaten to tear the oxygen mask from his face. The altimeter at his wrist read twenty-five thousand feet and began to count down rapidly.

* * *

Sweet lost sight of his fellow jumpers almost instantly. This was no mere static-line jump, wherein the operator's parachute deploys immediately after he leaves the aircraft. This would be a HALO insertion, High-Altitude, Low-Opening, so to better approach the drop zone with all due stealth. Recon marines and Navy SEALs practice such insertions regularly, and become expert at them. But Sweet knew that did not make the procedure any less dangerous. The two biggest risks stemmed from hypoxia (a lack of oxygen to the brain) and the deadly subzero temperatures encountered at high altitude. He had faith his extensive training and top-of-the-line equipment would protect him, but still the risk remained.

He fell through the inky darkness, plummeting. The roar of the engines had fallen far behind him. He consulted his altimeter, noting he had less than ten thousand feet to go before his canopy deployed automatically.

Seven thousand, six thousand. Five thousand. The numbers tumbled away, diminishing rapidly, and Sweet was out of the clouds, and bathed in wan, haze-deflected moonlight.

The altimeter neared one thousand feet. There was a quick shudder at his back. The altimeter had measured the air pressure and altitude to a preset limit, and automatically severed the ripcord.

Sweet felt the sudden deceleration as his parachute spilled from its container, nylon snapping in the wind. His teeth rattled as the risers went taut, jerking him to a relative standstill. He could feel the canopy billow wide, a good jump, he was going to make it, Thank you, Jesus! A vast, darkened shadow that could only be the ground rushed up to meet him with unseemly haste.

He hit hard, and felt the breath torn from his body. He tucked his legs, rolling with the impact. Seconds later he was down, half-buried in fluttering parachute nylon but otherwise unhurt.

Off came his mask. The air tasted dry, dusty, and at the same time eerily familiar. He tugged on his night-vision goggles to note he was in a deep valley, rock-cluttered, and bordered by a line of dry wadis to the north and west.

First things first: Sweet unlimbered his rifle and cleared away the tape over the muzzle and magazine well. He locked a magazine into place and brought a green-tipped 5.56mm round into the chamber.

Now to swat down his parachute, and bundle the mass of fluttering green nylon until it formed a more convenient package. He wadded it into a nearby hollow and buried it amidst some rocks, concealing it.

He made for a jumble of boulders a few hundred meters on. Once hidden amidst the cairn's darkened flanks he withdrew a compact GPS set. Sweet took a reading from the navigation satellites far overhead, fixing his location, and compared it to the plastic-coated terrain map he carried. He found that he was nearly twelve kilometers southeast of the team's chosen rally point.

* * *

0435 hours: Sweet crept cautiously to the edge of a low rise and peered to the north. Vague illumination appeared in the distance, strung out like far-off Christmas lights. They were headlights, he decided. Sweet counted a dozen trucks, both military and civilian. Some were headed west, some east, on the major, two-lane blacktop highway that stretched for two hundred miles between Ar Rutbah and Amman.

The sudden growl of jet turbofans sounded in the sky overhead. They were probably U.S. aircraft, Sweet thought. He wasn't worried about enemy aircraft. Saddam's fixed-wing air force had been grounded as part of the UN-brokered ceasefire, whilst his surviving helicopter fleet was still busy putting down twin insurrections in both the north and south.

Sweet pulled back from the ridge and continued on his way. He moved cautiously for the next thirty minutes or so, stopping often to survey his back trail. Time was running out. He'd hoped to arrive at the rally point before dawn. Otherwise he'd have to go to ground during the daylight hours, delaying the mission. The sky was just beginning to show the first faint shades of pink when he reached the spot he was looking for. Drawing up another low rise, Sweet keyed his tactical radio and transmitted a single code phrase. He was answered immediately, and told to come forward.

Sentries intercepted him almost immediately. He recognized them as British Special Air Service, the best of the best, kitted out in desert ghillie suits and carrying night-vision equipped semi-automatic rifles.

The camp beyond was small, desolate, austere. Known as a forward refueling point, or FRP, the camp was a Special Forces-manned way station for Coalition personnel operating in the wilds of Iraq. Carefully sited camouflage netting covered the small collection of GP tents and spider holes, rendering the camp nearly invisible to any observer situated more than a hundred meters away.

At the moment the camp was getting ready to bunker down for the rest of the day. Sweet found Jerome, Torres and Gehren squirreled away in the camp CP, taking morning chow with the FRP's senior officer, Captain Southby-Taylor. The SAS commander was pale and sunburned, and seemed, overall, to have little to say.

He was told that Griggs had still not showed up. Little else was said as Sweet was handled an MRE and told to take it easy.

He ate in silence, and felt his finger trace the diamond ring he kept in one pocket.

Petty Officer Griggs made it to camp just as the first harsh light of dawn colored the sky. The team rode out the heat of the day in the sandbag-reinforced bunker that was the camp's main billeting area. Sweet and his teammates hydrated themselves, slept. Occasionally he would awaken abruptly, bathed in sweat and thinking of Jessica. The hours passed slowly, like the crawl of a rattlesnake across a dirty wooden floor.

CHAPTER 40

Rally Point November – Iraq
(1930 hours – Monday, 15 April 1991)

"Gunny Sweet."

David Sweet rolled over and saw Lt. Jerome standing over him. The SEAL team leader had his face cammied over, his Heckler & Koch sub-gun slung crosswise against his torso.

"Sir?"

"On your feet."

The flat tone in the other man's voice stirred Sweet into action. He grabbed his rifle and pack. The fall of twilight had brought rapidly cooler temperatures to the desert. He looked skyward to see that the heavens were filled with stars, legion upon legion of them, in an endless pinwheel that hovered over his head like a sea of fine lace.

Jerome was a dim shadow against the night. "Okay, let's go. Mount up."

The team clambered into what the U.S. armed forces called Light Strike Vehicles, or LSVs. Sweet knew the LSV was basically a product-improved dune buggy with heavy armaments and a three-man crew. Force Recon sometimes used them in the desert.

"Gunny, you ride with me." Jerome settled into the front passenger seat, directly behind a pintle-mounted general-purpose machinegun. Sweet dutifully clambered up behind the vehicle's primary armament, a Browning .50-caliber heavy machinegun.

He fitted a belt of AP mixed with tracer into the feed tray and racked the bolt. Petty Officer Gehren took the wheel and started the engine. Torres and Griggs settled into an LSV of their own, and soon the steady rattle of 125-horsepower engines carried across the night-dark terrain.

Sweet slipped his night-vision goggles into place, and tied an Arab head cloth, known as a *shemagh*, around his nose and mouth. SAS men with flashlights guided them up and out of the FRP.

The camouflage netting would be back in place promptly, he knew, as if the SEAL team had never existed. The ride was rough, forcing Sweet to grit his teeth and hold on for dear life. He checked his watch and noted the time. The team was twenty-five miles from the border, and another five from the meet-site with the other ops team, codename Banjo.

* * *

The land here proved to be as flat and empty as the Texas Panhandle. According to the pre-mission brief few people lived in the area, save hardy nomads who made their living herding livestock between the few precious waterholes scattered between Ar Rutbah and the Jordanian frontier. The team crossed the border at precisely 2015 hours, with another twenty minutes passing before the team arrived at the agreed upon rendezvous. They stopped about two thousand meters in, and Jerome ordered Chief Torres and Sweet to reconnoiter the area.

The pair moved forward cautiously, one man covering the other, until they had crossed the intervening distance. Torres was a good field man, Sweet thought, and covert-minded, cautious, and nearly silent while on the move. Once they had come close enough, the pair hunkered down in a dry wadi at the edge of a low, rocky escarpment.

"Looks clear." Torres scanned the distant valley through a pair of night-vision optics.

Sweet checked his watch. "It's about that time."

"Go for it."

Sweet keyed his tactical RT. "Banjo, this is Sandpiper five. Over." Static crackled in his headset almost immediately.

"Sandpiper, Banjo Actual. Signaling now." A dim light flickered three times at the far end of the escarpment.

"I have a visual. En route." Sweet stood up, leaving Torres in place. The wiry little SEAL peered over the sights of the heavy M-14 rifle he carried, commanding an excellent view of the surrounding terrain. Sweet headed off with his weapon held ready.

He picked his way carefully amongst the rocks, and soon found himself at the deepest end of the ravine. A steady wind blew at his back, chill enough to raise the sparse hairs at the nape of his neck. Torres was one hundred meters back, just within night-vision range. Sweet waited with one thumb tight against his rifle's selector-switch.

Seconds later he saw shadowy movement against the rocks. The figure wore a U.S.-style ghillie suit and cradled a suppressed MP-5.

"Hey there, old man." Sweet saw the guy's smile, vivid in the NV glow. "You get your taxes filed yet?"

For a second Sweet wasn't sure he'd heard correctly. "Bill?"

Staff Sergeant Bill Marino's smile grew wider. "I never thought I'd be the one to sneak up on you. Must be getting soft in your old age."

"Shit, yeah. I guess so." Sweet peered at the surrounding darkness and shrugged. "The rest of the team here?"

"I've got Ahern on overwatch. The others are around. Are you and the squids ready to move out?"

"Let me call it in."

* * *

Jerome wasn't interested in needless introductions. Instead he ordered the combined Recon/SEAL unit to get back on the road and head west. The men of Recon 2/4 were mounted up in LSVs identical to the mounts used by the SEALs, so the group made good time, even considering the need for caution. An hour of steady driving brought them the thirty-odd miles to the point Peter Vermeer believed the Iraqis would use to get James Detloff out of Jordan.

It wasn't much to look at. Just a rutted track, a few scraggly palms, and an old police way station that hadn't been manned since Britannia had ruled much of the known world. The main building was stone-walled, one story, and partially buried in drifting sand. The highway Sweet had spotted earlier was about fifteen kilometers to the north, cloaked now by a series of folds in the arid terrain.

Jerome ordered the vehicles hidden away, bundled under camouflage netting. Then the group got to work at digging in, preparing fighting positions and spider holes for the coming ambush. The SEAL commander decided to keep the two units separate, with Recon 2/4 assigned to hold the high ground just to the north of the old police station.

Sweet requested permission to bunker down with his old team. Jerome didn't seem to care either way. It was just after 0030 hours. Sweet got out his E-tool and began to dig. The ridge offered an excellent view of the road below, while the main outbuilding was a little over a hundred and fifty meters to the southeast. From here Sweet could just make out the SEALs prepping their fighting positions.

It was hard work. Sweet was bathed in sweat despite the cold night air. Four hours of steady effort allowed the group to finish, however, with another three hours remaining before daybreak. Sweet took a moment to rest, spotting Corporal Rackley on the overwatch position. He took a swig from his canteen and peered north toward the lights on the distant highway.

They were high up enough now to make out the road. He could see a set of headlights move against velvet darkness, headed east toward the Iraq border.

He felt a hand on his shoulder. Sweet turned to see Lance Corporal Ahern, who told him the digging was complete. He nodded, and hitched up his pack. He would share a fighting hole with Marino. Together the two rigged a camouflage tarp over the hole, hiding them from view.

Bill indicated he would take the first watch. Sweet nodded and settled in, drawing a rain poncho over his head. Within seconds he was asleep, resting peacefully. He did not dream.

CHAPTER 41

Ar Ruwayshid – Jordan
(1100 hours – Tuesday, 16 April 1991)

The building looked old, abandoned, as if it had not been occupied in decades. Grime was smeared at its shuttered windows, and gathered in the spaces between the rusted rollup doors that covered the broad front entrance.

Major Hasim Awad climbed from his sand-pitted Toyota Land Cruiser and surveyed the street around him. His eyes were protected from the sun by mirrored sunglasses. He saw nothing out of the ordinary. The only movement came from a trio of young boys playing football in a dusty alley just down the street. Awad fingered the pistol holstered beneath his blazer for a moment before turning away.

He leaned inside the car. "Stay here. I'll be back in a moment."

The fat American said nothing in reply. He merely sat, sunburned, perspiring, as Awad opened the lift-gate and removed the folding-stock AK that was hidden inside. He strolled up to the building and peered through one of the cracked windows facing the street. His men sat in the car, waiting. Awad fished a key from his jacket and unlocked the door. Unlike the rest of the moldering remains of the building, the lock had been carefully maintained, and gave way with little difficulty.

He quickly surveyed the front room, and the storage spaces beyond. All was silence filled with dusty ruin. He went back outside and gestured for the others to join him.

He had brought two of his best men. Both were armed, of course. One escorted James Detloff inside while the other brought the car around back.

"I still don't see why we can't cross the border now." Detloff's tone was petulant, like that of a spoiled child.

"I told you before." Awad set his weapon on a nearby table before lighting a cigarette. "We wait here until our escort arrives. It's possible your old friends may try to stop us at the border."

Awad did not like this American. At best he considered Detloff to be a lazy parasite, as well as a coward and a traitor. He would be happy to deliver the fool into the hands of the Mukhabarat, and be done with him.

One of his men, a hulking sort of fellow by the name of Majed, entered the building. "We're set."

Awad nodded. "Take Sami and watch the street."

Majed picked up the rifle and left to do as he'd been told. Awad turned his eyes to Detloff and forced himself to smile.

"Not much longer, I promise."

* * *

The men Awad were waiting for arrived less than an hour later. They were hard-eyed types, local Abbadi tribesmen for the most part, and were armed with an assortment of Kalashnikov rifles scoured from the illegal arms markets of Amman and Az Zarqa. They rode in three battered Toyota pickup trucks that had seen better days.

Their leader was a Palestinian by the name of Marouf Mohammed. Awad sincerely doubted that was his real name. He was known to the CIA and Mukhabarat both, and had been PLO once, until he'd been caught siphoning off funds to one of Arafat's special overseas' accounts. Until very recently he had made a living smuggling hashish across the border into Syria and Lebanon.

Awad greeted the man like a long-lost brother. The two sat in a corner, bemoaning the lack of hot tea and the other accoutrements of civilized society before getting down to business. Detloff sat and seemed to watch them with sullen disinterest.

"You wish an armed escort to the border?" Marouf considered this for a moment before nodding. "Of course. But my men and I shall require five hundred U.S. dollars, per man, per day."

Awad lit another cigarette. "Fifty dollars per man, no more. Half now, and the rest once we reach our destination."

"No, my friend! No. You bleed my children dry."

On it went, until the price was agreed upon. Marouf commanded a party of twelve men. Awad decided it would be more than enough to deal with anything the CIA might try to throw their way.

The two shook hands, and Awad told Detloff what had transpired.

"You didn't tell them where we're going, did you?" The American sounded appalled at the thought of having anything to do with Marouf and his men.

"Not exactly, no." Awad fought the urge to roll his eyes to the Heavens. "You worry too much. I have done this before. Soon you will be in Iraq, and all will be well."

"I'll believe it when I see it." He sat down and returned to his sulking.

Awad looked to the gold Rolex at his wrist. A few hours more, he thought, and they would move out. He felt eager to be away from this place and back amongst his own kind once more.

* * *

The daily courier arrived while Peter Vermeer was taking afternoon chow. He signed for the classified items under his name before retiring to his quarters. There he began to read.

It had been difficult for him to acquire even a heavily censored copy of the original Backgammon files. Reading on, he noted most of the senior personnel involved had their names stricken from the official record. Details, dates, and even the locations of specific Backgammon operations had been removed, leaving Vermeer with little concrete to go on.

Something, however, leapt out at him on his second go-through of the file. It was a name, Benjamin H. Stanton, listed as a military officer stationed at the U.S. embassy in Baghdad throughout the middle 1980s. The man had been a major in the

United States Army at the time, with a specialty in Middle Eastern culture and languages. Part of his duties had been to act as liaison between the U.S. and Iraqi militaries during the height of cooperation between the two countries.

The name jangled around at the edge of Vermeer's memory. He frowned and set the file aside, and began digging through the litter of paperwork atop his desk. Most of it was from the papers the FBI had seized from Gunny Sweet. Soon he found what he was looking for: a copy of an Interpol file dated 12 October 1987. Inside was the murder case file of Major B.H. Stanton, United States Army. At the time Stanton had been serving with the 10th Special Forces Group (Airborne), headquartered out of Bad Tolz, West Germany.

Included were police evidence photographs showing Major Stanton laying facedown in a pool of blood. Probable cause of death, a gunshot wound to the back of the head. A partial service record had been included as well. Here Vermeer found that Stanton had been the operations officer for the 10th Special Forces Group. It also seemed that he'd been assigned there after a stint at European Special Operations Command. His senior-most commanding officer at the time of his transfer: Brigadier General Mitchell Abernathy.

One other item caught his eye, a photo that had seemingly been tacked on to the record at the last moment, almost as an afterthought. It was a unit photograph, the kind taken for the permanent record, pure rah-rah bullshit designed to stoke the egos of staff weenies and other rear-echelon types who'd never heard a shot fired in anger.

He looked over it now, scanning faces, looking for details. It was odd how some things never changed. The young men, with young faces: the hard eyes, the too-serious expressions. How many of these kids had been killed shortly after the picture was taken? The date on the back read 17 February 1987. Most of the operators wore modified civilian attire, blue jeans, black field jackets and civilian hiking boots, plus navy watch caps. Their faces had been blackened against the night. They were all armed to the teeth of course: thinking on it a bit he decided they were probably Delta or Army Rangers, the best of the best. The tag at the bottom read "Operation Jackhammer." Nothing more. He was just about to set the picture aside, unsure why it had been included, when he spotted a familiar face. Major Stanton stood in the very front of the group, third from the left.

And beside him, another familiar visage.

Vermeer considered this a moment and reached for the phone. He dialed the special number he'd been given, and waited for the man on the other end to pick up.

"I've been waiting to hear from you."

"I'm sorry for the delay, sir. Until now my investigation hasn't been going as well as I'd hoped."

"Oh?"

"I think I've found something to connect Mitch Abernathy to Bed Check." Vermeer briefly outlined what he had discovered. "But I need more information. That includes researching documents I can't get to without raising undue suspicion. Do you think you can help me?"

The pause on the other end of the line told Vermeer a great deal. "I hear you, Peter, but I'm not sure if this is the best time to tip my hand."

"None of that will matter if I'm right." Vermeer lit a cigarette. "I'll do as you ask, of course. But I think we should move now. Especially before the ops team has a chance to interdict Detloff and his new friends."

"All right, give me what you have. I'll see what I can do."

CHAPTER 42

The Syrian Desert – Jordan
(1411 hours – Tuesday, 16 April 1991)

Insects buzzed in the thick, still air.

David Sweet sat sweating as he peered through a set of high-power binoculars. The road leading to the abandoned police outpost stretched out beyond his line of sight, empty. The sun baked all underneath a silent, blazing eye, malicious and uncaring.

Satisfied that all was well, he sat back and wiped the perspiration from his face with his headscarf. Bill Marino sat in one corner of the fighting hole, chewing away quietly on a pack of MRE barbeque meatballs.

Recon etiquette in the desert: no one speaks. Ever. The more you flap your mouth, the more likely it is the enemy will hear you, and zip you up tighter than a brand new sleeping bag. Recon marines would rather shit or piss into little plastic baggies than break noise discipline. But there was so much that Sweet had to tell his old friend. About Jessica, about the Painter. About what they were doing in this godforsaken wasteland. After a moment's thought he pulled out his field notebook and a black government-issue ink pen, and began to write.

Bill watched for a time, but did nothing more. Sweet tore off the pages and handed them over. Bill read quickly, his lips moving silently as was his habit. Sweet saw his expression harden, his eyes turning blackly inward.

Once the other man was finished Sweet silently mouthed the words: you didn't know? Marino shook his head in the negative. His expression was hard. He wanted to talk, obviously, to ask Sweet for clarification, but dared not. Sweet leaned back against the cool walls of the fighting hole, feeling oddly detached. He was just reaching for his canteen when a sound reached them, a tiny clamoring that seemed oddly out of place.

It was the sound of bells.

The two men exchanged glances, and went for their guns. Sweet readied his 9mm service automatic, fitted now with a sound suppressor. Bill had his submachine gun similarly equipped.

The sound was coming somewhere from the hilly terrain behind them. Sweet edged up and peered over the lip of his fighting hole. The rocks to the north shimmered with waves of displaced heat. A series of figures moved below them now, one hundred meters out and closing.

It was a kid, he saw, leading a string of shaggy goats. The boy wore Bedouin robes over Levi jeans, his shemagh grimy and patterned with dust.

There were tufts of tough, dry grass on the hill leading to their position. Even as he and Marino watched, some of the goats turned and headed lazily up the slope to take a nibble.

The kid was thirteen, maybe fourteen years of age. Sweet traded another look with Marino, who shrugged.

Sweet didn't want to shoot a kid. No fucking way! He didn't want to deal with the grief, the night-sweats, the bad Karma. It was a no-win situation as well. You kill a local, his people miss him, and come looking for him. Mission compromised. He sees you, and you let him go, and suddenly half the Jordanian army is swarming over the place, intent to kill.

Mission fucking compromised.

He gripped the Beretta tighter and began to pray. The kid was coming closer now, following his animals. A goat bleated, close enough for Sweet to make out its smell, a pungent, damp odor. He watched as Bill eased up and put the MP-5 to one shoulder. There was a muted click as he took the selector from "safe" to "semiautomatic." Sweet joined in, aiming down the white-dot sights of the pistol.

A voice came to them, calling in Arabic. The boy stopped, turned back. An older man appeared, also clad in Bedou attire, complete with white headscarf. He had an old bolt-action Lee Enfield slung across one shoulder.

Sweet heard another shout, angrier this time. The boy called back, and hustled to collect his animals. Dust hung in the air, barely stirred by the hot wind. The older man cuffed the boy at the back of the head, hard, and shouted once more.

Ah, Sweet thought. That explains it. The kid had probably wandered too far from where they usually pastured their animals. Moments later both had disappeared, the slight tinkle of bells the only thing remaining to mark their passage.

Sweet exhaled and lowered the pistol. Marino did likewise. The flies continued to buzz around his head as Sweet settled in. His hands were still shaking a bit as he returned the Beretta to its holster.

* * *

"Sorry to wake you."

Peter Vermeer came awake instantly. He removed his hand from the .45 underneath his pillow before sitting up to face Lt. Colonel Andrew Kiley.

"What is it?"

Kiley held out a sheet of paper. "The sixteen-hundred SITREP from Sandpiper."

Vermeer took the paper and read it, struggling to shake the last vestiges of sleep from his mind. He'd been flaked out in Kiley's minuscule office, having spent the night waiting for word, any word at all, from Jerome and his party. Now he found little of note, save that the team had encountered civilian traffic in the immediate area. He handed the flimsy back.

"Thanks. I'll be up in a little while."

Kiley offered him a tired smile. "Take your time. We've got a few hours until nightfall anyway. Awad's not likely to move until then."

"Andy? Wait a second, all right? I need to talk to you about something."

"Go ahead." Kiley riffled through the desk in the corner and pulled out a bottle of something the local imams would never approve of. He found two glasses, and poured Vermeer a good stiff drink.

"To the good old days." Vermeer held up his glass.

"They weren't that great, but what the hell." Kiley drank, poured himself another. "So. What can I do for you?"

"I came across something in my travels. Something that's not in the official records. I was hoping you'd know something about it."

"Shoot."

"Operation Jackhammer, 1987. I know it was deep black. Beyond that I have nothing. What can you tell me about it?"

"Jackhammer?" Kiley stared into the depths of his glass. The long, searching look in his eyes spoke volumes. "I remember it, yeah. It went down just after I finished my hitch with Delta. Thank God for small favors! There's a reason one never made it into the official record."

"Go on."

"It was SOCOM's show, Peter. I guess they were trying to make up for the mess we made of things at Desert One. I don't need to tell you morale was pretty bad back then. We needed a victory, even a manufactured one, and Jackhammer was supposed to be just the ticket."

Vermeer drained his glass. Ugly memories lurked just beneath the surface, threatening to bring him to places he had no wish to go. Desert One: it had been SOG-Delta's first real-world mission, eleven years ago now. Iran's mullahs had challenged a politically feeble U.S. president, leading to an ill-advised attempt to rescue American hostages held in Tehran. The final result had been more good men dead and nothing to show for it.

He'd been there, yeah. In some ways he had never left.

"Go on, I'm listening."

"Mitch Abernathy ran the show then. As I recall the plan was to take out a Red Army Faction cell we knew to be operating in Bremen. The same group had just bombed a dance club somewhere in Spain the year before, killing a dozen U.S. servicemen. The order came down to take them out, so Abernathy set up Jackhammer with Agency assistance. Only things didn't go quite the way they'd originally hoped.

"The assault went down without a hitch, SEALs and Delta working together, a joint operation right out of the Special Operations Command playbook. But their intel was shit, Peter. The people in that tenement weren't terrorists. Hell, they weren't even German. From what I remember, they were political refugees from somewhere, Libya or Syria, I think."

"Could they have been Iraqis?"

Andy seemed to think on this for a moment. "Sure. Yeah, that's it. They were Iraqis, people on the run from Saddam. I think something like a dozen people were killed, including children. It's fucking ironic when you think about it, especially now."

* * *

Once Kiley had gone, Vermeer leaned back on the cot and stared at the ceiling. His cigarette was a cherry glimmer against the darkness, flaring and diminishing with each draw. He checked his watch. Two hours remained until the fall of night.

He considered things for a bit, and reached for the phone. The NCO on duty in the commo shack answered on the first ring.

"This is Vermeer."

"What can I do for you, sir?"

"Get Element Bravo on the line. Tell them to initiate Plan Zebra. Got that? Plan Zebra."

"Yes, sir. I understand."

Vermeer returned to his cot. Sleep would elude him, he knew. But he had to try nonetheless.

CHAPTER 43

Somewhere over northern Saudi Arabia
(2201 hours – Tuesday, 16 April 1991)

The converted Boeing 707 had been aloft for ninety minutes when the contact that Captain Katherine Bonaventura, USAF, had been waiting for came up on radar.

The plane was a Boeing E-3C Sentry, the Airborne Early Warning and Control System aircraft so prominently featured in Operation Desert Storm. Its primary claim to fame was the massive, rotating dome above the main fuselage, housing a sophisticated AN/APY-2 phased-array radar antenna. Data-links allowed Bonaventura and her fellow radar-intercept officers to sample, collect, and collate aircraft contacts observed by any friendly military aircraft from hundreds of kilometers out.

On spotting the contact she keyed her mic: "Airborne contact, designate as Sierra Four-seven. Hand-off to Thumper Two-four."

"Thumper Two-four, roger."

Bonaventura watched as a pair of F-15C Eagle jet interceptors peeled off from their designated patrol station and rolled in, shedding altitude and accelerating to something in excess of nine hundred knots. The data-link fed exact course information to the two fighters, including estimated altitude and speed.

She rechecked the data on the screen before her. She decided the contact was a low-flying aircraft, probably a Russian-built transport helicopter. It had taken off from the Iraqi military complex near Ar Rutbah known as K2, its speed 120 knots at an altitude of less than two hundred feet. A soft chime sounded in her headset as the lead Eagle locked up the slower-moving aircraft with his radar.

"Victor One-six, Thumper Two-four. Target acquired. Waiting for further instructions. Over."

Bonaventura was quick in her reply. "Thumper Two-four, take heading two-four zero, Angels five. Make visual confirmation." It wouldn't do to splash the wrong aircraft, she knew.

"Thumper copies."

"Getting kind of tight, Kate." Another of Victor One-six's radar intercept operators was looking over her shoulder.

Bonaventura eyed the helo's rate of closure with the Jordanian border, now only fifteen miles off. "No. We'll make it."

"Victor One-six: visual confirmation. Iraqi air force rotary aircraft, designation Hotel India Papa. Request permission to engage."

The Eagle driver sounded almost bored, Bonaventura thought. She keyed the mic: "Thumper Two-four. You are cleared for weapons free."

"Weapons free. Roger." Seconds later Thumper Two-four was back on the horn. "Fox One."

Another signal lit her screen, if only for a moment. The single AIM-7M Sparrow radar-guided missile angled in, tracking the distant helo, before slamming home after a journey of nearly fifteen nautical miles. The track designated Sierra Four-seven flared briefly, and was gone.

As if it had never existed at all, Bonaventura thought. She hailed Thumper Two-four and told him he could return to his regular CAP station. She pulled off her headset and turned to the lone man dressed in civilian attire seated in the rear of the cabin.

"Well?" He sat quietly, a leather briefcase balanced across his knees.

"It's done," she told him.

"Good." He sat up, accepted the coffee an airman handed him. The guy had Agency written all over him, she thought. "How close did he get to the Jordanian border?"

She thought a moment, remembering the track as it disappeared from her scope. "Two, maybe three miles, sir. No more."

"Good. That will be all, Captain." She nodded and went back to her chair. As she did so, she saw the man get to his feet and head to where the secure-com satellite gear was stowed.

* * *

2230 hours, near Ar Ruwayshid, Jordan: Michael Litke checked his watch one last time and sighed.

"I should go."

"Be careful." Elise Shilling sat stiffly behind the wheel of the hired Land Rover.

He smiled. "Just be ready to move when I signal."

He climbed into the night to find Malik already waiting for him. Lights from the dusty little Arab town glimmered as the two headed down the street, past shuttered buildings. A dog began to bark angrily somewhere to the right. He moved on, mindful that hostile eyes could be watching.

Litke zipped up his jacket and adjusted the native shemagh that hid his features. "What about the local contact you told me about? You're sure he'll be here?"

"Yes, he'll be here."

Soon they came upon a darkened building huddled at the far end of town. Malik had a key, and unlocked the door in the back. The room beyond held a rank, musty odor. An older man waited for them there. He was nearly seventy, Litke saw, and dressed in full Bedouin attire.

Money changed hands, and he and Malik spoke for a time, the old shepherd gesturing animatedly. The words were too fast for even Litke to follow. Malik smiled, exposing tobacco-discolored teeth.

"He says he saw your Americans, here." The old shepherd indicated a spot on the map that Litke had provided him. "They were well hidden, with firing positions designed to sweep both the road and the fields beyond."

Litke told Malik to pay the shepherd something extra before heading back outside. He took out a hand radio and tuned it to the unit's agreed upon master-frequency.

"We're done here."

"Understood. En route now." Elise sounded relieved. Litke lit a cigarette and stood gazing at the sky overhead. Stars glimmered far above, even as the wind rose to stir the sands into a growing frenzy.

* * *

Hasim Ibrahim Awad had been out taking a piss in the desert when he discovered something was amiss.

Marouf Mohammed was waiting for him when he got back, as was James Detloff, Majed and Sami. Detloff and Awad's two assistants lay on the ground, bound and gagged, disarmed. Their features were covered with burlap hoods. He could actually see the American's rotund body quiver in terror.

The small convoy had stopped at Marouf's insistence. One of the vehicles had something wrong with the engine, a leaky radiator hose, or so Marouf claimed. Whatever the truth, two of his men had leaned over the Toyota's exposed guts, arguing who would hold the flashlight. Precious time had been wasted, and Awad had been tempted to order the damn thing abandoned. But then his bladder had called to him, taking him away from the others.

"What is this? What are you doing?" Awad was careful to keep his hands away from his holstered pistol.

Marouf drew his own weapon. "Drop the gun, Hasim. And keep your hands where I can see them. No sudden moves."

Awad let the Russian Makarov drop to the sand. His heart pounded in his chest, thundering majestically.

"There's no reason to do this! I will double your pay. Triple it! The Americans cannot be trusted, I promise you."

"Who said I was working for the Americans?" The bastard actually laughed. "I think this American is worth much more than you are willing to pay me directly. So perhaps I should find a new patron, one willing to give me what he is worth."

"Think carefully before you act. You are all dead men if you cross us now." It was hard to keep his voice from stammering, and Awad hated himself for it.

Marouf laughed once more. "Think on this, my friend. Iraq is in ruins. The world pities you, and thinks you impotent! Even now Saddam is losing control of his people. I doubt he will last much longer. The Americans will see to that."

Marouf raised his pistol and shot poor Sami in the back of the head. Blood splashed across the cracked earth, only to be soaked into the ground, drop by precious drop. Awad found that his mouth was as dry as the dust at his feet.

Marouf aimed in at the back of Majed's head, but seemed to reconsider. He kicked the Iraqi operative's foot, hard, and told him to get to his feet. This Majed did, awkwardly, and one of Marouf's men cut him loose.

"For now you and the American will stay with me, Hasim. This man here will go and report what he has seen to your masters in Baghdad. The price for your freedom will begin at fifteen million dollars."

CHAPTER 44

The Syrian Desert
(0150 hours – Wednesday, 17 April 1991)

The wind had picked up steadily with the coming of night, stirring dust, rising skyward, to finally send the very desert against them. David Sweet sat in his carefully camouflaged fighting hole, wrapped in a thermal blanket to ward off the stinging sand and grit. He wore protective goggles and a tightly-tied shemagh to keep the sand out of his nose and mouth.

A message had come over SATCOM several hours before: "Wildman. I say again, Wildman. Stand by." It was the call they had been waiting for: the Iraqi extraction helo had been shot down, exactly on schedule. Detloff's party was en route, and it had been time to perform the final preps on the planned ambush.

That had been nearly three hours ago. Sweet knew it was only ten miles by road from here to Ar Ruwayshid, a drive of just minutes if you went straight on through. Something was wrong, he decided. Something Lieutenant Jerome didn't seem to want to deal with despite the steady approach of dawn.

"This ain't right."

"No shit." Bill Marino huddled over his bolt-action Remington, goggled and masked as well. "What do you think we should do?"

Sweet never got the chance to reply. Instead his earpiece crackled with fresh static: "Banjo Six, Banjo Three. Contact report." Lance Corporal Ahern had been positioned at the far end of the ambush line, and commanded a telling view of the road into the desert. "Unidentified Victor inbound, five hundred meters and closing."

"Solid Copy." Sweet could just make out the headlights of the suspect vehicle, visible now through a dirty filter of sand and dust. He pulled his rifle into his lap and waited, suddenly eager to get on with the business of the day.

* * *

Lieutenant Walter Jerome saw the headlights as well. "We're up, Senior Chief. Lock and load."

"Aye, sir." Chief Torres shouldered his rifle and squinted down the sights.

"Fire only to disable."

"Yes, sir."

The lone vehicle was now three hundred meters distant. Jerome readied his weapon, and sighted downrange. He keyed his mic.

"Sandpiper Lead to all Sandpiper elements. Stand by to initiate on my signal."

* * *

Sweet jacked open the grenade launcher mounted beneath the barrel of his M-16 and loaded a white-nosed 40mm shell into the breech. Bill huddled close at his side and sighted in on the road below.

"All set?" Sweet whispered.

"Roger that."

"Banjo Six, go now." Jerome's voice was loud in his earpiece.

Sweet raised the M203 and fired, sending a lone parachute flare ranging skyward. Seconds later it flickered alight, sending a garish white glow across the scene.

"Banjo Five. Initiate." Bill leaned into his rifle, tracking the still-moving vehicle. There was a deafening crack, and Sweet saw the big rifle go into recoil against him. The driver jerked the wheel, skidding as his left front tire disintegrated.

Bill threw the Remington's bolt, settled in, and fired once more. The left rear tire blew out, slowing the guy even more. There were more gunshots, this time from the roadblock below. Seconds later the vehicle—it was a civilian jeep of some kind, Sweet saw—had come to a complete stop, its radiator ventilated and smoldering. Shadows emerged from the nearby roadblock to approach on foot, armed and moving cautiously forward.

"I'm going down there."

Bill pulled at one corner of his shemagh and grinned. "Mister Jerome's not gonna like that. This is supposed to be his party, remember?"

"He'll get over it." Sweet pulled aside the camouflage netting over the fighting hole to half-run, half-slide down the sandy incline to the roadside, where the bullet-riddled jeep sat, steaming silently. The SEALs had already opened the driver-side door and pulled the driver into the night.

"No shoot! No shoot! I give up!"

There was no sign of Detloff, just a big Arab who jabbered to them in fractured English. The man's face was pale, and cut by flying glass. Sweet stayed out of the way as the SEALs moved in to secure their prisoner.

"How is he?" Jerome asked. Petty Officer Gehren was cross-checked as the team corpsman.

"He'll be fine, sir. His wounds seem superficial."

"He has ID, Lieutenant." Torres had already riffled through the guy's pockets. "His passport is Iraqi."

Jerome spent a moment surveying the ruined Toyota jeep. "Strap him into my vehicle. We're moving out."

* * *

Peter Vermeer was in the commander center with Admiral Mollar when the call came in.

"Give me the handset." Vermeer keyed the mic. "This is Lima Actual. Send your traffic, over."

"This is Sandpiper Actual. Stand by for situation report. Over."

It took Walter Jerome a few minutes to outline the team's current situation. He was just finishing up when Mollar reached out to take the radio handset.

"Sandpiper Six, this is Sierra-Charlie Actual. How firm is this new intel?"

"Our confidence is high. The source was part of the team sent to escort Wildman across the border, over."

"Stand by." He glared at Vermeer. "Do you think there's any chance of finding them now?"

"I'm not sure." Vermeer stared back, his gaze unflinching. "But I think I agree with Lieutenant Jerome. We need to get in there and try and get Wildman back, no matter what."

Mollar's eyes were dangerous, remote. "I have to wonder if you're seeing this situation clearly, Peter. I understand Detloff is an important asset. But those are my men out there. I'm not willing to throw their lives away on a whim, or the words of some abused prisoner."

Vermeer felt his face color with fresh ire. "I'm not ready to throw in the towel just yet. I'll take full responsibility if you like. But we have to try. We can figure out what went wrong later, once things have quieted down."

Mollar turned to stare at a nearby copy of the ops map. "I don't like it. Our footprint there is already too blatant as it is."

Vermeer stepped forward and fixed Mollar with a steady glare. "I don't believe we have a choice, sir."

Still Mollar hesitated, his expression unsettled. "All right, do it. But you'd better be right about this."

Vermeer took back the headset. "Sandpiper, this is Lima Actual. Stand by, go to Hide One. Retasking orders to follow." He signed off before turning to Mollar. "I don't think there's anything to keep you here, Admiral. Why don't you hit the rack for a bit? I'll have someone call you once we know more."

Mollar looked to the wall clock for a moment, as if weighing his options. He shrugged. "I think we both remember when this wasn't such a young man's game, Peter. Call me in an hour."

CHAPTER 45

The Syrian Desert
(0222 hours – Wednesday, 17 April 1991)

The bullet-savaged Toyota had Saudi license tags. The paperwork Elise Shilling's team found in the glove box suggested the car had been hired at a rental agency in Riyadh. Michael Litke played his flashlight across the ground beside the vehicle. Numerous boot prints were visible, most partially blotted out by the hurried desert wind.

"They wanted prisoners, Elise. There'd be more blood otherwise."

"The Americans?"

"I think so." He dug into a pocket, and handed something over to her. Elise turned the brass cartridge casing over in her hands and frowned.

"It's a NATO Match round," he said. "Designation M118, generally issued to American snipers. I found it up there, amongst the rocks."

"Major Shilling?" Klaus Reinhardt appeared from out of the shadows. "There is a message for you on the satellite uplink."

They found the team RTO huddled in the lee of the main building. The miniature communications dish on his SATCOM receiver pointed skyward.

"This is One-seven. Send your traffic, over." Elise waited as garbled com-chatter filled her headset. A few minutes later she signed off and turned to face Litke once more.

"Trouble?"

"You could say that. A third party has taken Detloff. It's not the Americans. Control was very adamant about that. They're working on relocating him now. For now we're to head back to town and wait for further instructions."

* * *

The latest updates had arrived via data-link just the hour before. Peter Vermeer and Andrew Kiley stood sequestered in an air-conditioned briefing room, subsisting on bad coffee and stale cigarette smoke. The mission now was to find where Detloff's erstwhile protectors had taken him. One of the most likely candidates was an old industrial facility located at the northern periphery of Ar Ruwayshid. Vermeer had found mention of the place in an OPEC listing of all current and former commercial oil installations in Jordan, Iraq and Kuwait.

"You have something?" Kiley looked up from the National Reconnaissance Office briefing he'd been reading, his eyes red-rimmed from lack of sleep.

"Possibly." Vermeer showed the other man what he had discovered. "It's an old British Petroleum pipe-storage lot. According to this it was closed down in the 1970s."

It took Kiley and Vermeer a few minutes to go over satellite photos of the facility in question. The latest overhead pass by a KH-11 had been at 2300 hours local. Vermeer's interest was piqued by what he saw outlined in distance-blurred black and white. Numerous parked vehicles were visible in a lot situated near the main entrance to the place.

"That's a lot of activity for somewhere that's been shut down for fifteen years," Kiley said. "Do we have any recent data on what the place has been used for in the time since?"

"No, nothing." Vermeer lit a cigarette. "But it's the best we're going to get on such short notice. Do you want to brief the admiral, or shall I?"

"I'll do it." Kiley smiled. "You should get some rack time, though. When was the last time you had any sleep?"

"I'm fine." Vermeer stubbed out his cigarette. The ashtray at his elbow was filled to overflowing. "Wait a second, will you? There's something I've been meaning to ask you."

"What is it?"

"How well do you know Lieutenant Jerome? Professionally, I mean."

"Not well." Kiley seemed to search his memory, as if peeling the years away like the skin of an onion. "I know he's been with the Teams for five years now. He has a sterling record, top of the line. The latest word is he goes to the top of the promotion list once all this is over."

Vermeer did not remember lighting the Pall Mall he now found in his right hand. "What about Operation Jackhammer? Did you know he was in on that one?"

"No, but I'm not surprised. Jackhammer was a high-profile operation, despite the outcome. More than a few of my friends in Delta had their stars hitched to that wagon. Some of them didn't come out of it in one piece, career-wise."

"What about Jerome? He seemed to do all right. More than all right, by the sound of things."

"You'd have to ask him about that." Kiley scooped up the sheaf of papers he was going to need for the coming briefing. "See you later, Pete. I've got work to do."

* * *

0425 hours: The Sandpiper mission team had settled in a new hide, located ten kilometers from their original post at the abandoned police station. Lieutenant Jerome had seen to it that the vehicles had been laagered down, well hidden, spider holes dug, and camouflage netting put in place against the steady approach of dawn.

At the moment the prisoner sat in David Sweet's freshly dug fighting hole. He stood with a red-lens flashlight in hand as Corporal Rackley made sure the Iraqi's bindings were tight.

"All secure, Gunny."

"Get on overwatch. I'll send someone out to relieve you in two hours."

After Rackley had gone Sweet settled in beside the bound prisoner. The Iraqi sat and glared back with a mix of fear and sullen hostility, his eyes black in the moonlight. The right side of his face was mottled with fresh bruises, and swelling rapidly with each passing hour.

Sweet now knew his name was Majed al-Fawzi, his rank, that of a lieutenant in the Mukhabarat. Torres and Marino had beaten that much out of him, and more.

The crunch of boots in the soft sand heralded the approach of another of his teammates. Moments later Bill Marino peeked in around the shelter half overhead, his features masked by both darkness and expertly applied war paint.

"Dave? Briefing in five mikes. Lima Actual is sending us a mission update."

* * *

Sweet waited tensely as the final portion of the tasking order came in. Then the initial planning began, with Jerome and Torres doing most of the work. Soon they were finished, however, and it was time to move out.

"Banjo Six. Take point."

"Solid copy." Sweet keyed off his radio and waited as the other three LSVs crept up the hill, shadowed now except by dying moonlight filtered by patches of highflying cloud.

"Move out."

"Aye, Gunny." Rice sat behind the wheel, with a bound and gagged Majed al-Fawzi seated beside him. Sweet felt Rice put the buggy in gear, downshifting on the slopes, and then their tires were biting into the dirt, and throwing up rooster-tails of sand and gravel. Fifteen miles of empty desert lay between them and the suspected enemy safe house, Sweet knew, with dawn drawing closer with each passing second.

* * *

The sun peeked above the far horizon in shades of crimson and gold as Sweet, Marino, Torres and Jerome clambered up the ridge that overlooked the Jordanian town of Ar Ruwayshid.

The skyline beyond was a gray, greasy smudge against the rising heat of the day. Sweet scowled at the thought of being this close to a major population center. He remembered well the stifling closeness of his time in Basra, the wet dog smell of the place, the milling troops, and the rumble of military aircraft as they circled remorselessly overhead. Oily sweat stood out on his exposed flesh as he scanned the distant cityscape through a set of binoculars.

"Break out your E&E gear," Jerome told him. "You're going in on foot."

"Yes, sir." Sweet pulled a set of civvies from his pack: blue jeans, a plain white T-shirt, Chippewa hiking boots and a faded GI-surplus field jacket. It was all part of the team's Escape and Evasion kit, kept in case their mission was compromised, and the team was forced to blend in with the locals until help could arrive. This was the part of the plan Sweet had no use for: head in to town on foot, and recon the supposed safe house at close range. Sweet got dressed quickly, glad that he'd let his hair grow out a bit.

Even their field packs were of commercial origin, and stocked with civilian supplies: Oakley sunglasses, al-Ghadir mineral water, the tasteless protein bars hikers used, and forged Canadian passports that would never pass muster if the investigating authorities spent even a moment examining them properly. The guns were strictly mil-spec, of course. Sweet kept his Beretta at the small of his back, covered by the tail of his T-shirt. The MP-5 he'd borrowed from one of the SEALs would be harder to keep hidden. For now Sweet decided to stow it in his pack, wadded beneath a spare set of clothing.

* * *

The sun was hot against their backs as Sweet, Marino and Torres made their way into town, walking along a dust-choked road already crowded with cars, pollution-spewing buses and the occasional donkey cart.

Most of the buildings were of decaying brick, with sand-pitted metal rollup doors that covered each broad storefront during the hours of nightfall. Pepsi signs lettered in spidery Arabic glittered in the sun, mixed with the occasional Kentucky Fried Chicken franchise or street vendor selling counterfeit Nikes. Slat-ribbed dogs sulked in the sultry heat, begging for scraps. Looking westward, down a street crowded with burgeoning traffic, a pair of local cops could be seen listlessly directing traffic.

Few seemed to pay them any mind at all. One guy came up to Torres, chattering energetically, and pointed to a taxicab parked nearby. The SEAL waved him off, smiling, and the trio moved on, eager to be lost in the crowd. Soon they found a quiet back alley and paused to recheck Torres' map.

"Here it is," Torres said. "Come on. It's just a few blocks over."

They found the place a little over an hour later. It was as Vermeer had promised: the site was an old oil company storage lot, ringed with crumbling brick walls topped with concertina wire. A sign still showed the BP logo, faded now by years of exposure to the merciless desert sun. The front gate was locked, with no guards visible from the street. It was Marino who first noticed that a building a block over stood empty, as if it had been vacant for years.

They performed a slow, careful recon of the area, noting any local merchants, traffic patterns, and police presence. Nothing out of the ordinary seemed to present itself, and less than thirty minutes later the three reunited at the confluence of al-Amir and Salwa Boulevards.

Time now to investigate the building Bill had noted earlier. Sweet took point, pistol ready, as the group entered via the door just off the small alley out back. The rooms beyond were dust-strewn, filthy. Cobwebs clung to everything, while the floor was cluttered with rat droppings and bits of torn paper. A wooden staircase fed onto the second floor, where a shuttered window overlooked the street.

"Staff Sergeant Marino? Watch the first floor. Gunny, you're with me." Torres eased open the shutter and peered outside. Sweet handed over his binoculars and watched as Torres scanned the compound below. After a moment he handed back the optics and moved over to let Sweet have a look-see.

Sweet saw a half-dozen or so white stone buildings huddled amidst a flat compound of sun-baked concrete. There stood a cluster of civilian pickup trucks, a Mercedes sedan, and a pair of timeworn Daihatsu panel trucks.

A few men stood near the vehicles, all heavily armed. No one else was visible. He focused on the guards, and counted three men total, with lean, hungry faces, bearded and dirty from a life spent in the deep desert. Most wore semi-traditional Bedouin attire, white robes or Levis mixed with bits of cast-off military apparel.

"There's not much security visible right now," Sweet said. "But I bet they have men with NVGs cover those walls after the sun goes down. It's what I would do."

Torres gazed out at the distance compound, his expression thoughtful. "Be that as it may, I don't think we should hit them hot and heavy, like the night we pulled you out of that prison in Iraq. We don't have enough people for that. They'd just pop Wildman before we could get twenty paces beyond the main gate."

"Yeah." Sweet handed back the binoculars and pulled out his field notebook and a pencil. There would be more than time enough, he decided, to put together a thorough briefing before their next scheduled report to Higher.

* * *

Elise Shilling settled her spotting scope on the lip of the roof and focused on the building just up the street. From her vantage point, the Americans could just be made out through the window of their hastily prepared observation post. Objekt-74 had had them under surveillance the entire time they'd been on their reconnaissance mission, unseen and unexpected.

A moment later she saw a face briefly outlined in a distant window. "Confirm the secondary target is present, Peter." Until now she hadn't been positive that Sergeant Sweet had been a part of the American team. She felt herself smile at the thought of seeing the man squirm a bit before he died.

"Understood." Sergeant Fanger readjusted the scope mounted atop his precision sniper rifle, and settled into a more comfortable shooting position. At this distance he couldn't possibly miss. "Do I go now?"

"No. For now we wait."

CHAPTER 46

King Khalid Military City
(1135 hours – Wednesday, 17 April 1991)

Peter Vermeer had been in Ops, checking the latest satellite intel when he overheard the air tasking officer discussing plans for a coming air strike. Its location: Ar Ruwayshid, Jordan. He had been told the attack was scheduled for 0100 hours.

"You've got to be kidding me."

Vermeer now stood in Norman Mollar's office, feeling like a schoolboy brought before his disapproving headmaster. The office wasn't actually the admiral's, of course. It belonged to the base exec, a Saudi prince, who insisted Mollar use it while His Highness took a well-deserved holiday on the French Riviera. The place was a collage of high-end designer office furniture, all glass and chrome, a hideous display of affluence run riot.

"As ease, mister." Mollar sat behind the space age desk, clad in starched service khakis. A cigarette smoldered in a glass ashtray. "The decision was made above your pay grade."

"Meaning what?"

"Meaning Nick Farraday and I now agree this thing has played itself out. We'll never get Detloff out of there, not with the people holding him waiting for us like they are. I've seen Jerome's latest reports, Peter. The complex they're holding him in is a fortress. We'd need a marine rifle platoon to dig them out."

Vermeer found a seat without being asked. "Admiral, please. We can have Delta hit the place, quick and quiet. If Jerome's source is right, they have what? Twelve shooters? We'd be in and out of there so fast the locals wouldn't know a thing until our people are back in Saudi, safe and sound."

"It's not going to happen." Mollar took one last drag on his cigarette. "I've already looked into it. The Saudis were squeamish about this op from the start. There's no way they'd sign off on U.S. forces launching a direct action mission from their territory, not into Jordan at least. The political situation here is still far too tenuous for that."

"So don't tell them."

"Forget about it. By this time tomorrow it'll all be over, and you can go home." Mollar offered up a wan smile as he ground out his butt.

"Any air strike will leave obvious telltales, Admiral. The Jordanians are far from stupid."

"We've thought about that," Mollar replied. "There's already a cover story in place, something to forward to their chief intelligence service. It seems the PLO was running a bomb factory in Ar Ruwayshid, kitting together improvised devices from U.S. bombs salvaged in Iraq. Apparently they're going to have an accident tonight. It's all very tragic, and very easily explained."

Vermeer had nothing more to say to that. Instead he took his leave of the admiral, and headed back to the joint Special Operations command post, thinking quickly. A few minutes later he arrived at the base commo center and wrangled up the use of a secure-com satellite uplink. The man he needed to talk to came up on the line quickly, despite the distance between them.

* * *

The video camera was a huge, bulky thing, and mounted on a tripod like some menacing infantry support weapon. Marouf Mohammed had bought it in the market here in town for two hundred dollars.

At the moment his chief lieutenant stood, focusing it on the two bound prisoners, while another man adjusted a light source. Hasim Awad held a copy of today's newspaper to prove to his employers (and, if necessary, the American CIA) that he and James Detloff were still very much alive.

"All set."

Marouf pulled a nylon balaclava over his features before stepping in front of the camera. "Okay, ready."

"You're on." The light on the camera glowed crimson.

"I will make this very simple. I hold these men hostage. Pay me, and they live. Fail to do so, and they die." Marouf held a long-bladed knife to Awad's throat. "Contact information has been included with copies of this tape. Do not delay overlong. I am not a man known for his patience."

The light blinked off. "Okay."

Marouf tore off the mask and ordered the prisoners back to their cell. "Make two copies. Send one to the Iraqi embassy in Amman. The other goes to the Americans. It should be interesting to see which of them takes us up on our offer first."

* * *

1355 hours, Ar Ruwayshid: The two Jordanian police officers were clad in pristine service khakis, loaded submachine guns slung over their shoulders. Neither seemed to pay Walter Jerome any attention as he loped casually across the crowded city street. A cabdriver honked angrily at him in passing. Burqa-clad women eyed him before allowing their attention to slide elsewhere. The straps of the heavy backpack he carried dug into his shoulders, making his muscles ache.

He reached the building the team was using as an OP and entered cautiously, hands held low at his side.

"Glad you could make it, Lieutenant." Staff Sergeant Marino lowered his weapon and nodded. "Sweet and Torres are upstairs."

"Thanks."

Jerome found Sweet seated at his post by the window. Torres was stretched out on the floor, catching some shuteye.

"No movement as yet, sir."

Sweet offered his binoculars to Jerome, who declined. "Later. I want to get set up first."

Jerome had brought one of the team's SATCOM transmitters with him, as well as other specialized equipment. The first item he set up was the AN/PRC-104 field radio, complete with burst transmitter and satellite uplink. Working now with an ease brought by long experience, Jerome soon had the RT up and running. Next he keyed in the freq for KKMC and sent out a test transmission.

"Lima Six, Sandpiper Actual. Come in."

"Sandpiper, send your traffic. Over."

"Commo check. Alpha, Bravo, Charlie. Break."

"We read you, Lima Charlie. Out."

The other piece of gear was the team's laser designator, known as a MULE, short for Modular Universal Laser Equipment. When used properly, an operator could use the MULE to place a red-dot laser directly on his chosen target, thus giving an approaching aircraft an aiming point for a laser-guided missile or bomb. This he entrusted to Sweet, who went over the device with an expert's eye for detail. Recon marines were famous for calling in both indirect fire and air strikes using the exact same equipment.

"Good to go, sir." Jerome watched him carefully as he replaced the laser-designator back in its carrying case. His movements were slow and deliberate, almost apprehensive even, as if the gunnery sergeant had something very important weighing on his mind.

"Something you want to say, Gunny?"

Sweet stood and brushed grime from his trouser leg. "Why the change in plans? I thought we were supposed to bring Wildman back in one piece."

"You saw the place they're holding him in." Jerome stood and crossed over to the window, and peered outside. "We'd never get him out. Not with just nine men. Higher isn't about to ship in a large body of troops to help us out. So Detloff dies, end of story."

It was obvious to Jerome that Sweet wanted to say more, to argue. But instead he nodded, and returned to his place at the window, binoculars in hand. His expression told Jerome nothing, save that he was tired, and badly in need of a hot meal. As where they all, the SEAL commander supposed.

"Get some rest, Gunny. I'll take over here, and have Chief Torres relieve Marino downstairs. We're expected to be up and running by midnight tonight, so I want everyone operating at their best."

CHAPTER 47

Khamis Mushyat Airbase, Saudi Arabia
(2350 hours – Wednesday, 17 April 1991)

To an outside observer, the aircraft looked sleek, black, as if filled with equal shares of malice and evil. It squatted on the tarmac like some giant cockroach, all blunt angles and menacing functionality. In Air Force technical journals it was the Lockheed F-117 Nighthawk, a single-seat ground attack plane that until recently had been classified Top Secret. To the world at large it was simply the Stealth, famous now after a stellar term of service in the Persian Gulf.

This particular aircraft had flown from this very airbase, performing missions that had struck deep behind Iraqi lines. The pilot, Major Thomas Iacobelli, USAF, was a veteran of Panama and Desert Storm both, and knew the airspace leading to his current mission area very intimately indeed.

He performed his preflight walk-around carefully, never missing a step. Fuel state: fifteen thousand pounds gross. Inertial and GPS navigation systems: check. Loadout: twin GBU-10 Paveway laser-guided bombs, weighing in at an even 2,103-lb apiece. Both warheads were contained within the Nighthawk's integral weapons bay, safely closed off from the outside world to help preserve the aircraft's tiny radar cross section.

Satisfied that all was as it should be, Iacobelli signed off on the bird and climbed aboard. His crew chief sealed the canopy, and Iacobelli performed his final instrument checks before calling in to the tower, and requesting permission to roll.

"Bandit One-six, you are number one for the active. Clear for departure on Runway Seven West."

"Roger." Iacobelli rolled out, extending his flaps, and put the throttle forward to full military power. The end of the runway came up fast, the ground hurtling by, and he let slip the bonds of hearth and home, winging skyward. Seven hundred kilometers of nearly empty airspace lay between him and the culmination of his assigned mission.

* * *

"Bandit Flight outbound now."

Peter Vermeer stood in the command center, watching as the F-117 departed friendly airspace and headed north. He'd tried to get Nick Farraday on the phone, to get him to put a stop to this, but at the moment no one at Langley seemed to be interested in taking his calls.

It was a sure bet the Jordanians would eventually figure out what had happened. Any competent bomb damage assessment team would know the difference between an air-dropped bomb and an improvised device almost immediately. Vermeer knew the Dairat al-Mukhabarat al-Ammah, Jordan's premier intelligence service, had a great deal of experience with terrorist bombings, mostly as a result of decades of conflict with the nation's large population of Palestinian refuges.

The F-117 had reached its optimal cruising altitude. Moments later the blip winked out of existence as the Nighthawk's IFF transponder was shut down, rendering the plane largely invisible to conventional radar.

"What's his estimated time on target?" Vermeer asked a nearby radar officer.

The man paused a moment to check with his senior operations NCO. "TOT in one hour, sir. The ground team has already reported that they're in place."

"Thanks." Vermeer decided to head down to his room and turn in, secure in the knowledge he had done everything he could to see this thing through.

* * *

"Team One, Team Four: movement at the main gate."

Michael Litke opened his eyes at the sound of Hans Eberbach's voice over the tactical channel. He crawled from his bedroll, eager to see something—know anything of interest at all.

"It's a bit late to be headed to market, Herr Hauptmann." Klaus Reinhardt had the duty, and sat glued to the tripod-mounted night-vision scope Litke had left atop the roof of their mutual observation post.

"Let me see." Litke took Reinhardt's place at the scope. He spied the departing Mercedes, and focused on the man seated behind the wheel. The range was far too great to make out his facial features, of course. But he was fairly certain the driver was alone.

"Log it in, and let Major Shilling know," Litke said. He stood, and pulled on a jacket to cover the sidearm holstered at his side. "And get the rest of the team ready. We should be ready to move on an instant's notice."

"Yes, sir."

* * *

"Battery check."

"Status green. Going hot now." David Sweet peered through the designator's sight aperture and keyed the activation switch. Instantly a beam of infrared radiation lanced out to strike the distant target building.

"Good to go."

Jerome checked his watch. "Thirty minutes, give or take. It won't be long now."

* * *

0105 hours: Iacobelli crossed the Jordanian border without incident. He had maintained a cruising altitude of thirty thousand feet. He now dropped down to twelve thousand, and checked his datalink with an AWACS aircraft circling over Saudi territory. No obvious threats presented themselves, suggesting he'd entered the mission area without being detected by Jordan's air defense command.

He switched over to the frequency used by the men on the ground. "Sandpiper, this is Bear Trap. On station now. Please confirm."

"This is Sandpiper. We read you, Lima Charlie."

"Illuminate when ready."

* * *

"Now, Gunny."

Sweet pointed his designator downrange. "Target's painted."

Jerome keyed his mic. "Bear Trap, this is Bagman. You are cleared hot."

* * *

The night was humid and still. Warm air from the west stirred at the trees lining al-Amir Boulevard, rustling palm fronds lazily. The sky was clear and bright, and illuminated by the light of the crescent moon. Then there was the dim rumble of far-off aircraft engines, the sound all but carried away by the snarl and grumble of late-night traffic.

There was a sudden flash, a roar. Then there came a wall of heat and sound, blotting all before it, shattering windows, scattering brick and mortar. Killing indiscriminately, a wall of force swept outward from the decommissioned oil facility, flattening its outer walls and spilling broken masonry into the street. The light of the blast was visible for miles, and well out into the desert, where it showed up as a bright spike of hellish incandescence before fading away altogether, as if it had never existed at all.

* * *

The world outside the ad-hoc observation post was a sea of fire, a billowing ash cloud that rose to heaven on a pillar of dense black smoke.

Sweet had never been danger-close to the detonation of a two-thousand-pound bomb before. Even now his ears rang, and he felt slightly dizzy, maybe even nauseous, as if he'd been squeezed by some gigantic hand, and tossed aside with a brisk, contemptuous wave.

The room was filled with clouds of pale dust. He turned to see that Jerome's face was white, kabuki-like beneath a growing coat of pulverized concrete. The SEAL waved at him, gesturing for him to go ahead, nothing's changed, get moving, damn it! Sweet broke down the MULE and stowed it in its carrying case in record time.

"Go, go." Jerome's voice echoed strangely, as if coming to Sweet through a string stretched between two tin cans. He gathered up the case containing the designator and stuffed it into a field pack. Jerome did the same to the SATCOM, and then the two were moving fast down the stairs, eager to be away from this place of misery and disaster.

* * *

"I've got movement." Peter Fanger had been glued to his riflescope all evening long.

Elise Shilling panned right, scanning the street below. It was hard to see. Clouds of powdered chalk filled the air, choking her. After a second she spied Sweet, however, moving eastward down Samir Boulevard, on a direct route that would take him and his team away from the fire-seared horizon.

"I see them." She keyed her radio. "All units: break contact. I say again, break contact. Team Five, get ready to move. Everyone else form up at Rally Point Sierra and wait for further instructions."

* * *

The streets were crowded with the wounded, the terrified. Sweet pressed through the throng, taking point, and moving onward as quickly as he was able. Marino, Jerome and Torres followed behind, lugging the team's equipment between them.

Sweet fingered the Beretta underneath his jacket as a pair of Jordanian cops dashed by, running up the street. The crowd surged forward. Sweet locked eyes with a young woman, clad all in black, a squalling toddler clasped to her chest. Her eyes were big and brown, and bright with horror. Sweet pressed on by, gently shouldering her out of the way, and continued up the street.

There were sirens now, and the crowd parted, slowly, like a wave rolling in upon some distant beach. It was an ambulance, Sweet saw: one stinking ambulance for this entire disaster. He'd seen dead bodies in the street back there, a dozen or more at the very least.

"This way." Jerome grabbed him by the shoulder, steering him to the left. Sweet saw an alley just ahead, and angled toward it. Less than two hours later the group had made it to the spot where the remainder of the team had laagered down to sit out the night, waiting for their safe return.

* * *

0250 hours: Sweet made sure Majed was tied securely to the passenger seat of his LSV before clambering into the gunner's chair.

Rackley took the driver's seat and Sweet keyed his RT: "All set here."

Answering calls came over the team channel. Jerome ordered Sweet to move out, and he held on for dear life as the LSV lurched up and out of the rocky hollow they had been using for cover, and sped north. Sweet's vehicle stayed on point. Two hundred meters beyond the road into Ar Ruwayshid lay a long, rutted track that fed directly onto the primary LZ. He ordered Rackley to take the road, and waited for the sudden jolt as their tires crossed onto loose gravel. The engine roared as the corporal opened his throttle all the way, making their speed just shy of fifty miles per hour.

He checked his watch and noted the time. Next he hit the transmit button on the Motorola and called out Tim Rice's call sign.

"Banjo Three. Go."

"Call X-Ray Papa." Sweet paused, gasping for breath as Rackley hit a rut that sent the LSV rocketing skyward. "Tell them we're on our way."

CHAPTER 48

"LZ Canada" – The Syrian Desert
(0310 hours – Thursday, 18 April 1991)

The primary LZ was situated twenty miles to the north. The night sky to the south and east was darkening, David Sweet saw, the stars suddenly hidden, as if heralding the coming of an early season sandstorm.

Lieutenant Jerome shot a quick GPS fix as soon as his vehicle stopped moving. He called out that the group was right on target. The others dismounted, gathering weapons and equipment and stripping the now-abandoned LSVs of anything of value. Sweet paid special attention to the Iraqi they had captured. He was fully awake and alert, his features bloodied and swollen.

Sweet left the prisoner with Griggs and Jerome and went over to where Corporal Rice had set up his SATCOM set. The distant clatter of helicopter rotors came to him, carrying far on the stiff desert wind.

"X-Ray Papa, this is Banjo Actual. Do you copy?" Sweet's heart leapt as the radio crackled in reply.

"Banjo, I read you, Lima Charlie. Send your traffic."

"X-Ray, we are at LZ Canada, and need seating for ten. Over."

"Roger. Pop IR strobes."

The slap of rotor blades soon split the air, ruffling Sweet's clothing, and raising clouds of windblown dust. A shadow hovered large, outlined in his NV goggles, and he saw it was an MH-60G Pave Hawk, a Special Ops-modified version of the Army's standard Blackhawk troop carrier. Sweet knew such aircraft carried FLIR navigation aids, terrain following radar and chaff/flare dispensers. Even as he watched, the big bird began a steady descent to the desert floor.

* * *

Michael Litke watched as the extraction bird thundered in low, its rotors stirring up great clouds of dust as it settled to the ground. Some sort of ground-deployed beacon glimmered in his night-vision optics. Objekt-74 had sped to this location as fast as their vehicles would take them. They had arrived just as the first rumble of jet turbines split the night, forcing Litke to set up his firing positions with undue haste.

They were five hundred meters out, maybe more. Now the American team was up and running for the helo's open side door.

"Open fire, Hermann. I want that helicopter destroyed."

"Yes, sir." Hermann Thiele knelt at Litke's side, the surface-to-air missile launcher cradled in his fists. Litke put the night-vision binoculars to his eyes once more and watched as the last American clambered into the idling helo.

* * *

Rackley and the crew chief helped drag Sweet aboard. He felt the pilot hit his throttle, adding to the cyclic. His stomach dropped away as the helicopter gained altitude, clawing skyward and fighting against the infernal bonds of gravity.

"Wait, Goddamn it." Chief Torres clutched at his arm, nearly frantic. "Wait!"

"What is it?" Sweet could barely hear the man over the chopper's engines.

"It's the lieutenant. He didn't get on with us, Gunny!"

"Damn." Sweet did a quick headcount, and saw the truth of the matter: somehow they had forgotten Jerome in the darkness and confusion.

Torres' grip was like steel. "We need to go back for him." The SEALs' well-known, almost religious statute against leaving a man behind was nigh absolute. More than one SEAL had died to uphold that stricture, Sweet knew.

"Roger that." Sweet took the crew chief by the arm, and leaned close to shout over the roar of the turbines. He never got the chance to get his point across, however. Through the starboard window he saw a sudden flash, followed by a raising contrail of smoke and fire.

No! Sweet shouted a warning, too late, damn it, too late by far. He followed the flash as it neared them, heard a dim *CRACK-CRACK-CRACK* as the pilot began spitting out decoy flares.

It had to be a shoulder-launched SAM, Sweet thought. He looked away, already expecting the worst, and saw the captured Iraqi glaring at him with hate-filled eyes.

* * *

Litke saw the Igla-1 missile strike the Blackhawk just behind the cargo compartment, puncturing flimsy aircraft aluminum with childish ease. Aircraft rarely explode into great oily fireballs as if they were in the latest Hollywood action drama. Instead the warhead penetrated deep into the body of the Sikorsky before detonating, shredding steel and human flesh alike. The pilot lost power as his engine was damaged, his hydraulics shot, and his aircraft leaking fuel.

Litke watched as the bird spun in to crash. It bellied in, hitting hard and rolling over, where the whirling rotors tore up great hunks of sandy earth before failing and tearing themselves to pieces in the process.

The Blackhawk had barely settled to earth, smashed and burning, before Litke ordered his men to close in for the kill. Instantly the assault teams were up and moving, hitting the hillside at a hard lope designed to cross the killing ground as quickly as possible.

* * *

Jagged shards of pain lanced through Sweet's left forearm as he struggled to pull himself from the crashed helo. Something was burning, he knew. The bulkhead behind him was hot enough to blister the skin at his back.

A dead man, Lance Corporal Ahern probably, lay across his legs. Someone reached in and grabbed him by his undamaged arm. He looked up, eyes stinging from the smoke, and saw Bill Marino's dirt-smudged face.

"Jesus, Dave! You okay?" Bill shoved Ahern aside and pulled Sweet from the wreckage. Moments later they were standing in the chill desert night.

"Ugh! My arm. I think it's broken." Sweet cradled his limb and tried to sink to his knees in the sand.

"No, damn it! Come on!" Bill pulled him back to his feet. "We gotta go! They're com—"

Sweet looked up and saw a trio of armed men standing just a few feet away. All wore splinter-pattern camouflage and carried Israeli Galil assault rifles.

"Bill, no. Don't do it." Marino still had his MP-5, tangled on its assault sling. Sweet saw his friend reach down, grasping for the weapon.

The lead gunman shouldered his weapon and fired a short burst, and Bill's chest exploded in blood. Sweet was dragged down beside him, exhausted, spent. The man came forward, his features covered by a black balaclava. His eyes were flat, emotionless.

Sweet looked at Marino, whose eyes stared heavenward. All he could think of was Suzy and the girls.

Men grabbed him, and bound his hands. Someone kicked him, hard, sending another wave of agony lancing through his already shattered arm.

The lead shooter stood above him and ground the muzzle of his Galil into the fleshy part of Sweet's throat. For a second it seemed as if the guy was going to pull the trigger, and end it all then and there. The metal of the flash suppressor was hot against his skin.

Instead he pulled the weapon away, and summoned one of his men. When he spoke it was in English, with only the slightest Germanic accent to be found.

"Bring him, Willi. Sergeant Sweet and I need to talk."

* * *

Two others had survived the crash, Litke was told. It was the Sikorsky's copilot and one of the marines. Both men were badly injured. He ordered them shot before turning his full attention to Sergeant Sweet.

Willi Krenz had made sure someone collected Majed al-Fawzi's charred remains from the chopper. He now lay on the sand, covered by a blanket. Insects were already beginning to buzz around the corpse.

"His knife, Elise. Give me his knife."

Elise Shilling handed over the big fighting knife Sweet carried on his webbing. It was a Ka-Bar, the storied Bowie-style fighting knife that had been in Marine Corps service since the Second World War. He pulled the blade from its sheath, testing its edge with his thumb.

It was razor sharp. He turned to Sweet, who sat on the sand beside al-Fawzi's body, with hands bound. Blood ran down one side of his face from a nasty cut on his right temple.

"I don't normally approve of torture, Sergeant." Litke eyed the 7-inch blade of the knife before handing it back to Elise. "It takes much too long, and in the end the subject usually just gives you the answers he thinks you want anyway."

The prisoner stared off into nothing, his expression fixed, lifeless. Elise took a moment to use the Ka-Bar to slice away Sweet's sweat-soaked T-shirt.

"Fuck you."

"Please! Let me finish. The only use I see for torture is as a punishment, you see, or for revenge. Luckily you fit into the latter category." He gestured to Shilling, who bent low and applied the blade to the pale, freckled skin on Sweet's broad chest.

The American screamed as the blade sliced his flesh, delicately, minutely. More blood flowed, and two of Litke's men had to come forward to keep him still so Elise could work properly.

The screaming continued, the knife scribing flashing circles in the glow of the burning helicopter. Now the fleas buzzed around Sweet, eager for a fresh source of nourishment. Litke waved Elise away.

"I am going to ask you this once, Sergeant, and once only. Please pay attention."

Litke drew out his sidearm and made a show of checking its magazine. "Your friend, the lovely Ms. Seeley? Surely you spoke to her about all this? Your meeting Colonel Halabi, his involvement with James Detloff. How much did she know, Sergeant? What, exactly, did you tell her?"

Sweet looked up at Litke, his face clouded by pain. He looked confused, Litke thought, confused and defeated. "What? What difference does it make? She's dead. Dead and buried."

"Please, Sergeant. Answer the question." He nodded once again to Elise. The blade flicked once, and Sweet screamed.

"How much did she know?"

"Okay, damn it. Okay." Sweet asked for water. Willi held a canteen to his lips and watched as the American drank greedily, gagging a bit at the end.

"Now. What did she know?"

"Everything." His shoulders sagged and bloody spittle hung from his mouth. "I told her everything I knew."

"Thank you. That is all I needed to hear." He leveled the Glock and began to take up the slack on the trigger.

* * *

CRAAAK!

A high-pitched snap made Sweet's ears ache. The sound was followed a heartbeat later by the thud of a 7.62mm bullet punching into human flesh. He saw a ragged crimson stain spurt from the base of his questioner's torso, just below the right armpit.

Sniper! Sweet was throwing himself to the dirt almost before his mind could comprehend what was going on. He heard startled shouts, followed by cries of anger and alarm. The German slumped to the ground, spurting messily.

CRACK!

The woman with the knife grunted as another high-velocity slug struck home. The bullet hit her squarely in the chest, right above the heart. She pitched over and went still as raw arterial blood jetted from the wound.

* * *

Litke sought cover even as the first strobe-hot tracers stabbed downrange, punctuated by the crisp chatter of a belt-fed machinegun. Some of the incoming fire skimmed by, mere centimeters overhead, while other rounds slammed into a nearby Land Rover, rocking it on its springs, shattering glass and puncturing metal.

The pain in his chest was terrible, staggering him, making it hard to breathe. He could taste the blood in his mouth, coppery and warm.

The roar of outgoing gunfire deafened him as his men began to return fire. Litke looked to his right, not daring to raise his head above cover, and saw Willi Krenz firing an FN light machinegun from the prone position. His tracers lanced out toward a distant, unseen enemy. Willi fired again, spitting out a long, angry burst, before a copper-jacketed slug caught him in the face, tearing away his jaw in a torrent of mangled, bloody skin.

* * *

The guns went on for what seemed an eternity, with bullets punching into automotive steel or ricocheting amongst the sand and rocks all around Sweet. He huddled beside al-Fawzi's corpse, his hands still bound tightly behind him.

He saw muzzle flashes twinkling from the surrounding hills. There was no way to tell how many men were firing. At least a dozen, he supposed, although it could be more. Dead men lay scattered all about him, stiff, unmoving.

The firing began to taper off as quickly and stunningly as it had begun. The enemy began emerging from behind cover, a few survivors only, to raise their hands, and proclaim, loudly, that they were surrendering. Almost immediately figures in dun-colored fatigues came from the rocks, armed, dangerous, and shouting orders in Oxford-accented English.

One figure in particular detached itself from the main group and came toward him. Captain Southby-Taylor crouched at Sweet's side and gently rolled him over onto his back. A quick flick of a knife cut away his bonds.

"All in one piece, Sergeant?"

"More or less, sir." Somehow Sweet found the strength to speak.

"Corporal Hansen!" The shout summoned an SAS medic. "Wounded man here, lad." He turned back to Sweet, patted him on his uninjured shoulder. "Good thing your man Vermeer sent us to find you. You'll be all right. We'll talk more on the drive back to civilization."

* * *

Seventy-two hours later Sweet was aboard an Air Force C-9 "Nightingale" medical transport aircraft, bound for Rhein-Main Airbase in Germany.

He had a morphine drip in his arm and was feeling no pain. They'd boarded at KKMC, with only a few other patients in attendance. At first, it seemed as if Sweet was the only patient on the flight.

His broken arm was in a cast. The knife wounds inflicted on him at LZ Canada were still raw, and ached each time he shifted his weight on the gurney. The docs had told him he'd retain the scars for life.

The young Air Force lieutenant tending to him came by, offered him the latest issue of *Time*. She was pretty, he thought, with big dark eyes and an open smile. The nametag on her battle dress uniform read: Fernandez.

"Is everything okay, Sergeant?"

"Yes, ma'am. Thank you." He took the magazine. "Say. Do you know who that guy is?"

He gestured to the only other gurney patient in this section of the converted DC-9. His face was swathed in bandages. Two grim-faced men in plainclothes attire stood post near the guy, who had been handcuffed to his bed.

"We were told not to ask," she replied. "And that goes for you, too." She smiled once more. "I'll come by later. Try to get some rest."

Sweet thanked her, and settled back to do as he'd been told. As he did so, however, he saw the injured man look at him through the holes cut in his bandages.

They were dark eyes, Sweet thought. Angry eyes. And he had seen them before, just days ago now. He lay back, trying to let the drugs take him somewhere, no, anywhere else.

* * *

Litke felt himself jostled awake. The pain in his chest was a dull, roaring ache . . . Whatever they had given him had kept him asleep for a very long time. He'd opened his eyes to find himself being taken off the medical transport.

Words now came to him, someone speaking German. Home? They'd brought him to Germany?

Of course. The Americans had bases there, with top of the line hospitals for treating their wounded from the Gulf. Another jolt sent daggers of pain rolling through him. He opened his eyes, and was promptly blinded by brilliant sunlight. They were in an aircraft hangar of some sort, occupied by the plane that had brought him here, as well as a pair of ambulances and numerous men dressed in civilian attire.

"Get him loaded." The leader was a tall, balding fellow, thin featured. He looked more like an accountant than an officer in the Central Intelligence Agency.

"Herr Litke? Can you hear me?" The man leaned so close that Litke could smell the cheap aftershave that hung around him like a cloud.

"Yes."

"You're going into a hole now. A very deep, dark hole that few men have ever managed to climb out of. Do you understand?"

"I understand, yes." All he wanted now was sleep. His wounds ached so!

"Good." The American lit a cigarette. "Cooperate, and things will go easy for you. Fuck with me, and you go deeper into the hole. Do you understand?"

"Yes. I understand all too well." He was just beginning to drift back to sleep when men came to put him on the ambulance, and begin his long trip into captivity.

CHAPTER 49

Arlington National Cemetery, Virginia
(1125 hours (EST) – Wednesday, 1 May 1991)

The casket was empty, of course. Too little of the dearly departed's corporeal remains had survived for it to be otherwise. Now Peter Vermeer stood, only half-listening to the words of the Navy chaplain performing the ceremony. Instead he was watching the crowd. The man beside him took a quick gander at his watch before speaking.

"Nick isn't here?" The Director for Central Intelligence was a thin, washed out sort of individual, and vague in both appearance and manner.

"No, sir. He's not." Vermeer fought down the urge to scan the crowd once more.

"You intend to go ahead then?"

"Unless you say otherwise, yes, sir."

"It's too risky, Peter. I'd rather we just have the Bureau bring them all in now, before this can get out of hand."

"There isn't enough evidence to make it stick, sir. Maybe if we'd been able to find Jerome, of if the people we captured in Jordan had known more. But I think you know what has to be done."

The other man sighed. "All right, do it. But for Christ sake, be careful. The last thing we need is for this to go public."

* * *

McLean, Virginia – 1345 hours: David Sweet stood and regarded himself in the bathroom mirror. By now many of his cuts and bruises had healed nicely, leaving only scar tissue and sullen memories. His left arm still throbbed dully, no matter how much of the prescription codeine he took. It now hung at his side, bound tightly and encased in the sleeve of his service dress blues.

He'd decided not to wear the sling today. He didn't want it to ruin the cut of his uniform. A little discomfort was a small price to pay for looking good, he thought. Especially considering that soon he might not be allowed to wear the uniform of a United States Marine ever again.

He picked up his cover and made his way into the upstairs hallway. It had been nice of Peter Vermeer to let Sweet bunk here for the past few days. Barbara Vermeer had been nothing but kind to him. As a former RN she had been more than happy to help change his dressings and whatnot, a kindness Sweet was determined never to forget.

The hallway was filled with mementoes, photographs of both family and friends and events long past. He saw the Painter as a young man, in high school, at Fort Benning, and the highlands of Vietnam. Pics of their wedding, of cousins and nephews, and of the teenage daughter they'd sent to Texas A&M just a few short months before.

Sweet made his way downstairs and into the kitchen. There he found Barbara busy with trays of hors d'oeuvres for the coming party.

"Hello, ma'am." She looked up at his approach. Merely handsome now, she had been beautiful once, with clear hazel eyes and shoulder-length brunette hair shot through with a touch of iron.

"Hello!" She smiled brightly. "Did you find everything you need up there?"

"Yeah. No problem. Need some help?"

"Oh, no." She pulled another tray from the oven. The smell of freshly baked manicotti made his mouth water. "You sit, rest. Peter should be back any minute now."

She hustled him off to the living room and handed him a cold soda. A buffet with snacks, myriad appetizers, lined the bar near the door to the back deck. CNN was on, showcasing a feature on some big tropical cyclone in Bangladesh. The talking head was going on about casualties, likely to be in excess of 120,000 souls. Sweet stuffed his face and watched, only half-interested.

The first guests began to arrive fifteen minutes later. Sweet, like Barbara and the Painter both, had been at the final ceremonies at Arlington earlier in the day. It still galled him to think that a prick like Detloff would be given a plot in such hallowed ground. But Jim Detloff had died without family, without friends. So the Painter and his lovely bride had offered to throw a wake for the guy, with only top-flight Washington brass invited. For his part, Sweet still wasn't sure what he was doing here.

The first guests came in limousines, in POVs. Many had bodyguards of their own, who eyed Sweet curiously before dismissing him as a non-threat, a non-entity.

Of note were the Director of Central Intelligence, several big shots from the Justice Department, a caller from NSA and even some old guy from the Soviet Embassy. Detloff's death had seemed to play out as a great tragedy, a loss in the never-ending battle America played in the great Shadow War, the covert world of cloak and dagger.

Sweet stood in one corner, sipping his Coke. A few of the guests nodded politely, and he nodded back. His junior rank and a relative lack of importance kept most of them from interacting with him at all.

"Hello, Gunny."

Norman Mollar was in civvies, Sweet saw, a Brooks Brothers suit with a lapel pin denoting him as a holder of the Navy Cross. He had to fight down the urge to come to the position of attention.

"Admiral."

"Peter sure knows how to throw a party." The admiral nodded affably to Barbara as she circulated amongst her guests.

"I suppose so, yes, sir."

Mollar sipped at his scotch and soda. "Did you know Detloff well?"

"Just from the Gulf, sir. Not socially." Sweet wished the guy would go away.

"Did you know I'm retiring soon?"

Sweet nodded. "Mr. Vermeer mentioned something about it, yes, sir."

Mollar drained his glass. "I want you to know there are people in Washington who are very aware of all you've lost because of this. Your sacrifice has not gone unnoticed, I assure you. And I, for one, am going to be in a position to do something about it."

"Yes, sir."

Sweet wasn't sure what the older man was going on about, not really. But he did recall something Vermeer had told him earlier, about how Mollar was headed over to Fort Meade for a top spot with the National Security Agency.

"You've lost a lot, Gunny. More than anyone else here. But maybe it's not as bad as you think." The admiral reached into a pocket, withdrew a small slip of paper.

"Admiral?"

"Take it."

Sweet did as he was told. On it was a woman's name he did not recognize, as well as an address on the outskirts of Baltimore.

"Sir?"

"Good luck, Marine." Mollar set his empty glass on a nearby table before angling over to speak with someone Sweet had no hope of recognizing, another Suit. He stood, staring at the slip of paper, trying to puzzle out its meaning.

"Everything okay?"

Sweet looked up to see the Painter standing there. He held two beers, one of which he offered to Sweet.

"No thanks. It'll clash with my meds."

"Right." He set the extra beverage next to Mollar's glass. "What did the admiral want?"

"I'm not sure." Sweet concealed the note in the palm of his hand. "I think he was trying to offer me a job."

"He's expected to head the NSA next year." Vermeer grunted, then sipped at his Budweiser. "You could do worse."

"I'm happy where I am."

"Ain't we all." He drained his beer before setting the can on the table. "See you later, Gunny."

"Sure." Sweet watched him go, and chugged down the last of his drink. A few minutes later he was headed upstairs to change.

* * *

Nancy Marie Stopa: the name swirled in his mind like stale smoke.

The address belonged to a building in a small industrial park just outside of Baltimore. The sign outside suggested the place was a private medical clinic, with office hours from 8 a.m. to 5 p.m., Monday thru Friday. He parked in the lot outside and made his way to the front entrance.

It was already well after nightfall. Peering inside, he saw the lobby area was shadowed, ill-lit. He reached out, tried the door, and found it unlocked.

Sweet pushed on through. He'd found a .45 Combat Commander in the nightstand in Vermeer's bedroom, and taken it, along with several spare magazines. He now carried it hidden inside his sling, close to his body. The pistol was a cold, solid presence as he approached the front desk and peered down corridors to both the left and the right.

Vermeer had told Sweet the name of the goon who had killed Bill Marino, and had questioned him out in the desert. Michael Litke, former Stasi operative. He had wanted to know about Jessica, and what she had known about Detloff and Halabi. It had seemed odd at the time. Now the admiral was handing him a piece of paper with a name and an address on it. The name of a young woman he had supposedly never met.

The latest issue of *Popular Mechanics* had been left open at the guard station, and a cigarette smoldered in a nearby ashtray. The cup of vending machine coffee on the desk was still warm.

Sweet paused, looking at the floor at his feet. He'd stepped in something that made his shoes squeak.

Something wet. He knelt, and worked at the tacky swatch of blood with one finger. It was fresh. He resisted the urge to ease the .45 out of its hiding place.

A corridor led deeper into the facility. He found a log book at the nurse's station just down the hall. It showed three patients in residence, including Nancy Stopa, who was housed in the second floor ICU.

He headed for the stairs leading up. He paused, however, at the janitor's closet on the other side of the hall. Another patter of fresh blood marred the waxed linoleum at his feet.

He opened the door, looked inside. Felt the door thump against something soft and unyielding.

Sweet pushed harder and saw a woman's hand fall limply to the floor. He pushed all the way in, and saw a tangle of blood-smeared bodies inside, all jumbled together in death.

The smell made Sweet's stomach tighten. He counted two men and two women, most dressed in hospital scrubs. All had been shot at pointblank range with a small-caliber weapon. Only one guy was clad in a suit, he saw, JC Penny standard and easily affordable on a government salary.

He rolled the guy over to check his wallet. The name was James Brothers, U.S. Federal Marshal Service.

Sweet shut the door and headed upstairs. He pushed on through, and entered the second floor hallway leading to ICU. No one was at the nurse's station there either. He checked the log book and noted Ms. Stopa's room assignment, Number 14A.

Butterflies danced inside him as Sweet headed down the hallway. Could Jess be alive? He dared not even pray it was so, as he approached the end of the hallway.

Here it was: Room 14A. Sweet entered, checking to the left and right. The place was empty, it seemed, save for the slender form huddled on the bed. The soft *beep-beep-beep* of a heart monitor was the only sound in the room.

He stepped forward, looking at her face. It had to be a trap, of course, and yet he did not care. His hands were shaking as he bent low to look the young woman over, measuring her, searching her silent features for any sign of recognition.

"Don't feel bad, Gunny. I thought it was her, too."

Sweet turned slightly, and looked over his left shoulder. "Hello, Mr. Jerome," he said, and pulled the trigger.

The Combat Commander was still hidden inside Sweet's sling, pointed backward between his broken arm and his bandaged torso. His right fist was wrapped around the pistol, and he felt it recoil against his side, the heat of the shot burning him, jarring the broken bones inside his cast.

A hit! Walter Jerome staggered back, smearing bright crimson across pristine hospital walls. Sweet saw it was a through-and-through stomach wound, and already bleeding badly. The suppressed .22 Ruger Jerome had in his hand clattered uselessly to the floor.

Sweet saw the man lurch into the hallway, clenching his injured belly. His fingers were sticky with blood. Sweet pulled his pistol and prepared to give chase.

He noticed the .45 had jammed, with a casing stuck in the breech. He jacked the slide to clear it, and headed into the hallway. A smear of fresh gore decorated the linoleum there. There was a window to the left, overlooking the street. Red police flashers glimmered below. He heard men shouting and the tramp of running feet.

"No, Gunny. Please. Don't." Jerome was bleeding out, Sweet saw. He'd managed to crawl to the nurse's station before running out of gas, and now lay on his back, clenching at his ruined stomach.

His fingers, Sweet saw, were black with gore. He raised the pistol, aimed in at the other man's forehead.

"This is better than you deserve. Fuckin' traitor." He began to take up the slack on the trigger.

He heard footsteps, and the squeak of shoe leather on waxed tile.

"Federal agents! Drop your weapon!"

Sweet looked up, saw men in black tactical gear carrying German submachine guns. The lead shooter had an FBI logo stenciled on his body armor.

"Don't do it, Gunny." Another agent stepped forward, also dressed in tactical gear. He let his MP-5 hang by its sling. "My name is Special Agent Bozak. We need him alive, all right? Put down the gun."

Sweet's first instinct was to fire. Memories of poor dead Bill came to him, memories of everyone he had lost, so many dead, but years of Marine Corps training and discipline were still strong within him.

"It took you long enough to get here." He set the .45 aside before putting his good arm on top of his head. The SWAT boys stormed forward to take charge of the situation.

* * *

Special Agent Bozak, surprisingly, did not put Sweet in handcuffs. Instead he had orders to escort him to the nearest FBI field office and hold him securely until further notice.

"There's something I need to do first, sir," Sweet said as a wounded Walter Jerome was taken away, under guard, for treatment. "Do you mind?"

"That depends," the man replied. "What is it?"

"I just need to say goodbye to someone first."

The two went into the only occupied room on the floor, guarded now by FBI agents. The heart monitor continued its steady pulse, the hiss of oxygen moaning softly in the otherwise silent room. Medical personnel were en route, Sweet was told, to take her somewhere safe.

"You know her?" Bozak asked. Sweet leaned in once more to gaze at the girl's slumbering features.

"No. I guess not."

Nancy Marie Stopa, age 28. She looked a bit like Jess, he supposed. Dark hair, slender features. It had been a good match the Painter or whoever had made to play games with his head. Sweet struggled for a moment to remember where he had seen her before.

Then it came to him: Nancy had been the name of their waitress at the Monterrey West.

"Okay," Sweet said as he awkwardly pulled his jacket on over his cast. "Let's go."

CHAPTER 50

Falls Church, Virginia
(2135 hours (EST) – Wednesday, 1 May 1991)

Rear Admiral Norman Mollar returned home late, exhausted in every sense of the word. It had been a long day: first the farce at Arlington followed by yet another dog-and-pony show at Peter Vermeer's house. Then there was more pressing the flesh afterward, at both Fort Meade and with old friends at the Pentagon.

The house was empty, of course. Corinne had left him years before, when he had still been with the Teams. Norman Jr. and both of the girls were up at school, so Mollar had the house all to himself. He headed straight for his office on the first floor, seeking bourbon. There he would be surrounded by wood-paneled comfort, models of 18th Century sailing vessels and specially commissioned paintings of John Paul Jones and David Farragut. Framed certificates displayed copies of his Navy Cross citation, as well as pictures of his time in Vietnam complete with tiger stripes and camouflage war paint.

He was just reaching for the Woodford Reserve when he realized, however belatedly, that he was not alone.

"Good evening, Admiral." Mollar turned to find Peter Vermeer seated in the comfortable leather armchair near the window. He was still clad in the suit and tie he'd worn to Detloff's funeral.

"Jesus, Peter! You startled me." Sudden anger filled Mollar as he set down the bottle.

Vermeer shrugged, the gesture casual, offhand. "Sorry. I'm afraid this couldn't wait."

"What the hell are you talking about?"

"I was worried when Nick didn't show up today, so I sent someone to check on him."

"And?" Farraday hadn't been at the funeral, Mollar knew. But his absence had been commented on, questioned.

"You remember Gene Farrell? My ops manager for Wishbone?"

"I suppose so, yes." Mollar's anger was building to a dangerous head. "What of him?"

"He found Nick, Admiral. In his study, shot through the temple with his own gun."

"My God." Mollar poured himself that drink. "So he's dead?"

"Yes." Vermeer fidgeted with his necktie for a moment before tugging it off. "The Bureau's over there now, of course. They've already found something you might be interested in."

He crossed over to Mollar's desk, and placed a crisp manila file there. Mollar sat to take a look at it.

"What is this?" He opened the file and saw the NSA photographs of James Detloff in the desert, serving the interests of Saddam Hussein.

"Master copies of the classified files we found in Ian Trucco's possession," Vermeer replied. "And now somebody's tried to make Nick's death look like a suicide. But it was very sloppily done, by an amateur, I suppose. I think Shilling and her people would have done a better job. But you already know that."

Mollar closed the file. "What are you getting at?"

"The Bureau is going over Nick's house with a fine-tooth comb. They've already found bank transfers and account numbers on his computer to several off-shore accounts. There was enough money there to outfit another dozen teams just like Objekt-74."

"My God." Mollar leaned back in his seat.

"Nick has been running Shilling's team the whole time. He was part of Bed Check, perhaps going all the way to the start."

Mollar drained the last of the bourbon, and wished for another. "So what do you intend to do now?" he asked. "If the FBI is involved it will be impossible to keep a lid on this. Somebody's going to have to take the fall."

"You're right. I—" Vermeer was interrupted by a harsh electronic clamor. He checked his pager and grunted.

"Can I use your phone?"

"Go ahead."

Vermeer picked up and began to dial. He waited for several long seconds as whoever was on the other end answered.

"This is Vermeer. You did? Excellent. And how is . . . ? Good, good. Keep me informed."

Vermeer hung up. "Great news! Walter Jerome is in FBI custody. He's been badly wounded, courtesy of Gunny Sweet, but he's expected to live."

"Walter's here? Alive? I—I thought . . ." Mollar's mind was reeling, moving full tilt. He eased a hand beneath his desk, and found that his old J-frame Smith & Wesson was right where it was supposed to be.

"It was clever, the way you suckered the gunny into going to our facility in Baltimore. Making him think Captain Seeley was alive, setting him up for Jerome. It's just too bad for you that Sweet is so good at putting steel on target."

"Is that supposed to be some kind of joke?"

"Not at all." Vermeer sighed. "Your first mistake was not killing Sweet in Iraq. Of course, none of us knew he was in that Iraqi prison, but that's another matter. The fact remains we got him out in one piece, despite someone planting a couple of kilos of Semtex on the primary extraction helo. It cost seven good men their lives, but at least it got Halabi out of the picture before he could give us anything useful."

Mollar felt his fingers tighten on the snub-nose revolver. "You're not making any sense."

"Oh, but I am." Vermeer stayed right where he was, stock-still in front of Mollar's desk. "Halabi died trying to tell us something about General Mitchell Abernathy. As far as I can tell the two had never met, never had anything to do with each other in the slightest.

"So what was the connection between the two? I didn't have a clue, Admiral. Then you handed me the next piece of the puzzle, whether you meant to or not."

Mollar did not reply. Instead he released the clips holding the revolver and prepared to ease it out of its hiding place.

"Operation Jackhammer was the bit that got my attention. Three players in our little drama were all involved there,

Abernathy, Major Benjamin Stanton, and Walter Jerome. What caught my eye was the fact that all of the civilians killed that night happened to be Iraqi. Members of the outlawed Islamic al-Dawa party, to be precise. They were Shi'a political refugees, on the run from Saddam Hussein."

"What happened that night was an accident."

"Bullshit. They were targeted intentionally, as a favor to Mohammed Halabi and his friends in the Mukhabarat. You took good men, the best our country has to offer, and turned them into contract murderers."

Vermeer reopened the file and shuffled through the papers within. After a moment he found the crime scene photos taken at Major Stanton's apartment.

"There is one thing I'm not sure of, Admiral. Why kill your own people? Did Abernathy lose his nerve after Jackhammer? Did the blood of so many innocent people finally get to him, and leave him with doubts about what you and your people were doing?"

A cold knot had begun to form in the pit of Mollar's gut. "You still haven't offered me one solid piece of evidence to any of this, Peter."

"I'm guessing that Stanton helped 'arrange' for Abernathy's helo to crash. After that he had to go, too. No witnesses left behind, am I right? The rest of it will come out, of course, now that Lieutenant Jerome is in custody."

"You have no idea what you're dealing with, Peter."

"Wait, Admiral. There's more. A lot more. At first I couldn't imaging why Nick would send those files to Trucco. But now it seems clear to me: you did it. And by involving Trucco, letting him know there was some truth to the rumors about Bed Check, you eventually put our attention on Farraday. You set up your own co-conspirator, right? Getting Nick to take the fall would keep you out of the limelight very nicely, I think."

"I'm not the only man who had access to those files, you know."

"Of course not." Somehow Vermeer managed to smile. "But you do have something in common with at least one of the known conspirators: a hatred of Iran. We know Jerome had a brother in Beirut, a brother who was killed in the bombing back in '83. A bombing the Iranian-backed Hezbollah was responsible for.

"But you lost someone there as well, didn't you? Your oldest boy, Thomas. He was a platoon leader with Bravo Company, Second of the Eighth Marines."

Memories came to Mollar then, burning like sticky black oil: memories of a tri-folded American flag, and another burial at Arlington. His wife, crying bitter tears.

He tightened his grip on the revolver. "I have nothing more to say to you."

"You may want to reconsider that." Vermeer leaned forward. "Tell me about Bed Check. I want to know the names of the other men involved."

Somehow Mollar found the strength to chuckle. "You're fishing, and I'm not going to bite. I want to speak with my lawyer."

"There aren't going to be any lawyers. Not this time. Eventually we'll get Jerome to talk. So you might as well come clean, before—"

Mollar drew the .38 and centered his sights on Peter Vermeer. "You're not making me disappear. I've played this game too often to not know where this is headed."

"If you say so." Vermeer pulled something from his pocket and held it out for Mollar to see. Five rounds of .38 Special +P ammunition slipped from his fingers to clatter across the surface of Norman Mollar's desk.

The admiral pulled the trigger. The revolver clicked dry, once, twice. Three times.

"I was hoping you wouldn't take it this way. Now come on. Put the gun down, and come clean with me."

"It's too late for that, Peter." Mollar dropped the Smith & Wesson and stepped away from his desk.

"What are you doing?" Vermeer calmly drew his .45 and watched as Mollar crossed over to a lovingly crafted model of the frigate USS *Essex*. There he began fiddling with a large hatch on the ship's forecastle.

"What do you think you're doing?" Vermeer repeated, stepping to one side for a clearer shot.

"Ending this." A small handgun had been hidden inside. The weapon was a Seecamp .32, tiny, and designed as a last-ditch backup. And this, he thought, was about as last-ditch as he was going to get.

"Don't be an idiot." Vermeer aimed in, finger on the trigger. "Come on. Put it down. Think of your children, and what this would mean to them."

"I am, Peter. I am." It took surprisingly little effort to put the gun in his mouth and press the trigger.

* * *

Vermeer looked at the dead man sprawled at his feet. Blood speckled a painting of some long-dead admiral on the wall behind him.

Things would probably be better this way, he thought. There would be less to clean up, and less in the way of unwanted attention on certain high-level activities on Capitol Hill. After a moment he grabbed the phone and dialed. Special Agent Bozak picked up on the second ring.

"It's me," Vermeer told him. "I found the admiral. He's dead. Gunshot wound to the head. Send a team over as soon as you can."

Bozak told him he would. Vermeer hung up and stood, considering. With a shrug he headed over to the admiral's wet bar and helped himself to something strong to drink.

EPILOGUE

Mountain View Cemetery – Denver, Colorado
(1205 hours (MST) – Monday, 16 September 1991)

The people at the head office had been very helpful. A woman actually drove him out to the plot in question, and then stood, respectfully removed, as he approached Jessica's grave, hat in hand.

It was a beautiful day, a bit crisp maybe, but still clear enough to see the snowcapped Rocky Mountains to the west. David Sweet set the pot of flowers he'd purchased at the cemetery office on the ground near the site, and crossed himself, a legacy of a distant Catholic upbringing.

"Hey, babe. Sorry it took me so long to get here. I've been busy."

He knelt on the grass, mindful of the other graves nearby. He pulled a paper grocery bag out of one pocket.

"Things are going good for me right now," he told her. The cool wind tingled at the naked skin at the back of his head. "Mr. Vermeer saw to it that the Corps took me back without any complaints. I guess he told them I'd been serving the common good, or some such shit."

He opened the bag and took out a Budweiser. He popped the top, and drank down a silent salute to her, believing somewhere inside she would not only understand, but approve.

"I've reported in for that instructor's slot over at Little Creek. I suppose it's good duty. Not the same as working in the field with the bugs and the dirt, but it'll do. And I reenlisted too, right on time."

He slammed back the rest of the beer, and set the empty can on the grass. He pulled a few other items from his pockets, one at a time.

First in line was the Silver Star they had pinned on him the week before. It was marked down in his service jacket as a "black" award, given for services during an operation not officially recognized by either the Secretary of Defense or Headquarters, USMC.

Next he added his Purple Heart, the one award no sane man should ever covet. This too had been offered to him, for injuries suffered in both Desert Storm and during the course of Operation Sandpiper.

"It's all crap, Jess. I'd give it all back for one more minute with you. But you know that, don't you? That's why I wanted you to have this."

It was the engagement ring he had meant to give her, all those months before. It meant nothing to him now, despite the fact it had cost him a great deal of money. He set it beside the medals and climbed to his feet. His pants were soaked with dew.

He stood for a moment, gazing down at that lonely rectangle of granite, before policing up the beer can and the tattered paper bag.

"Goodbye, Jess. I love you."

Sweet turned and headed back to the car. As he did so the cool autumn wind picked up, tugging at his clothing as if trying to pull him back to the gravesite for one brief, final embrace.

* * *

Ahvaz, Iran: Amina Jabouri stood at the bus stop, cloaked head to foot in black.

She watched the cars and buses rumble by, emitting dirty fumes, polluting the air, making it hard to breathe. People pressed in on her, pushing, shoving. The streets were more crowded than usual. She was one of the many Iraqi Shi'a in the city, forced to flee due to Saddam's most recent purges. The identity papers in her pocket were forged, of course. She found herself wondering, idly, if she would ever be allowed to live under her own name again.

Another rumble of venomous diesel, and then the bus she had been waiting for appeared, chugging resolutely toward her. She climbed aboard last, allowing others to go before her, and took a seat in the back. The bus lurched into motion. She sat, looking out the window at the grimy city streets as they passed on by.

Her stop was the outdoor market just off Sahel Street, just across from the cinema. Amina disembarked and walked east, toward the river. There the White Bridge stood, silhouetted against the haze-gray sky. The market swarmed with people.

The shop she was looking for was just off the main drag. She entered. Inside it felt dark and close, and smelled of musty cloth. The owner sold mainly *hijab* apparel.

A woman stood at the counter. Amina approached her and spoke, her voice pitched low.

"My name is Tal'at. I understand you have a package for me."

"Come with me."

The man she had come to see waited in back. He was tall, heavyset, with expressive brown eyes and a firm, unsmiling mouth.

"When do you intend to cross the border?" he asked.

"Tomorrow morning."

"You are very brave." He handed over a small envelope. "This goes to our usual contact. See that it is delivered sometime in the next three days."

"I understand." Amina was left alone then. From her bag she withdrew one of her few remaining possessions from her life before al-Dawa: a photo album, salvaged from the ruins of their former safe house in Amarah.

Working quickly, she opened the book and secreted the thin envelope in the middle, between two photographs. The border guards would be unlikely to find it there, she knew. As she finished something fell to the floor at her feet. She bent low to pick it up.

It was a tattered strip of cloth, lovingly cleaned and folded. Part of a camouflage uniform, U.S.-pattern. It had been part of the field jacket David had been wearing when he'd broken into her apartment, a seeming lifetime ago now. She knew better than to begrudge the fate that God had decided for her, and yet she still found herself thinking of him often. Would she ever see him again?

In the end she supposed it did not matter. Her life, as always, would be as God willed it.

CPSIA information can be obtained at www.ICGtesting.com
Printed in the USA
LVOW08s0618090514

385057LV00001B/158/P